"I suppose on the ghost, too!"

Sarcasm dripped from Holly's words. It was just her luck that she was stuck in the garage with this very attractive—and very disturbing—man.

"Ghosts aren't responsible for the house being in disrepair. The owner is," Zach retorted.

Holly sighed, stamped her feet and hunched herself into her coat.

"Cold?" Zach asked.

She shook her head.

"You can sit in the car if you want to."

"What I want is to get out of here."

"Oh, you will." Zach remained infuriatingly calm. "You know, maybe you were brought here to restore this home. Fix it up. You aren't going to wreck it to put up a video store or something, are you?"

"I won't be able to do anything if we die of the cold," Holly snapped.

Zach smiled and leaned toward her. "Trust me, Holly. You were brought here for a reason, but I doubt it was to freeze to death in a garage."

Dear Reader,

Each and every month, to meet your sophisticated standards, to satisfy your taste for substantial, memorable, emotion-packed stories of life and love, of dreams and possibilities, Silhouette brings you six extremely **Special Editions**.

Now these exclusive editions are wearing a brand-new wrapper, a more sophisticated look—our way of marking Silhouette **Special Editions**' continually renewed commitment to bring you the very best, the brightest and the most up-to-date in romance writing.

Reach for all six freshly packaged Silhouette **Special Editions** each month—the insides are every bit as delicious as the outsides—and savor a bounty of meaty, soul-satisfying romantic novels by authors who are already your favorites and those who are about to become so.

And don't forget the two Silhouette *Classics* at your bookseller's every month—the most beloved Silhouette **Special Editions** and Silhouette *Intimate Moments* of yesteryear, reissued by popular demand.

Today's bestsellers, tomorrow's *Classics*—that's Silhouette **Special Edition**. And now, we're looking more special than ever!

From all the authors and editors of Silhouette **Special Edition**,

Warmest wishes,

Leslie Kazanjian,
Senior Editor

ANDREA EDWARDS
Ghost of a Chance

Silhouette Special Edition

Published by Silhouette Books New York

America's Publisher of Contemporary Romance

To John and Kathy, Ken and Judy,
for their welcome,
To Mary Ann, Dottie, Sue, Joyce and Nancy,
for their acceptance,
And to Krishna, Krystal, Christina and Colleen,
for their smiles.
Thanks.

SILHOUETTE BOOKS
300 East 42nd St., New York, N.Y. 10017

Copyright © 1988 by Ean, Inc.

All rights reserved. Except for use in any review,
the reproduction or utilization of this work in
whole or in part in any form by any electronic,
mechanical or other means, now known or
hereafter invented, including xerography,
photocopying and recording, or in any information
storage or retrieval system, is forbidden without
the permission of Silhouette Books, 300 E. 42nd St.,
New York, N.Y. 10017

ISBN: 0-373-09490-6

First Silhouette Books printing November 1988

All the characters in this book are fictitious. Any
resemblance to actual persons, living or dead, is
purely coincidental.

®: Trademark used under license and
registered in the United States Patent and
Trademark Office and in other countries.

Printed in the U.S.A.

Books by Andrea Edwards

Silhouette Special Edition

Rose in Bloom #363
Say It with Flowers #428
Ghost of a Chance #490

ANDREA EDWARDS

is the pseudonym for Anne and Ed Kolaczyk, a hus-
band-and-wife team who concentrate on women's
fiction. ''Andrea'' is a former elementary school
teacher, while ''Edwards'' is a refugee from corporate America, having spent almost twenty-five years
selling computers before becoming a full-time writer.
They have four children, the oldest now a student at
the University of Chicago, and live in a house they
built themselves on a hilltop in northeastern Illinois'
horse country. The house and grounds are patrolled by
three guard cats, two old dogs and occasional toads,
rabbits and birds the cats adopt.

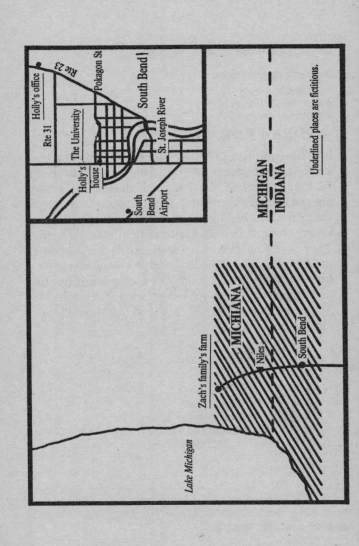

Holly's office

Rte 23

Rte 31

The University

Pokagon St

Holly's house

South Bend

St. Joseph River

South Bend Airport

Lake Michigan

Zach's family's farm

MICHIANA

Niles

South Bend

MICHIGAN

INDIANA

Underlined places are fictitious.

Chapter One

"Afternoon, ladies."

The man's voice was warm as brandy sipped before a blazing fire, but Holly saw nothing but the car he was getting out of. Actually, she could see only the bump on the snow-covered roof that told her this car was a taxi. Hallelujah! she thought. Even in this deserted, frozen wasteland of northern Indiana, prayers were answered. She grabbed the hand of her daughter, Jenny, and the pair hurried across the snowy pavement outside the airport terminal before another traveler materialized to steal their taxi.

"You can't imagine how glad we are to see you," she said to the cabdriver, forcing the words out between her chattering teeth. "We were freezing to death."

"You weren't waiting outside this whole time, were you?"

He stopped to stare at her, which was not the reaction Holly wanted. She wanted efficiency; she wanted warmth.

"Of course we were," Holly said, tugging at the cab's back door, but it wouldn't open. "Our luggage was out here and we couldn't leave it."

Even as she said the words, the barren landscape mocked her. The only other person even remotely near to them was the snowplow operator and he was all the way over at the far end of the parking lot. Who did she think was going to swipe their luggage? The abominable snowman?

Her cheeks flushed with sudden heat. "Well, I had no idea we'd be waiting out here for hours," she told him.

"Actually, it was only about ten minutes, Mom," Jenny said.

The man came around to the door. "But a cold ten minutes, I bet. I'm really sorry I'm late," he said, pulling hard on the handle. The door opened and Jenny rewarded him with a smile.

"That's all right," the girl said loudly, with a side glance that dared her mother to continue her grumbling.

Holly's heart sank. She'd done it again. She'd wanted everything about their move to South Bend to go perfectly, then she irritated Jenny by grumping at a cabdriver. All right, so it was silly to have waited outside in the freezing cold. She wasn't thinking all that clearly. She was nervous about this promotion—though when she looked across the mountains of drifting snow to the street at the far edge of the airport, promotion wasn't the first word that came to mind.

They climbed inside the cab, which smelled faintly of pizza, while the driver went back to the curb for the luggage.

"He's the cutest cabdriver I've ever seen," Jenny whispered after a moment of silent punishment was over. "And he's friendly."

"I had a friendly cabdriver once in New York."

Jenny made a face. "Psychos don't count, Mom."

Holly grinned and wiped a bit of frost from the window so she could watch the man carry the luggage to the cab. He was in his early forties and startlingly handsome, though she was sure it was his down jacket that gave that bulk to his shoulders. He glanced her way and winked, as if he could read her thoughts. She quickly looked away, turning back to Jenny.

"Sure is different from La Guardia, isn't it?"

"I'll say," Jenny agreed. "Nobody yelling and swearing. Nobody threatening to run you over if you try to cross in front of them. Nobody about to steal your purse."

Holly squeezed Jenny's hand. "It's going to be a great place to live. I really feel good about the move."

Jenny's long brown braids bounced as she nodded. "Me, too. It's kind of neat having hardly anybody around."

Holly smiled, though she actually found it eerie, having come from the throbbing hustle of New York, where you were never alone, never free of suspicions, to this quietness. A sudden fear welled up inside her. Should it be this quiet, this empty? All they'd seen were the cabdriver and a few airport employees. No other passengers had gotten off the commuter plane. Maybe it had landed at the wrong place. Maybe this was really Siberia, she thought irrationally.

Don't be silly, she scolded herself. Panic did not become the rising young executive or the single mother. She took a deep breath and watched the small snowplow slowly clear an ever-widening strip of parking lot. Things were just different here. Slower. Less frantic. They didn't need massive snow-clearing equipment because there weren't masses of people trying to get to the airport. They didn't need a huge fleet of taxis waiting around because there weren't many people to wait for. The change would be good for her, good for Jenny and good for Grandma Ruth. Her mother had been wanting to move out of the city for years.

Buoyed by her refound optimism, Holly resolved to behave as politely as Jenny could wish. The driver got into the front seat.

"I hear you got some snow last night," Holly said brightly.

"Oh, just a little bit." The man turned around, resting his right arm on the back of the seat.

"It looks like about three feet," Jenny said.

"That is a little bit for around here," he said. "A real snowfall is over ten feet."

Jenny dissolved in giggles; Holly's good intentions dissolved, period. How could a stranger, in a matter of minutes, get Jenny to sound like the ten-year-old she was, while Holly always brought out the mother hen in her daughter?

The man offered his hand to Holly. "Welcome to South Bend. I'm Zachary Philips," he said. "Zach to old friends and lovely ladies."

Jenny giggled again and Holly's spine stiffened. "I'm Holly Carpenter," she said. "And this is my daughter, Jenny. Now, could we please go? Our flight landed more than an hour late and I'm sure my mother will be worried."

His brown eyes widened just a fraction, and their smiling depths grew suddenly murky, making him look surprised. "Sure thing," he said, turning around. He revved the motor. "Warm enough back there?" he said coolly.

"Yes, it's fine," Jenny said quickly, with a definite scolding look at her mother. "It's nice and warm."

Holly refused to feel guilty. She hadn't really been rude. All she'd done was ask their cabdriver to get started. Should she have sat around chatting with him until snow drifted over the cab? And how did they know that friendly cabdrivers weren't psychos in South Bend, also?

She slipped off a glove and pulled a card from her purse. "We need to get to 109 Pokagon Street," she said.

"Po-KAY-gon," Zach corrected her as he drove down the exit drive toward the street.

Apparently afraid Holly would react to the mild correction, Jenny jumped headlong into the conversation. "How did they come up with a name like Pokagon?"

"He was an old Indian healer."

"Is he dead?" Jenny asked. "People don't usually name anything after somebody until they're dead." She slid forward in her seat.

Holly wondered if Jenny had moved out of interest in Zach's answer or to stay between him and her mother. She felt fingers of guilt close around her heart and turned to stare out the window. An assortment of fast-food restaurants dotted either side of the street, dwarfed by mountains of plowed snow, but it was the sky she noticed most. There was so much of it, and it made her feel small. Lost. The way she'd felt five years ago, when Joel had been killed in an auto accident and everything had fallen onto her shoulders. She returned her gaze to the safety of the cab's interior.

"Officially Pokagon's dead, but he still keeps an eye on things. Especially on his street."

Jenny frowned and Holly decided things were going a bit too far. "We don't believe in ghosts," she told Zach.

"Won't bother him none," he said, shaking his head. "Pokagon's a liberal sort. 'Live and let live' is his motto."

Holly sighed. She was sure this man's silly superstitions didn't bother Jenny, but she sought to reclaim her daughter's attention nonetheless. "Look at all the room around here. It's going to be a little hard to adjust to this much breathing space between buildings."

Jenny looked out her window, then spun back to her mother, braids flying and brown eyes glowing. "Are these regular houses along here?" she asked. "You know, not apartment buildings?"

"A few are boardinghouses," Zach called back. "But most of them are single-family homes."

Jenny stared back out the window. "Look at the yards, Mom. Will we have a yard like that? Oh, and look at that house. It's got' a porch that goes all the way around. Wouldn't it be great to have a porch like that?"

"We'll have a yard," Holly assured her, looking over Jenny's shoulder at the clapboard houses along the street. Windows stared back at her like watching eyes. "We won't have an all-around porch, though. These are older homes. Grandma got us something newer."

Zach had stopped at a stoplight and she saw him look back at her briefly. The glance gave her only a glimpse of his eyes, but they had a puzzled expression. What's so strange about getting a newer house? she wondered. Then the light changed and Jenny caught sight of an enormous fake cow and chicken parked in an empty lot.

"Wow, those pictures of farm animals in my social studies book sure made them look smaller," Jenny said with a laugh.

"Hey, we do everything bigger out here," Zach said. "Farm animals. Snowfalls. Backyards. And just wait until you see what Indiana considers homework."

Jenny groaned into a pile of giggles that brought the ache back to Holly's heart. She spent the rest of the trip staring out the window. They drove through the downtown area, then north over a river and into another section of older homes. Holly frowned at a street sign. This was Pokagon Street, but where were the new houses?

Zach pulled to a stop. "Here we are," he said. "Pokagon's favorite."

The first things Holly noticed were the trees in the parkway—huge, substantial, ancient trees, not the spindly sticks she'd expected. Then her gaze went beyond to the green cyclone fence. A green cyclone fence? When did cyclone fences start coming in colors? Towering above the fence was an evergreen hedge, but if anything towered above that, it was blocked by the roof of the cab.

A certain horror clutched her stomach. A relatively new house—that's what she and Ruth had agreed on. A new house for their new start. That's what kind of house Holly had thought she was buying when she signed those papers Ruth had expressed to Holly's New York office. Holly didn't want a house with a past, with memories in every corner—a house like she and Joel had dreamed of having one day. She was vaguely aware that Zach had spoken, and her gaze darted to the front seat.

"I beg your pardon?" she asked.

"This house here is where Pokagon always stays when he's in town," Zach said.

Jenny frowned. "I thought you said he was dead."

"I said officially," he said with a huge grin.

Holly's horror began to ebb. This wasn't their house; they were on a tour as part of his ghost tales. But just as her heart started to beat again, Zach got out of the car.

"Is this it, Mom?"

Holly shook her head. "I don't know."

"It has to be. Why else would Mr. Philips be getting out?" Before Holly could say a word, the girl was scrambling out her side of the cab.

Holly could hardly do less. Besides, the trees and fence meant nothing. True, it was an old lot, but the house could still be new. Ruth had agreed on a new place; she wouldn't have picked something else. Holly climbed from the car and stopped in horror. Towering above the hedge was an old house, or was it a castle?

"I thought you said it would be new." Jenny had stopped in midstride as she was crossing the snow.

"This can't be it," Holly muttered, and with careful, cautious steps went up to the gate.

The house was three stories high, three stories of light brown brick with granite blocks along the corners and covered with a green tile roof. The wide front door was framed by massive stonework and at one corner rose a turret. All the place needed was a moat and a drawbridge.

"Sort of takes your breath away, doesn't it?" Zach said, coming up behind her.

Holly discovered he was carrying their suitcases. "Look, there has to be some mistake. We were getting a new house."

He shook his head. "This is 109 Pokagon." As he went through the gate, he nodded at the mailbox. Small but clear numbers repeated his claim.

"Then I must have the address wrong." She hurried after him into the yard. "I need to get to a phone."

Jenny came up next to her. "You know, Mom, it looks like something out of one of Grandma's horror books. Maybe Pokagon does live here. It's spooky enough for a ghost."

Holly squeezed Jenny's hand. "There's no such thing as ghosts."

Zach put the luggage at the foot of the steps. "Just don't say that too loud," he whispered. "Pokagon might take it as a challenge."

Jenny laughed, but Holly glared at Zach. "It hardly matters who hears, since this is obviously the wrong house."

Even as she spoke the front door burst open and Ruth bustled out. But for once, her short, plump figure was not a reassuringly familiar sight. If this wasn't their house, Ruth shouldn't be here.

"Hey, you two," Ruth called from the porch. "I thought you'd never arrive."

"Grandma," Jenny cried out, and rushed into Ruth's arms. Holly slowly followed her daughter up the few steps.

"Wait till you see the place. You're going to love it," Ruth assured Holly over her shoulder as she ushered Jenny inside.

But Holly's feet stopped short of the door. She just couldn't bring herself to enter. Joel was gone; he no longer haunted her dreams. But she wasn't the same person she'd been when he was alive. She didn't have the emotions to waste on a house. She wanted something bland, something that wouldn't take a toll of her time or her heart. But her mother's excitement was in the air, and that enthusiasm made Holly almost as happy as the house made her worried.

"Something wrong?" Zach asked, then smiled. "Or you waiting for me to carry you over the threshold?"

Like a Roman candle, his smile seemed to shower sparks over Holly, warming her heart in ways that she didn't expect and certainly didn't want. She had enough problems with a new job and an old house, with a worrywart for a daughter and a mother who deserved better breaks in life than she'd gotten, and with the chore of keeping them all balanced and happy. Holly didn't need a man to curl her toes inside her boots.

But in one split second, the fuse was lit, burned, and Holly exploded. "No, I don't want you to do anything but give us back our luggage and go." Realizing that their luggage was already sitting on the sidewalk, she whipped a ten-dollar bill from her purse and handed it to him even as she stomped toward the door. "Here. Keep the change."

"I beg your pardon?"

Holly turned. He was still there. She took a deep breath, sending orders to relax all the way down to her toes. "Now what?"

"What's this for?" He held up the money.

"For the fare." She was comforted to see that friendly cabdrivers were the same the world over. "And the rest is your tip."

He shook his head slowly. "What fare and what tip?"

Holly wrapped her arms around her chest, to ward off the cold, not his smile. "Look, things are different in New York, but they can't be that different. You ride in a cab, you pay a fare. Someone carries your luggage, you give him a tip."

Zach's smile started to inch back across his face and she tightened her hold on herself. "What cab?" he asked.

The man was obviously insane; there was nothing to fear in his smile. She waved her hand toward the taxi, visible through the gate. "That—" She stopped. Most of the snow had been blown from the auto's roof and on top was not a taxi roof light, but a Luigi's Pizza sign. "Oh, no," she muttered, her heart sinking into her stomach.

"The alley wasn't plowed yet and I couldn't get my car out," he said. His voice was quiet as if he was holding back his laughter, but he wasn't quite successful. "I borrowed this from a friend of mine."

It was an explanation, but not one that explained much of anything. "To do what? Hang around the airport and pick up strangers?" Had she made a complete fool of herself? She couldn't remember everything she'd said since she got in the car. At least, the smell was explained.

"But you and Jenny aren't exactly strangers," he pointed out.

"Zach, there you are!" Ruth was back at the doorway. "You can leave the bags here if you want. Lou's anxious to get his car back. The other one won't start and he's got a kitchen full of orders."

Zach nodded. "I'll just run the keys over to him now." He handed the ten-dollar bill back to Holly. "Lou lives just down the block. Any tips you want me to pass along to him?"

Zach didn't wait for an answer but half jogged down the sidewalk and disappeared behind the hedge. The wind must have died down slightly, for suddenly Holly's cheeks felt very warm.

"Holly?" Ruth was at her side, tugging her sleeve. "Come on in, honey."

"Mother, who is he?"

Ruth had her arm around Holly, leading her inside. "Zach? Didn't he introduce himself?"

"Of course he did. But why was he picking Jenny and me up at the airport?"

"Because I was afraid a cab would be hard to get." Ruth stopped in the entryway. "They clear the runways long before they clear the roads. Just look at this place. Isn't it wonderful?"

With a sweep of her hand Ruth drew Holly's gaze from the black-and-white marble floor to the brass light fixtures high up on the ten-foot ceiling. From the rough-textured plaster walls to the lead-paned window in the enormous wooden door. From the wide dark molding framing the doorway to the crystal doorknobs cut with diamondlike facets. This was not the safe, neutral decor Holly had been dreaming of. Certain questions began nagging at her, demanding answers. "Mother—"

"This banister is just made for sliding down," Ruth said with a grin at Jenny. "And there's a room upstairs that's perfect for a little girl I know. It's in the turret, the round tower on the side of the house, and the room is perfectly round."

"No corners?" Jenny asked. "Where will my desk go?"

But Holly was not distracted by this little byplay. "Mom, why was he—"

"And wait until you see this," Ruth said, waving them to follow her across the bare hardwood floors of the hallway and living room, the thump of their feet playing base to the higher notes of the creaking floors. She led them into a solarium that looked out onto the snow-covered garden. "This is our very own gargoyle and it's hooked up to spill water out of its mouth.''

"A statue that slobbers. That's really gross." Jenny tried to twist her face into an expression of disapproval but her voice gave her fascination away.

Holly gave up with a sigh. Her mother would explain Zach when she was good and ready. Just as she'd explain how they happened to get a ''newer'' house that seemed about eight hundred years old.

"So what do you think?" Ruth turned to Holly, a pleading note in her voice. "Isn't this place great? I mean, those new houses are like living in a motel."

"Speaking of motels," Holly said, suddenly exhausted, "which one are we staying in?"

"Didn't I tell you?" Ruth asked. "We're spending the night in our own home." Her eyes searched Holly's face for a moment. "Right here," she added.

"Hey, that's rad, Gran," Jenny cried.

Holly did not share her daughter's enthusiasm. "There's no furniture, Mother."

"No problem," Ruth said, bustling them back into the living room. "Zach got us some sleeping bags. They're down-filled and quite warm."

Back to square one. "Mother, just who is Zach?"

"Didn't I tell you about him?"

Why would Holly be asking if she had? "No, Mother, you didn't."

"Well—" Ruth's voice was quiet "—he's sort of your tenant."

Holly stared for a long moment, certain this was all a bad dream and none of it was happening to her. "My tenant? Since when do I have a tenant?"

Ruth smiled. "He came with the house."

"Really?" Jenny said. "You mean like a dishwasher or drapes?"

"The third floor is a separate apartment," Ruth explained. "And Zach's been renting it for a couple of years. The realtor said we could ask him to move, but I didn't see why. It's not like we need the space."

So Holly had a house she didn't want and now a tenant, too. What a great start this new "beginning" was off to. "Mother, what am I supposed to do with a tenant?"

"Whatever you like," a laughing male voice answered. "I'm easy to get along with, I pay my rent on time and I'm quiet."

Holly turned to find Zach leaning against the doorway. His jacket was open, showing a lean, trim figure and shoulders that she now knew needed no help from a down jacket to look broad. His brown eyes glowed mischievously; his smile was ready to devastate. She didn't want him in her house. He was disruptive. He was disrespectful. He was dangerous.

"I never have wild parties," he went on. "I let someone else give them. Saves me the trouble of cleaning up."

"That's good to hear."

"I'll pretty much stay out of your hair," he went on. "I have my own entrance and the only thing we share is the laundry room. You won't even know I'm here."

He could be as quiet as a cat burglar but Holly somehow suspected she'd still know he was around. A man like Zachary Philips didn't exactly blend into the woodwork.

"I'm afraid I wasn't expecting to own a boarding-house," Holly said, then stopped. What if he had a lease? Could she just throw him out? Maybe it was best to move more slowly, she determined, telling herself that the decision had nothing to do with his sparkling eyes. "Is there anyone else here I should know about?" Holly asked.

"Yeah," Jenny piped up suddenly. "Is there really a ghost?"

"Only when you need him," Zach said with a smile.

Jenny obviously didn't understand, but Holly did. Not his strange remark, but the fact that his smile, his glance, just his presence, toasted her insides. If he was promising to be so invisible, maybe it was time he started.

"It was nice to meet you," Holly said. "But we really are anxious to see the rest of the house."

"Let Zach show it to you," Ruth suggested. "He knows everything about the place."

More time with Zach was not what Holly needed. "I'm sure Mr. Philips has other things to do without showing us the house, Mother. Besides, I'm kind of anxious to discover it on my own."

"Actually, I was just on my way to do some chores," Zach admitted. "So I'll let you get on with your exploring. If you have any questions or need any tips, I'll be around." He took a step away, allowing Holly to breathe again.

"Yes, thank you," she said, ignoring Ruth's perplexed frown. "We'll remember that. I'm sure we'll see you again soon." How could they not if he was living with them?

He grinned. "Only as much as you think fair."

Holly could feel her cheeks glowing with heat at all his tip-and-fare remarks, but before an appropriate retort could spring off her lips, he was gone. Her attention returned to Ruth, who was now eyeing her strangely.

"Since when did you join the ranks of Lewis and Clark?"

"Why shouldn't I want to explore the house on our own?" Holly asked bravely, and walked into the middle of the living room. "It's not like we're going to get lost or anything."

"We might meet Pokagon," Jenny piped up.

Was that a smirk or a smile of uncertainty on her daughter's face? Holly's boots beat a brisk tattoo on the bare floor as she moved quickly across the room. "Mr. Philips was joking," Holly murmured as she fingered the stonework of the limestone fireplace. She'd never seen anything like it before. Garlands of flowers were carved along the edge of the mantel, producing a quiet, elegant effect.

She'd never had a fireplace before. What would it be like to sit in front of this one on a chilly winter evening? She could see herself here, sipping a fine, rich brandy as soft music played on the stereo. And next to her, his brown eyes reflecting the fire and the— She shut down the dream and marched to the open door next to the fireplace.

"Let's see what's in here," she suggested brightly.

It was a library, the walls covered with dark oak shelves that reached almost to the ceiling. Did anyone in these days of videos and tape cassettes have enough books to fill all that space? A sense of sadness seeped into her. Holly moved quickly to the nearest window. It reached from floor to ceiling and was taller than most doors she'd seen.

The mullioned panes framed the outdoors scene into multiple small pictures. She chose to look at the one containing a bird feeder hanging from the side of an old pine tree. A flock of smallish brown birds scattered with her movement at the window. They hadn't had a bird feeder in New York, since they hadn't had a tree or even a yard. She found watching the birds restful, although the birds themselves were anything but. Their pushing and shoving was causing seed to rain upon the snow, and Holly suddenly realized the feeder was full, the birds' feeding routine established. She hadn't known how old the house was, but she had known that the previous owners had left months ago. Zach must have been keeping the feeder supplied.

She moved slowly from the window, bothered for some reason by the knowledge that Zach was taking care of the birds. There was no reason to feel threatened by the knowledge that a man with a warm smile, a man whom she had thoroughly embarrassed herself in front of, was kind to birds. Especially since she had no desire to stay in this house where he lived.

"Mom! Jenny!" she called as she hurried out of the library.

"We're upstairs," Ruth called back.

Holly hurried through some sliding doors—heavy oak creations cradling thick glass panels—and up the stairs, her hands respectfully caressing the carved oak banister. She could certainly appreciate the craftsmanship evident in every nook and cranny even if the house wasn't for her.

"This is the room I thought you'd like," Ruth was telling Jenny as Holly caught up with them. "I think every girl dreams of having a bedroom in a tower. A place to pretend you're a princess, being held prisoner while you wait for your prince to come."

"A princess, Gran? Come on."

The words were sophisticated youth and the tone was big-city cynical, but what could one call the sparkle that grew in Jenny's eyes as she looked around the room?

"A princess, Mom?" Holly echoed, hurrying her words out. "Jenny's like me, and never in my weirdest, wildest dreams did I ever dream I was a princess."

A speculative look came into Ruth's eyes. "That's too bad. A person needs those kinds of dreams to accept romance in her soul." A gentle smile curved Ruth's lips ever so slightly. "But it's never too late. Maybe *you* should have this room."

"Forget it, Mom." Holly turned to wander back down the hall. Ruth followed her.

"I never said much when we lived in New York because it's the lousiest place in the world to meet men," Ruth said. "But Indiana's different. There are a lot of men here, real men. Or don't you ever think about anything but spark plugs?"

Holly opened up a door to find a linen closet. There was not so much as a doily inside to distract her mother. "REV is more than just spark plugs," she said. "We sell just about every replacement part an engine could need, plus the company gives me a very full life."

"Oh, sure," Ruth snorted. "How many dates has the company arranged for you? In fact, when was the last time you were on a date, period?"

Holly went into the bathroom and checked each faucet. Running water even. "What's that got to do with anything?"

"Must mean you haven't had one since Joel died," Ruth murmured.

Holly had to laugh. "Mom, stop trying to find a fairy tale in everything. My job is all the happily-ever-after I need."

"Mom! Gran! Come here!" Jenny called. "There's a secret hiding place under the window seat."

Ruth and Holly trooped back to Jenny's room to exclaim over her discovery, but Holly found herself too restless to stay for more than a minute. She left them searching for other surprises. Wandering back down the hall, she passed doorways trimmed with polished oak, walked under brass light fixtures with equally ornate switches and entered a large bedroom with its own fireplace.

She knew what was wrong. This *was* a haunted house. Once it had been a castle that had promised a magical prince and princess a happily-ever-after, but now it housed only the memories. Loneliness lived here, along with a sense of waiting and expectation for another prince and princess to come and find joy. That's why it wasn't suited to her. She didn't believe in happy endings anymore. She hadn't for many years now. Those kinds of dreams were from a time long past, a time when love brought joy, not pain. Life was different today and she needed a different type of house.

She opened a far door and stepped out onto a porch that was probably above the library. Snowflakes were floating down from the leaden sky, but it was pleasant compared to the brooding silence of the house.

The evergreen hedge, which edged the whole property, had snow clinging to it, like in a scene from a Christmas card. Birds chattered in the trees, yelling at her to go inside so they could go back to their eating, while a squirrel scampered boldly over to the bird feeder. There was a strong sense of peace here, but Holly could build that wherever she went. Who said happiness couldn't be bought? Every hardware store in the world sold bird feeders.

On that thought, she hurried back into the house. The first step was to get her family into a motel for the night. Her mother was too old to be sleeping on the floor, anyway.

"Mom? Jenny?" she called, retracing her steps. But the hallway and the tower room were empty, and no voices drifted toward her.

She fled down the stairs into more silence. They wouldn't have just left her here. Smashing the ridiculous thought that this was Pokagon's doing, Holly rushed to the kitchen, where a window framed a set of snow-filled footsteps leading to the garage.

Rising irritation grappled with the frantic tone sneaking into her voice. "Mom? Jenny?" She hurried across the yard to burst into the garage. "You out here?"

"Nope, it's just me," Zach said, straightening up as he wiped his hands on a rag. His smile faded when she didn't return it. "Something wrong?"

"No, of course not," she assured him, not about to admit she had lost her mother and her daughter. "As long as we were exploring the house, I thought I should check out the garage."

She busied herself first by peering at some shelves filled with rusted odds and ends of garden tools, then by inspecting the windows. When she had circled around to the snowblower in the corner she found herself in a position to check out something a little more interesting: Zach leaning over the engine of his car as he poured in a bluish solution. Why wasn't he married and in a home of his own? she wondered. With that fiery smile he must have women falling all over him.

He stopped pouring and replaced a cap, then turned suddenly, catching her unexpectedly. "You're very thorough," he said.

She wondered if he referred to her inspection of the garage or of him. She lifted the handle of the snowblower and peered at it intently. "I'm sorry about the misunderstanding earlier," she said. "When I thought you were a cabdriver."

"Nothing wrong with driving a taxi."

"No." She stopped and wrestled for a moment with her habitual reticence. "I had a cabdriver once in New York who was friendly. He kept his pet python underneath his seat."

Zach laughed, banishing the last traces of her embarrassment and letting something warmer, softer, into its place. "Well, that certainly explains it," he said. "How many times did you check under the seat?"

"One eye was on it constantly."

He chuckled again, and she watched him work in a comfortable silence that let her relax.

"How is it you happen to be living here?" she asked.

"I like the neighborhood and the house," he said simply. "And it's very convenient to the university."

Even though he'd spoken softly, his voice seemed all the more powerful out here. She could feel a tingling deep in her soul and grew wary. "You work there?" She told herself it was the eeriness of the garage with its dark beams and the bare bushes scratching at the windows that was affecting her.

"I'm a professor. American history. I specialize in Indian lore, but I love anything that's old." He paused a moment to let his smile grow. "Although on occasion I've made exceptions for young women."

She looked away. "This house should certainly meet your criteria for old."

"It's been here for over a hundred years. That's a lot of time to throw away for something slicker and shinier. This house was standing when Teddy Roosevelt was charging up San Juan Hill. No new house can make that claim."

"No." Guilt sliced at her heart, but she wasn't advocating tearing the place down. She just wanted to live somewhere else.

"I'm glad you bought it," he went on, twisting the knife. "It needs somebody who'll take the time to care for it, who won't rush in and change it into condos."

"I'm not sure I'm going to keep it," she felt bound to admit. "It's not really right for us."

"Your mom loves it."

"She loves anything that looks haunted."

"Jenny seemed interested."

"The house just isn't us."

"You seem afraid."

She tried to laugh, but the sound echoed strangely in the small garage. "What's there to be afraid of?"

His gaze seemed to envelop her, inviting her to drown in his eyes and find peace. But wasn't that how predators mesmerized their prey?

"Nothing." He paused to wipe some liquid off the motor. "Don't fight it. The fates intend this house to be yours."

A sound halfway between a gasp and a laugh escaped her lips. "What are you talking about?" she asked, broadly gesturing with her arms. As she did so, unfortunately she bumped some shelves along the wall. A bottle of bug spray fell and overturned an oil can, which caused a chain reaction that didn't end until a bag of lawn fertilizer toppled over and hit the open door. In seeming slow motion, the door moved on rusting, creaky hinges until it shut with a resounding thud.

Holly groaned. Another first-class performance for his benefit. Was the house, the move or his presence having this effect on her? "I'm not usually this clumsy," she pointed out, righting all the spilled containers. "It's just that I've had a long string of full days the past few weeks."

"It just shows you need this house," he said simply. "Pokagon will heal your wounds."

"Is that right?" she snapped. "Well, it just so happens I have no wounds, and if I did they'd be healed by central air conditioning, aluminum siding and every other maintenance-free feature known to man. If I barely have time enough to be a mother to Jenny, I certainly don't have time enough to play nursemaid to some old house."

Suddenly both angry and ashamed of her outburst, Holly turned to leave. She pulled at the door. It stuck. Clenching her jaw, she pulled harder. Fighting a growing panic, she grabbed the knob with both hands and pulled with all her strength. The door didn't budge, not even a hair.

Chapter Two

Zach stepped forward, drawn by the sudden tension in Holly's eyes, but he stopped when that tension was replaced by fear. What was she so afraid of?

"I want this door opened," she said. "And I want it opened now."

He raised his hands in a gesture of surrender. "I didn't close it." He tried the door anyway, slowly twisting the doorknob. "It's broken. No matter which way you turn it, the latch won't move."

Holly gasped softly. The sharp lines of her tension melted into a pale mask of weariness and Zach felt an inexplicable urge to hold her, to chase away the shadows that haunted her heart. He didn't move, though. He hadn't grown up on a farm without learning that a frightened colt had to be lured, not chased.

"The door's been this way for a while," Zach commented. "It only works from the outside."

"That could be dangerous," Holly pointed out. "Why hasn't it been fixed?"

"I don't know."

"You don't know? I can't believe it." Sarcasm dripped from her words, thick and slow, like sap from a sugar maple. "I was sure you were going to blame it on a ghost."

"Ghosts aren't responsible for the house being in disrepair. The owner is."

She looked stung, as if his words had been more than a casual comment. "Give me a break," she said. "I just got here. You can't blame this on me."

He allowed a gentle smile onto his lips. "I never intended to."

She looked away and he gave her breathing room, finishing his chores. He checked the oil level in the car, then closed the hood. Holly stamped her booted feet lightly and hunched herself deeper into her coat.

"Cold?" he asked.

She shook her head. "No, this is a down coat. It's quite warm."

A polite lie, he suspected, though cold wasn't likely to be causing the faint shadows he saw in her eyes. "I have a blanket in the trunk," he said as he wiped his hands on a rag. "You can sit in the car and wrap yourself in it, if you want."

"All I want is to get out of here."

"We will."

"How?"

Zach shook his head. "Trust me." He ventured closer, leaning next to her against his car and taking hope when she didn't move away. "Look, you were brought here for a reason, and I doubt it was to freeze to death in the garage."

Holly rolled her eyes heavenward. "How reassuring."

Zach pretended affront at her mocking tone. "You're not taking this seriously."

"And you are?"

"Pokagon was renowned for his healing and his wisdom. Maybe you're here because you're hurting and you need him."

"And he figured getting numb from the cold would be a cure." She ran her fingers through her short brown hair, rearranging the disarray. "Besides, I'm not."

"Not cold or not hurting?"

"Neither."

Her beautiful, soft features had turned rigid, so he tried another route to find her smile. "If you aren't in need of Pokagon's care, maybe you were brought here to restore his house. You're not going to wreck it so that somebody can put up a video store, are you?"

"This was his house?"

"A great-grandson built it, but Pokagon's ancestors used to live in this spot, too." He moved slightly closer, nudging her with his elbow ever so gently. "But you haven't answered my question."

She took a deep breath, closed her eyes for a long moment and then let the breath out. "I'm sure there are zoning regulations to prevent that kind of thing."

"But what if you were allowed to?" he persisted. "Would you?"

"No," she snapped.

Zach leaned back again, smiling. Anger, impatience, anything, was better than the fear he'd sensed in her earlier. "Then Pokagon will take care of us."

"But in our lifetime?"

He chuckled, but his rolling laughter didn't reflect the unexpected protectiveness in his soul. Ruth had told him that Holly had been working hard—too hard, according to her mother—and he could believe that. Holly seemed the dedicated type, which was all well and good, except that she didn't seem to know how to relax.

The silence settled over them, hanging lightly about their shoulders like a down comforter. Holly's beauty called to something deep inside him. She stirred as if she felt the strength of his thoughts and stepped away from his car.

"Can't we go out a window?" she asked.

"Nope." He shook his head. "The previous owners put those burglar gates on them. You can't get through them."

Her body began to cry out its tension again, from the glare in her eyes down to the impatient tap of her boot on the garage floor.

"Relax," Zach said.

"I can't," she snapped. "I have a lot of things to do and can't afford to spend the afternoon locked up in a garage."

He decided then and there that Holly definitely needed his help. She was a woman of gentle curves and dancing curls, but life had left battle scars on her soul that reflected in her eyes. She needed to learn to laugh, to relax and enjoy the gifts life surprised you with along your journey. He'd plan out a course of action for her and start lessons immediately.

"Holly?" someone outside called.

Zach sighed. It looked as though immediately would have to wait. Ruth was banging on the door.

"Holly? Are you in there?"

"Mother!" Holly rushed over and shouted through the windowpane. "Mother, open the door."

"What are you two doing in there?" Ruth asked.

"Open the door," Holly shouted. "The knob is broken and it won't open from the inside."

"Your mother's locked inside with Zach," Ruth told Jenny as loud giggles penetrated the garage.

Holly pounded at the door. "Mother, please open this up."

Ruth finally did and quickly came inside, Jenny following close behind. "Good heavens, Holly," Ruth said. "This certainly isn't like you. You should have been more careful."

"I told her Pokagon would take care of everything," Zach told them. "But she didn't believe me."

Jenny burst into laughter, but Holly looked close to losing what little of her temper she had left, so Zach backed off.

"I'm glad you're all here together," he interjected. "I'd like to take all of you out for dinner tonight to celebrate the New Year and your new home."

"That's very kind of you," Ruth gushed. "We'd be happy to come."

Jenny was looking at her mother.

"I know the best restaurant," he went on. "They have great fried chicken and homemade pie." Jenny's resolve was visibly breaking. "Cherry and pumpkin."

"Can I have ice cream on my cherry pie?" she asked shyly.

"Two scoops," he replied, then turned to Holly, waiting for her response.

"Thank you. It would be very nice," she said carefully.

Her manner was polite but a stiffness in her back told him she wasn't thrilled about being maneuvered into agreement.

"I'll pick you up around six-thirty," he said.

"Let's change into something nice." Ruth took her granddaughter by the hand. "That is, if you two can manage to stay out of trouble on your own."

Jenny giggled as they left the garage, her hand in her grandmother's as she talked excitedly about the house.

Zach stared for a moment after them. The sense of trust and love between Jenny, Ruth and Holly was obvious, almost a living thing that enveloped them.

Zach knew a moment of sadness. What would it be like to have someone who belonged to you, who knew all your strengths and your weaknesses and loved you not in spite of them but because of them? Someone to make dinner for. Someone to dream with. Someone he could wear his grungiest clothes in front of and who'd still think he was the handsomest man on earth. It had been a long time since he'd even thought about it, longer since he'd wished it for himself. Holly's movement brought him back to the present.

She stopped in the doorway and turned to him. "Have you been locked in the garage before?"

Zach nodded slowly, shaking off his moodiness. Being alone was his choice and he was used to it. "A few times."

"Did you just wait for someone to come by and let you out?"

He shrugged.

Suspicion moved boldly to the front of Holly's beautiful blue eyes. "What did you do?"

"I chanted an old Indian prayer," he replied.

"Is that all?"

Zach walked over to Holly. "No. Then I touched this sacred little button here."

The grinding noise of the automatic door opener filled the garage. Thunderclouds filled Holly's eyes, turning their heavenly blue to storm gray. She spun around, slamming the door behind her.

"I feel like such a fool," Holly muttered, sitting on the wooden radiator cover, the only place to rest in the empty living room. "I don't see how I can face that man again."

"Relax, Holly," Ruth said. "You've hardly ever been in a garage before. It was perfectly natural that you'd forget there was a big door."

"In a garage and forget there's a garage door?" Holly felt worse than embarrassed; she felt idiotic. She was obviously in need of more than ghostly assistance. "I don't think I'll go out to dinner with you tonight. Just say I'm tired or something."

"What good will that do? You can't avoid him for the rest of your life. The man lives in the same house as we do."

As a diversionary tactic it worked wonders. "Ah, yes, the house," Holly said. "The 'four-year-old house' that looks more like a hundred years old."

Ruth had the grace to look sheepish. "I know this isn't the kind of house we talked about," she admitted. "But as soon as I saw the place, I knew it was for us."

Now that she'd started, Holly couldn't back down. "Mother, have you noticed all the work it needs? We could spend every waking minute fixing this place up."

"It's not that bad," Ruth scoffed. "A little paint here and there and it'll be great."

"A little paint?"

"This is a solid, substantial house, meant to stand for generations. Just like the houses on Lawndale Avenue that I used to see on my way home from the bakery."

Ruth's voice was soft, her eyes seeing a distant time, but then suddenly she returned. "You probably don't remember them," she said briskly. "You didn't come to the bakery much once we moved onto Pulaski Street."

"No, I didn't." The bus ride had been long and Holly had spent most of her weekends baby-sitting neighborhood kids. But she did remember the old Victorian houses on Lawndale. Built with gray limestone or brick, they certainly were substantial and had yards that looked like the rolling meadows of an English country house to a little girl who'd always lived in third-floor walk-ups. She also remembered vowing one sweltering night, when her mother had returned, hot and exhausted, to their stifling apartment, that someday they'd have a house like that.

Holly frowned into the darkness of the yard. She'd forgotten all about that day until now. It had been Ruth's birthday. Holly had been eleven, so that would have made Ruth—Holly closed her eyes and figured—thirty-three. My age now, Holly thought, causing her conscience to squirm uneasily.

She'd made Ruth a cake, spending hours trying to rival the decorations on the ones Ruth sold all day, and then carefully wrapped the cloisonné initial pin she'd bought for a dollar. "All women love jewelry," the grandmotherly clerk had said. Holly had remembered the golden heart-shaped locket her father had given Ruth for her birthday the year before. Holly had seen her mother holding it and crying late some nights when she'd thought Holly was asleep. They didn't need her father—neither of them did, Holly had told herself as she wrapped the pin. He could stay away and never come back; she didn't care. She would give her mother everything she ever wanted and Ruth wouldn't need to cry again.

By the time Ruth had made it home that day, the apartment had been like an oven. They'd taken their cake out on the front stoop to eat, hoping to catch even the hint of a breeze, and Ruth had told her about the house on Lawndale that was having a party out on the lawn, with brightly dressed people eating ice cream. Holly had known that her little party was the best she could have done, but it wasn't without wistfulness that she lay in bed that night. Someday, she vowed, she'd get her mother a big house and they'd have a birthday party on the lawn. And she'd serve ice cream....

Holly was suddenly having doubts. What difference did it make what kind of house they lived in? If Ruth was willing to supervise the repairs, then it should matter little to Holly. Still, she couldn't escape the fact the house made her uneasy. It seemed to appeal to the little girl in her, to the little girl who still believed in dreams and romance, except that the little girl had long since grown up.

"Mom! Gran! Zach's here!" Jenny called, skipping into the room. Wonder of wonders, she was wearing a dress, but Holly knew enough not to mention it or it would be back to jeans for the next six months.

Zach followed Jenny into the room. He'd changed his slacks and sweater for another set—navy this time, with a white shirt visible at the neckline—and looked even more dashing. "Ready to go?" he asked.

"I guess." The response was not particularly gracious, but it was the best Holly's heart could muster.

She let her mother carry the burden of the conversation as they drove to the Country Manor, a restaurant across the border in Michigan. Once there, Holly found herself seated next to Zach at a table in a corner that seemed warm and cozy. She ordered fried chicken along with everyone else, not because it was what she really wanted, but because suddenly she couldn't think clearly.

The waitress soon returned with their wine, and Zach shifted his position so that his hand was next to hers. She couldn't reach for her water glass without running the risk of touching him.

"Have you forgiven me for the garage?"

"Somewhat."

His eyes grew soft. "I promise I'll never trick you again."

Uncertain what response to make, she said, "I'm not sure you'll have the chance."

"You're not still trying to avoid the inevitable, are you?" His voice grew deeper, and his eyes had relinquished their playful expression.

Holly quickly turned away. She didn't know what his eyes were saying and didn't want to. "I haven't made any decision yet," she said.

He shook his head. "There's no decision to be made."

There probably wasn't, but not in the way he meant. "We'll see about that," was all she said.

Holly saw that he was watching her intently as if he were hoping to read the secrets in her soul, secrets that she herself didn't want to know. She looked over at Ruth and Jenny, hoping to pull them into the conversation. But they were busy reading the chicken jokes on the place mats, effectively leaving Zach and Holly alone. Her eyes flickered back to his and her mouth suddenly went dry.

What was causing the tiny smile that flickered in his eyes? she wondered, and reached for her water glass. Did he find her attractive? The ice water cooled her overactive heart and brought back common sense. He was only flirting with her. Hardly the first time a man had flirted with her, and most likely not the last time. Hopefully not the last time, unless she'd had one too many pieces of cheesecake.

"What do you say we hit the salad bar?" Ruth suggested, and they all followed her across the room. By the time Holly had filled her plate with lettuce and tomatoes, she was feeling herself again.

"Have you lived in the house very long?" she asked Zach as she sprinkled green pepper on her salad.

"Long enough to be glad that you've bought it." He smiled at her. "You're going to be the perfect landlady."

She sent only quick glances his way, keeping her eyes on her salad fixings. "And what's your idea of a perfect landlady, may I ask? One who believes in your ghosts?"

He laughed. "The ghosts can take care of themselves. I don't have to fight their battles for them."

"Whose battles do you fight?" Jenny wanted to know.

"Jenny, you could take something besides applesauce," Holly scolded.

"Mom, applesauce is nutritional and high in fiber. It's better for me than all those calorie-laden salad dressings."

"There is a low-cal dressing," Holly pointed out as she put it on her salad.

"But it has no taste."

Zach chuckled. "Looks like I don't have to fight your battles anyway, Jenny."

"We studied proper nutrition in science last quarter, so I know all the things Mom's been eating that are bad for her."

"None of which we want to hear right now," Ruth quickly told her.

"Aw, Gran," Jenny groaned.

Zach laughed some more, and commented, "I guess I'd better be careful what I eat around her, too."

"Grandma's the worst, but she doesn't care," Jenny said with a sigh as they carried their plates back to the table. "I tell her that chocolate's loaded with bad things, but she keeps eating it anyway. It's getting discouraging."

"Do you see any chocolate on my plate?" Ruth demanded.

Jenny shook her head with such discouragement that Holly expected Zach to laugh once more, but instead he caught Holly's eye and smiled. When the girl went around to her side of the table, Zach stood closer to Holly.

"That's a very caring little girl you have there. You must be proud of her."

Holly wondered if this was part of Zach's flirting or if he really saw how special Jenny was. "I think she's turning out pretty nice," Holly agreed carefully.

Zach pulled her chair out for her. "Were you like that at her age?"

She'd probably been worse, but it wasn't a subject she ever talked about. "Oh, all ten- and eleven-year-old girls are busybodies," she said, forcing a short laugh and digging into her salad.

Zach's attention was all on Jenny, and Holly felt herself relax but was still uneasy that he had asked her about her childhood. She knew her father's desertion wasn't her fault; it was just the kind of man he was. But still, she hated anyone to know. It was a secret, something that as a child she always feared her friends wouldn't understand and something she still couldn't talk about.

For once luck was on Holly's side. Zach didn't prolong the discussion and Ruth kept them amused with stories of her friends in New York until the main courses came.

"Children's fried chicken?" Flashing a bright smile, the waitress put the plate and a bottle of catsup in front of Jenny.

"Thank you," Jenny said, returning the smile.

"You're welcome, honey." The waitress distributed the rest of the chicken, then left.

"She's a good waitress," Jenny said, and poured a huge blob of catsup next to her chicken. "I didn't even have to ask for the catsup."

"Maybe she's a Roman and knows that French fries can't be eaten without catsup," Zach said.

"What does being a Roman have to do with anything?" Jenny asked.

Holly shifted her weight, sliding her chair just fractionally over to the left to distance herself from Zach, as if it could protect her from his questions.

"Didn't you know the Romans invented catsup?" Zach pretended to be surprised. "Then you probably don't know that it was first made with anchovies, not tomatoes."

"Yuck!" Jenny cried.

"I'll second that," Ruth agreed. "And I'm not much of a catsup fan."

Zach went on with his discussion. "Catsup was also sometimes made with mushrooms or cucumbers, and it wasn't until the time of Thomas Jefferson that tomatoes were used."

"Somehow cucumber catsup on French fries doesn't sound right," Ruth said with a laugh.

"Boy, you sure know a lot of things," Jenny said to Zach.

Zach smiled at her and shrugged. "I'm a college teacher and read a lot. But there is a lot I don't know anything about."

"Like what?" Jenny's tone was disbelieving.

"I'm not too good at math," he replied.

"I'm pretty good at it," Jenny confided.

"I thought you must be good at figures," Zach said. "It didn't take you long to figure out what you wanted for dinner."

Jenny giggled into her milk.

Cutting off a piece of meat, Holly put it in her mouth and began chewing slowly, willing relaxation into every inch of her body. There was no reason to get so sensitive, so worried about a simple, innocent question. The move and the house still had her discombobulated. To say nothing of the ghost.

"This is ridiculous, Mother," Holly said as they squirmed into their sleeping bags that night.

"It's fun," Jenny protested.

"It's an adventure," Ruth agreed. "And tons more exciting than using Zach's apartment, as he offered."

"He offered his apartment?" Holly hadn't known that. That was nice of him, even thoughtful. Two things she wasn't sure she wanted him to be. Not that she was hoping for a psycho cabdriver or a member of a motorcycle gang, but a little colder and more aloof might be better. Safer. But she wasn't going to pursue that thought at all.

"Good night, all. Sweet dreams." Holly reached to turn off the light.

"We'll all have wonderful dreams in our new house," Jenny assured her.

"The best ever," Ruth called over to them.

Holly sighed, settling deeper into her sleeping bag. She knew that their first night in their first real home ought to be special, but she'd settle for a decent night's sleep. Tomorrow would be better once the furniture arrived.

Chapter Three

Here you are, fair lady," Zach said. "A touch of the grape to lift the weariness from your shoulders."

Holly brushed the back of her hand across her forehead and sighed. Was it only yesterday morning that the movers had delivered their furniture? It seemed like years since she'd been incarcerated in this medieval prison. They'd hardly made a dent in the unpacking, even with Zach's help. While she had to admit he'd been generous to spend his Sunday unpacking their odds and ends, she wished he was somewhere else. He made her nervous with the piercing quality of his eyes. It was just like her mother to accept his offer, even as Holly was politely refusing, and then assign him to be Holly's assistant.

Holly shook her head at Zach and his proffered glass of wine. "I don't think I should. If I relax now, I won't do anything the rest of the night."

A sympathetic smile warmed his eyes. "We've been unpacking all day. Is it so bad if you stop?"

"No, I really can't—"

"If you don't have a glass I'll have to drink both and it doesn't take much for me to get rowdy and obnoxious."

To her surprise, laughter flowed off her lips and she reached for the glass. After taking a sip of the wine, she leaned back on her heels and stared at the boxes piled about. "Can you believe this?" she said, indicating with a sweep of her hand the mess around the room. "My company paid good money for a complete moving job and I'm still left with this mess to clean up."

"Leave it until tomorrow. I've done my share of moving over the years and learned that the unpacking eventually gets done."

Holly opened another box and began removing tableware. "Did you travel a lot as a child?"

"Mostly from the dinner table when I stomped off in anger."

She looked up in surprise and found him grinning. Her heart told her to smile back, to accept the warmth he was offering, but her lips didn't find it that easy to obey.

"My dad and I didn't exactly get along," he said. "Actually, it wasn't until after high school that I became a wanderer. Went to college in California, then spent two years as a roustabout in the oil fields of Indonesia, six months biking through Europe and then another six months traveling around the world on a tramp steamer. After all of that, I was ready for grad school in Minnesota. Once the assistantships and study were over, I taught in Pennsylvania, Atlanta and London and have spent most of my summers on digs, searching for Indian artifacts."

"And here I had you pegged as a homebody." She unwrapped a bunch of knives, tossing the paper into a pile near the kitchen door.

"I am. Born and raised on a farm just over the Michigan border. I came back to the area a couple of years ago when my dad had a stroke."

"Is he still alive?"

"No. He died last year."

There was something in his voice that made her look up, but he was gathering the old wrapping paper and stuffing it into a plastic garbage bag. She told herself not to read so much into people's voices and took a sip of the wine as she glanced around her. The room was piled with boxes and crates all staring back at her.

"You know," she said, "the worst part of all this unpacking is that I'll have to repack most of this if we decide not to stay." Her doubts had only increased as she saw their furniture being moved in. Maybe Ruth would change her mind once she saw how much work an older home needed.

"Are you still under the misconception that you can leave?" Zach asked, stopping to glance at her.

"Anytime we choose," she said simply, but made the mistake of looking at him. Something lingered in his eyes— a warning, perhaps. Or maybe the warning was coming from her brain, telling her to squelch the little spark that just one look could awaken in her. She turned away, carefully lining up the knives in the drawer. "I'm sure this is a wonderful house, but I'm also sure it's not right for us."

"How can you tell? You haven't given it a chance."

Even his voice seemed able to do strange things to her heartbeat, but that was impossible. She must be tired, she told herself.

"If a pair of shoes doesn't fit, you don't keep wearing them to give them a chance to," she pointed out, and started on the soupspoons. "You find a pair that does."

"Ah, but how do you determine fit? By looking at them in the store window?"

He thought he was going to win this debate, but she could see where he was leading. "Some shoes you can tell won't fit just by looking, like I wouldn't try on baby shoes or men's oxfords. Others you try on, as I've tried this house on for the past forty-eight hours, and then can say they just aren't right."

"But you haven't seen the house in the spring, when the trees are in bloom, or in the summer, when the garden can renew the weariest soul. In the fall the place is a riot of color, and even the winter is great, when you're snuggled up warm and cozy inside while a storm is raging outside."

She refused to be moved by the pictures of beauty and security his words painted. "You should have bought the place yourself. Of course, you're likely to get another chance at it soon."

"Some of us weren't meant to own houses," he told her.

She had emptied the box and risked glancing at him. He was gazing at his glass, swirling the wine gently around and around. "That's a strange remark," she said. "Is there a law against you buying a house?"

He looked up, a grin on his lips that touched her heart. "Yep. Pokagon's law."

Holly groaned aloud. "Boy, you never give up, do you?"

"Mom?" Jenny flew into the room. "Do you know where I packed my backpack? I can't find it anywhere."

"Maybe Pokagon borrowed it," Zach joked.

Holly had had enough about the remarks and seen enough of his smile that seemed to make her heart turn somersaults. "Would you stop with the ghost already? Or do you enjoy scaring small children?"

"It's not scary, Mom," Jenny insisted. "I know there's no such thing as a ghost. Besides, I'm not a small child. I was the fourth tallest in my class."

"Yeah, but were you the toughest?" Zach asked.

"No, Megan Margaret Kennelly was. She's got a terrific bolo punch, but I could handle everyone else."

"Jenny!" Holly exclaimed, unable to hide the shock in her voice.

A look of tired patience covered her daughter's face. "Mom," she said. "It's a tough world out on those mean streets."

Stumped for a reply to that bit of fifth-grade wisdom, Holly jumped on Zach's chuckle with extra vigor. "I don't need that kind of help in raising my daughter."

"Hey," he said, lifting his hands in supplication. "I had nothing to do with Megan Margaret Kennelly. I don't even know what a bolo punch is."

"It's when you move your arm like this," Jenny said, moving her right arm in a complete circle, "and bop the other person on the top of the head."

Holly thought that somehow this whole discussion had gotten out of hand, like so many things around here lately. "Jenny, I think you'd better get ready for bed. I'm sure your backpack will turn up."

"Okay." Her voice resigned, Jenny shuffled up the stairs toward their second-floor bedrooms.

Zach's body filled the doorway behind Holly. Even without looking, she could feel his gaze on her. Her mouth seemed suddenly dry, her hands damp and sweaty. "I'll be up in a few minutes to tuck you in," she called to Jenny. *Change quickly so I can escape soon,* she added silently.

"That's all right," an uncooperative Jenny called back. "I can handle any ghosts that come around."

"Resourceful little lass you have there," Zach noted with a grin.

Holly wanted to smile back, which only proved how tired she really was. "We both know the best way to deal with the spirits is to deny their existence," she informed him. Maybe the best way to deal with Zach, too.

"Except that you can't deny Pokagon's existence. He was a real person, respected by both Indians and settlers in the area."

Zach had the most wonderful voice. It was soft but had a resonance that seemed to stroke her tensions away. She wanted to close her eyes and lie back, listening to it forever, which was just what she couldn't do. She pulled open a box of dishware.

"Well, I certainly hope Mr. Pokagon's eternal reward was adequate."

"Depends on what you believe in. Does having several streets, a few townships and even a county named after you count as eternal reward?"

She laughed, an unexpected chuckle that couldn't be denied. "It's not what I'm hoping for," she said.

"No?" He came closer, reaching into the box to hand her a plate. "Guess I'll have to scrap the plans to change the name of the street."

She hesitated, not certain that she wanted to unpack this box with him. What was to stop her silly heart from racing just because he was close by? But tomorrow was Monday and she had to start organizing her office. If she didn't finish unpacking tonight, the boxes would be around until next Saturday.

"Might as well," she said, and took the plate from his hands.

He didn't bother to ask whether she was replying to his statement about the street name or his offer of help, but he pulled out two more plates. "If you don't believe the gods brought you here, tell me why you think you came."

Holly looked up wearily. Just this box and then she was turning in. There were only so many explanations she could make in one day.

"I'm starting a branch office for my company," she said simply.

"Is that what your job is—moving around the country starting offices?" His voice was curious and politely interested but still somehow managed to tease her soul.

Holly yawned to show just how unaffected by his presence she was. "No. This is our first move. It's a big promotion for me and a lot is riding on my success."

"Ah, a dedicated career person."

He wasn't quite mocking her, but the old inner battle between motherhood and career reared its head. "I'm trying to take care of my family," she said sharply. "I'm all they have, so it's up to me to do the best I can."

"Hey, I wasn't criticizing," he told her, taking hold of her shoulders and turning her to face him. For once the laughing gleam was gone from his eyes. "I admire all you've done. You have to be a pretty strong person to wear all the hats you're wearing in your life. And then to be successful at them, too—it's nothing short of a miracle."

His eyes told her to relax, to not be so prickly, and she had no choice but to obey. "I'm not really sure how successful I am at any of my various roles," she admitted with a nervous laugh.

"Jenny's a great little kid," he pointed out. "And you must be doing something right to earn your big promotion out to South Bend."

"I guess." But why did there seem to be empty holes in her life all of a sudden?

"I'm not quite as dedicated to my career as you are," he said. "But I do have some goals I'm determined to accomplish."

The return of his smile warned her not to pursue the line of his conversation, but she seemed to have no choice in the matter. "Oh?"

He nodded, his warmth deepening until it danced in his eyes. "I'm determined to make you smile."

Holly stared into his eyes, at the fire that flickered in their depths, and struggled for the proper answer. "I smile sometimes," she said slowly, then thought how silly that sounded. "I smile a lot. It's just that—"

"I know. Your days have been busy and you're tired. But Pokagon isn't sure that's the only reason you're so serious. He said I have to keep trying."

"Oh, did he?" She should stop this ridiculous conversation. She should move away from the power of his eyes that both drew and frightened her. But still she stayed, loosely held by his hands. "And just how does he communicate with you? By—"

"Holly." Ruth came in, breaking into Holly's words and thoughts. "What do you say we call it quits? Let's send out for a pizza and find a basketball game on TV."

Normalcy returned with a crash around Holly's shoulders and she pulled from Zach's touch. What was she doing enjoying his nearness like that?

"You'll stay, won't you, Zach?" Ruth went on.

Holly's mouth opened to speak, to come up with some excuse—no matter how lame—to escape, but Zach broke in. "I'm sorry, Ruth," he said. "But I really can't stay much longer. I need to run over to my office to review some notes for a class tomorrow."

"Boy, you kids are real party poopers," Ruth said. "I guess I'll see if I can scrounge up anything in the kitchen."

Ruth left and the sound of her humming floated back to where Holly and Zach stood. The silence stretched until it was almost painful. What would have happened if her mother hadn't walked in at that moment? Holly wondered. Would Zach have kissed her? Had she wanted him to? All she wanted now was to be alone to rebuild her defenses.

"I'd better get to sleep," Holly said. "I really do have a busy day tomorrow."

"Me, too," he said. "Good night."

"Good night. Thanks for all your help today." She turned, slowly walking toward the stairs.

"Oh, Holly."

She stopped, a sudden quickening to her heartbeat. If just his calling her name had this effect on her, it was absolutely time to flee. "Yes?"

"Legend has it if you take care of Pokagon, he'll take care of you."

"I think I'm doing all right on my own," she said.

That potent smile curved his lips. "Are you?"

It could have been a simple, innocent question, but she could also read his doubt. Maybe a sudden quiver in her own soul told her that all her righteous speeches of independence were about to be toppled. The time for dignity had passed. It was the moment for retreat.

"Good night, Dr. Philips." She ran up the stairs.

Damn. Holly knew it was just a branch rubbing against her window, but the groaning sound was enough to make a zombie nervous. She rolled on her back, eyes wide open, to stare at the ghostly fingers of the tree branches that the moonlight cast on her ceiling. More than the groaning tree branch outside was keeping her awake. The old house was a virtual symphony of sounds—floors creaking even though no one was walking on them, wind whistling through cracks around the windows. This place ought to be a real zoo on Halloween, when the entire population of the spirit world dropped in to visit, Holly thought.

"Stop it, stop it, stop it," she muttered, out loud now. "No more ghosts. I am not going to think about ghosts anymore."

She clasped her hands behind her head. Work, that's what she'd think about. All the planning and plotting she had to do before the branch office would be ready. She'd be so busy that she wouldn't have time to act like a silly teenager over Zach.

Zach. Another item for the list of things she was not going to think about. Sighing, she sat up and swung her legs over the side of the bed, her feet recoiling momentarily from the smooth cold floor. If they were going to stay here, the first thing she'd do would be to cover these floors. She'd ignore Ruth's objections to masking the beauty of the beautiful old oak floors and cover them with soft, warm carpet.

She walked to the window, the creaks and groans of the floor marking her passage. "Will you be quiet?" she muttered. Certain religions believed in spirits inhabiting inanimate objects. Well, it wasn't her fault that some spirits were doomed to be floors.

What was with her tonight? she wondered, wrapping her arms around her chest. She was seeing demons and spirits everywhere. It's this stupid old house, she decided.

How was she going to convince Ruth to sell it? Maybe the best Holly could hope for was that it would collapse one day and she could use the insurance money to buy a real house. One that real people, not ghosts, could live in.

Looking out the window, she made a face at the bright moon. There was little chance the old hulk would topple over. It had stood on its stone foundation for over a hundred years and would probably stand another hundred.

Her gaze drifted down toward the garden, taking in the mounds of snow under which Zach said were statues. A soft smile touched her lips. Zach was right: a person could enjoy a garden like that in the summer. She quickly banished that thought with a frown. He was not going to enter her thoughts again.

A police car moved slowly down the back alley, and Holly was glad to see that the alleys, as well as the streets, were patrolled. She remembered how excited Jenny had been about the alley, calling it their little street in back. They hadn't had alleys in their New York neighborhood.

Suddenly, Holly frowned. Tomorrow was Jenny's first day of school. If only this job opportunity had come up last summer, then Jenny could have started her new classes at the beginning of the school year instead of after Christmas vacation.

Holly sighed. Jenny was a resourceful girl who did well in school. She should catch up with her classmates in no time flat. She might even be ahead of them already, since she'd done well in her school in New York. But what if her intelligence and good preparation worked against her? She could be a top student but totally friendless. Holly's heart was close to aching with worry for her daughter.

"Stop it," she scolded herself once more. Jenny was made of the same solid stock as herself. They both were tough and adaptable. Her daughter would march into that school wearing her favorite blue sweater and wow her—

Suddenly Holly froze in horror and clasped her hands to her head. "Oh, no." With all the turmoil of moving, neither she nor Ruth had washed clothes for days. Jenny's favorite sweater was in the laundry, waiting to be washed.

Holly turned on the light and began searching for her slippers. Some manager she was turning out to be. She went tongue-tied over the first handsome man who smiled at her and forgot half of her household responsibilities.

After frantically digging through boxes for several minutes in search of her slippers, Holly gave up. It was after two o'clock in the morning. She had to wash and dry some clothes and get some sleep before daybreak. Slippers were not a necessity.

She had to remind herself of that fact about every other step as she padded over first the cold floor of the bedroom, stairs and hallway, then the tiled floor of the kitchen. She stopped at the entryway to the basement and swallowed hard. The steps were as broad and wide as the stairs to the second floor above them, but the similarities ended there. Holly imagined that these stairs probably had hundreds of spiderwebs clinging to them and at this time of night all those spiders would be crawling about on the floor, looking for victims. A little voice told her to go upstairs and ask Zach to come down and show her how to use the washer.

"Not on your life," Holly announced, and grabbing the railing to steady herself, she started down into the dragon's darkened lair.

She was not going to let this basement defeat her. Jenny needed her favorite sweater for school and Holly would wash it for her. The demons and spiders of the house were no match for a mother. Clenching her jaw tight, she forced her reluctant feet down the stairs and over to the cabinet at the bottom of the laundry chute.

Zach quietly eased the front gate closed behind him, although there was no need for such care. The old house's walls were so thick he'd have to shoot a cannon in the front yard for anyone inside to hear it. But old habits were hard to break, and silent walking was one he'd had for a long time.

"Your mom's sleeping, kids. Keep it down," his dad had said a hundred times a day back when he and Zach had still been on speaking terms. Zach had then been around Jenny's age.

He and his brother and sister hadn't been noisy, but their mother had slept so lightly that the slightest noise would awaken her. They all knew that sleep was her only escape from the pain, her only source of replenishing her meager supply of strength, so the whole family gladly held their breath while she dozed. Not that she ever complained if they woke her. She always insisted their company was what she needed, that Zach's jokes made her feel better than twelve hours of sleep.

Pausing a moment, Zach gazed up toward the darkened windows of Holly's room. In a way, Holly reminded him of his mother, though the pain reflected in their eyes came from different sources. His mother's was from cancer, but what was causing Holly's?

She was hard to read. It wasn't that she was exactly cold, but there was a certain reserve about her. She didn't like to talk about herself or even admit that she was hurting inside. Maybe her husband's death still hurt. Ruth had said it had been five years since he died, but Holly might not be over it yet. Or maybe it was the strain of being a single parent and worrying over giving your child all she needed. Either way, Zach felt for her and wished he could replace that sorrow in her eyes with a smile.

It would give him something besides the moroseness that seemed to shadow his heart these past few months to concentrate on. Oh, he teased and laughed as much as ever—the mask had been in place too many years for it to slip now—but the laughter didn't quite seem to reach his soul anymore. Must be time to leave. Two years in one place was a long time for him. That was why the hours outside of work seemed so empty. He needed something new and fresh in his life, and that meant Paris. His application for a visiting professorship should have been processed long ago, and he should be getting the good word soon.

Zach stopped, his hand on the doorknob, a puzzled frown stopping his thoughts. A sliver of light shone under the other door leading into the back vestibule of the house. Had someone forgotten to turn the lights off?

He started up the back stairs to his apartment, then stopped after two steps. Maybe there was a problem. That boiler could be mighty cantankerous if you didn't know how to coax it into running. He let himself into the vestibule.

It was dark beyond the kitchen, so Zach turned toward the basement. Lights were on and he could hear sounds almost like the old washing machine grinding away. But no one would be washing clothes at two in the morning. He'd better check it out.

When Zach reached the door to the laundry room, he stopped in midstride. There was Holly sitting on a cement block next to the washing machine, staring off into space. Her hair was tousled and her bare feet were dusty from the dirt of the basement floor. Her face, scrubbed clean of all makeup, had a little-girl look of innocence.

Zach stared, almost afraid to breathe, fearing that the sound would destroy the magical moment. After a long minute, he decided it wasn't fair to intrude on Holly like this and cleared his throat loudly.

"Hi," he said.

Holly shrieked and jumped to her feet, snatching up an old broom handle. "Don't come near me." Recognition drove out the fierce and brought back the tired to her face. "Oh, it's you." The broom handle lowered to half-mast.

"This isn't New York City," he pointed out. "You can put that thing down."

"Why are you sneaking around?"

The little-girl innocence was gone from her face, completely covered by street-urchin tough. Zach fought a smile and finally won the battle, but only by a whisker. "Look, I've lived here for a couple of years and know how most of this equipment works. I saw the light on and thought somebody might need some help."

"Oh, yeah? What kind of help?" The tone was still street tough, but the expression was slowly changing to streetwise wary, and the broom handle went all the way down.

He allowed himself a smile but tried to keep it gentle. "My social life isn't desperate. I don't have to attack women in basement laundry rooms."

She put the broom back up against the wall. "Then don't go sneaking up on people," she said, an obvious attempt to salvage a little pride.

"I just walked down the stairs."

"Everything creaks around here. I would have heard you if you just walked down."

"They're cement," he said, pointing to the steps. "Indiana concrete doesn't creak."

Suddenly she sighed with sheepish embarrassment and flopped back onto the cement block. "I guess you can take the girl out of the big city, but you can't take the big city out of the girl. I've always been a bit suspicious." She nodded toward the washing machine. "I was washing Jenny's clothes. Tomorrow's her first day of school."

"Are all her clothes dirty?"

"Her very favorite blue sweater is."

"I see." When Holly let down her big-city veneer she looked vulnerable, not at all the self-assured businesswoman or the streetwise tough she usually put forward. He felt a stirring in his heart, deeper than expected, and wanted to stay.

"I guess you don't need my help," he said, hoping for her disagreement.

Holly shook her head. "No, my load's spinning now. After that's done, I'll stick the clothes in the dryer and head for bed."

His feet seemed unwilling to move. "I'll be heading upstairs then."

A crooked smile broke the thin line of her lips. "Sorry about the misunderstanding."

He could tell her smile was brought about by embarrassment, not joy. "You needn't have worried," he said. "Pokagon's got your best interests at heart."

Her grin died and so did the intimacy of the moment. "Good night, Zach." She turned to fiddle with the washing machine.

He wanted to say something soft, not quite an apology, but the steely stiffness of her back didn't invite further conversation. He turned and went upstairs. No use pushing anything now. He'd had a peek through the crack of her rigid control and that was a victory for him. He'd widen the crack another time. Besides, he didn't do his best work in laundry rooms.

Chapter Four

But the plans have already been approved by our corporate architect,'' Holly protested.

"You folks ought to get yourself a new architect, ma'am. The one you got ain't doing you right.''

Her first morning on the new job and she was spending it staring at the two tradesmen standing in her deserted office space. Her eyes went from Slim to Shorty. They shared a single smile between them and right now it was Slim's turn to carry it.

"I don't understand,'' she said. "The designs are according to code but they're not right?''

"There's a right way to do things and there's a stupid way,'' Shorty interjected, his features sagging under the enormous load of patience he was carrying. "And your architect picked stupid nine times out of ten.''

Holly shook her head and sighed. This move was supposed to be simple, but so far nothing had been easy, and today didn't look as though it was going to break the pattern. Tradesmen who wouldn't follow architectural plans if they didn't like them, old houses that creaked in the night, handsome cabdrivers who turned into handsome college professors...

"Look, I have to talk this over with my boss," she said. "I'll explain your concerns and see what he says."

Her decision seemed to satisfy them, at least for the moment, and they went back to laying subflooring. Unfortunately Holly had nothing to go back to. The lone desk in the place held only a telephone and the much-maligned blueprints. This left only her thoughts to occupy her time and they were too full of a certain male acquaintance to suit her.

She glanced at her watch; her boss wouldn't be available for another few hours. She might as well take that order over to the printers, then go home to pick up her files and review her personnel needs.

It sounded like a brisk, time-consuming plan for her first morning on the new job, but the stop at the printers took barely a half hour. As she pulled out of the printers' parking lot, she wondered if she should give Zach a bit longer to leave the house.

But that was a ridiculous thought, and the implication behind it was even more ridiculous. She wasn't afraid of Zach. Instead of going home, though, she ought to look at cars; she couldn't keep this rental one forever. Not that she was sure she was up to buying her first car. She hadn't even thought about what she wanted in a car and certainly didn't know what she needed. The traffic light switched from yellow to red, causing her automatic pilot to put a foot to the brake.

Snow covered her side-view mirror, so Holly rolled down the window and was rewarded with the sound of church bells pealing in the distance. She paused and smiled. Those were real bells, not an electronic gadget. She hadn't heard real church bells in ages. Her eyes closed and the sense of tradition, of history and permanence, surrounded her.

Then the jarring honk from the car behind brought her back to reality. "What's your hurry?" she muttered. "You want to be a horn jockey, go to Manhattan, where you'll have some real competition."

Holly turned right and the university's broad sports fields opened up around her, rolling off to meet the buildings on the far horizon. A ten-story, glass-and-steel library dominated the campus, although older buildings with beauty of their own refused to retreat to the background. Suddenly Holly was seized by a desire to go walking. A walk had always been good for relieving her tension. It wouldn't be Fifth Avenue, but walking on the university campus would be fun.

She parked near the football stadium and walked on campus. She noticed that the buildings near the center of the campus were older than those on its outskirts. As limestone gave way to yellow brick, a high-steepled church rose before her. The bells were now silent, but broad oaken doors beckoned to her.

The inside looked like a postcard of an old European cathedral. Tall pillars held up a canopied roof that seemed to reach for the sky. The smell of incense and flickering candles spoke of centuries-old rituals. She turned and was overwhelmed by the organ, whose pipes looked almost two stories tall. Feeling uncomfortably insignificant, she hurried outside.

Back out on the steps, Holly paused to let the door shut behind her, filling her lungs with the bitterly cold air. Students hustled along intersecting pathways, seeming oblivious to the towering trees, their empty branches rustling and creaking in the wind. Holly decided that although the campus was nice now, it would really be beautiful in the spring, when all the big trees leafed out and the broad expanse of lawn turned green.

Her eyes misted over slightly and memories of her own college days danced before her. She had been a commuter because the city college hadn't any dorms, not that she could have afforded them anyway. But instead of vast green lawns, there had been cement bunkers for sitting and relaxing. Instead of the worn softness of age, she'd had the stark harshness of modern brick and steel.

Holly sighed. It hadn't really been that bad; she did get an education. But this was the type of school that she wanted

Jenny to attend. Filled with traditions and fun. With football weekends, studying on the lawn and staying up all night to giggle, eat pizza and discuss Kafka.

Seized with a wave of nostalgia, Holly moved down the steps and looked at the church's cornerstone: 1871! This building was over a hundred years old. Their country wasn't yet a century old and this church was already here. And not too long afterward, her house was built.

Trying to shake that comparison from her mind, Holly took off briskly down one path, then turned onto another. Just because the age of the church brought her peace, it didn't mean she was changing her mind about the house. It was old and tired, and it was best to find a home that still had some life in its bones.

Holly suddenly found herself in front of the bookstore and she slowed to a stop by a student bulletin board. Tutoring needed. Chemistry book for sale. Campus movies. Some things never changed.

"Picking out a film?" a soft voice near her ear said.

Holly turned to find Zach behind her. She wanted to be annoyed that he'd found her, but somehow a smile formed on her lips instead of a frown. "Just bumming around," she said. "My office is under siege and I decided to go home to do some work." She realized even as she said it that none of that explained her presence here.

"Dare I ask how it was under siege? Your subcontractors breaking windows and making holes in the walls?"

A gaggle of young women pushed past them, knocking Holly up against Zach. The solid feel of him came as no surprise, but the rush of pleasure the contact gave her did. She felt herself wanting to stay there, in the safety of his arms. What was coming over her? she wondered. Her cheeks burned and she pulled slowly away.

"Uh, the siege," she stammered, feeling under siege herself from her errant emotions. She pulled her rapidly unraveling thoughts back under control. "No, the subcontractors think our architect is a jerk."

"Is he?"

She allowed herself a small smile, a reward for keeping her thoughts hidden from Zach. "I don't know, but there's a strong chance he is."

Zach took her arm, pulling her gently away from the bulletin board. Her feet, her legs and her heart followed along willingly, ignoring her mind's mild protest.

"Perhaps what you need," he said as they walked along a sidewalk that ran down the center of the quadrangle, "is a quick course in architecture."

"Know anyone willing to give one?" A gust of wind circled around her, pushing at her back so that she had no choice but to move just a tad closer to Zach. A group of fir trees near the walkway bowed and nodded as they passed.

"As a matter of fact, I do." His eyes were lit with laughter and something warm and inviting and full of promise. "Not that I can teach you lots of details, mind you. But I can point out a flying buttress, show you an arch and explain the art of laying shingles."

"Laying shingles?" She waved her hand at the nearby buildings, three and four stories of majesty and grace...and slate roofs. "You can't tell me that there are regular, ordinary shingles somewhere on this campus."

He grinned and led her around a corner. "Actually the shingle work is a remnant of my colored past. Along with pulling barbed wire and cleaning out a chicken house, it's the reason I'm where I am today."

"I know you grew up on a farm, but you lost me." Snow crunched under her feet, suddenly the warmest, friendliest sound on earth.

"Ever clean out a chicken house after a winter?"

She grinned at him. "Nope. Our chickens never had their own house. They lived in the apartment next to ours."

His eyes were just as teasing, but something in the air changed. "This is your first house?"

Her heart stopped laughing, but she didn't obey its command not to let Zach any closer to her secrets. The real trick to keeping your secrets was not to let on when they were exposed.

"Don't change the subject," she ordered. "What's it like to clean out a chicken house?"

"Disgusting."

His eyes seemed gentle and soothing as if he knew she had deliberately pulled her heart back into hiding.

"Chickens were never my favorite part of farm life," he went on. "Except for eggs in the morning, of course. But cleaning out the henhouse was the worst job. The place would reek after a winter of them staying inside, and it convinced me that I wasn't a farmer."

Holly breathed an inner sigh of relief as he abandoned his probing. There were no more eyes on her soul, no more gentle searching to read the mysteries of her past. "That surprises me," she said. "I would have thought you loved the land. All your talk of healing and Indian lore made me think you would have been natural for an occupation like farming."

He gazed ahead at some students building a huge snowman by the door of a dormitory. "You weren't listening. I do love the land. It was the chickens I hated."

Zach and Holly's laughter danced and flowed. And like a fire their good humor brought a glow to Holly's cheeks and a flicker of contentment to her heart. Then their laughter dwindled into embers and they walked in silence past the snowman and past a group of youngsters escaping from a student tour guide.

"Farms barely support one family these days," Zach said. "And our farm wasn't big enough to split three ways. So my dad made us all learn an occupation. My brother's a geologist in Nigeria and my sister's a schoolteacher, though when she married a farmer it seemed natural for them to take the farm when Dad couldn't work it anymore."

He grinned and was almost back to his former self except for a shadow deep in his eyes. "As I said, I like the land, but I love teaching about its history. I love the solid feel of knowing that I'm part of a long line of men who have toiled and worked and made a life for themselves. But I also love the freedom of not being owned by the farm.

"When I was a kid, I used to get these books out of the library. I don't remember much about them except that the covers were red and white and each one was about a different country. I read the whole series the library had, then I started over again. I was going to explore each and every one of those countries. Southwest Michigan and northwest Indiana were not where life was happening. I haven't seen all those exotic places yet, but I've made a start, and with a little luck my next stop will be Paris in the fall."

She felt her heart fall slightly at the knowledge that he might soon be gone, but at the same time her mind applauded the fact that she'd be rid of one tenant she hadn't wanted in the first place.

"But enough about me," he said. "What do you want to see first? My office, the cafeteria or the place where the students go to party?"

"None of the above, I'm afraid," she said, pulling away from him. Her heart protested, but she ignored the outcry. A pleasant few minutes of conversation was fine, but she wasn't in the market for anything else. She shouldn't give Zach, or her heart, the idea she was. "My break has long since ended. I've got to get going."

"How about if I throw in a tour of the classrooms I've taught in?"

She shook her head and took another step away. "Sorry. Maybe some other time."

"Right." His smile was gracious, his eyes understanding. "I'll see you at home in a little while then."

"Yes." Her feet wanted to run now, but she forced a slow pace. "I'll see you at home." The words were soft, though, too quiet for him to hear. But had her heart viewed them as a promise or a threat?

Holly watched as the garage door slowly closed. If she lived to be a hundred, she would never be able to see a garage door close without imagining a certain college professor bound hand and foot, lying in the door's path, his eyes pleading with her for mercy. She smiled thoughtfully, her eyes narrowing. She might weaken of course, if he pleaded enough, though he'd have to show his repentance in some other form.

Into her mind danced a vision of herself reclining on the sofa before a blazing fire. Zach entered with two glasses of wine, the burgundy catching the flickering of the flames. It seemed he was carrying liquid fire to match the smoldering in her heart. He came closer, his eyes promising delights, his lips in a secret smile—

The garage door hit the floor with its customary thud and Holly awoke from her daydream. This was ridiculous, she told herself, and spinning on her heels she hurried toward the house. She had had one loving relationship and its end had just about devastated her. There was no way she would let herself in for that kind of pain again and she had best remember that.

"Done for the day, dear?" Ruth asked as Holly stepped through the back door.

Holly shook her head. "Our offices are a mess and I thought I'd come home and get my files in order."

"Have you had lunch?"

"No." Holly hung up her coat and took off her boots. "Where did you have the movers put my office files?"

"In the basement. Go and change your clothes. I'll make you an egg-salad sandwich."

"You don't have to make me lunch. And why should I change my clothes?"

"It's a little dusty down there. Is whole wheat okay? I don't have any rye right now."

"Mother, I—"

"That's such a pretty white blouse, Holly. Don't get it all dirty."

Holly sighed and hurried upstairs. Ruth needed to feel needed. If Holly's changing her clothes and eating a sandwich would make Ruth happy, then losing a little time was worth it.

After donning a pair of jeans and an old sweatshirt she started for the stairs, but stopped. The back "servants' stairs" beckoned. Jenny loved using them, but Holly hadn't paid them any attention until now. She peered down them; they were steep, dark and narrow.

Suddenly the stairs took on greater importance. The house was testing her, mocking her, challenging her to prove that she could indeed own all parts of the house, even these back stairs. But could she make it down them? Holly knew it was crazy, but she wanted to try. She wanted to skip down them lightly.

With a frown to help her balance, Holly started down. The steps were too narrow for her whole foot to fit and too steep to allow her to stand on her toes. So she had to turn her foot slightly and go down sideways. She placed both feet safely on one stair before descending to the next one and clutched the rail all the way. But she reached the bottom in one piece, swallowing a giggle of triumph.

"Aren't those stairs fun?" Ruth laughed.

Holly somehow hadn't expected a witness to her silliness. "I thought it would be quicker to take them," she said. "You know, it's shorter than going around."

"Of course, dear," Ruth agreed, her eyes as calm as a lake on a still summer's day.

Holly relaxed, perching on a stool at the kitchen table. Why should she be embarrassed? Her mother had never laughed at her, never made her feel childish, even when she was. Why had she started hiding away little bits of herself like that?

"I wanted to see if my feet were small enough to make it down," Holly admitted, the words rushing out but followed by a grin.

Ruth looked astonished. "Well, of course they're small enough. You have lovely feet. Just right for your height."

Holly's grin grew. "Thank you. There's nothing like a mother's love, is there?"

Ruth brought over the snack plate with Holly's sandwich, cut in triangles and garnished with apple wedges. "I wasn't speaking as a mother. I was speaking truth." She poured them each a cup of tea.

"Yes, Mom." The first bite reminded Holly's stomach that she hadn't eaten since breakfast, and the following bites were gratefully accepted, washed down by the warm tea that took any lingerings of chill from her toes. With warmth came a feeling of euphoria.

She accepted a second cup of tea from Ruth and hunched comfortably forward over the table. The wind was picking up outside and the steam radiator hissed back at the chill in defiance. Holly sipped the tea.

It was silly, but thoughts of Zach made her panic. Well, made parts of her panic. Other parts rather enjoyed daydreaming about him. That was the problem. Good healthy panic would keep her safe, keep her priorities straight, but that ridiculous daydreaming would lead only to trouble. Daydreams led to discontentment, and that would lead to her heart's questioning the path she'd chosen. She had made her choices and wasn't deviating from them.

Listen up, heart, she silently commanded, and stop this foolishness.

"More tea, dear?"

"No, thanks. I still—"

Holly stared dumbly into her cup. It was empty. A momentary confusion twisted her stomach as she looked at her watch. Good Lord. She'd been sitting here, doing nothing but sipping tea, for almost half an hour.

"I have to get at those files," she told Ruth, and brushed her mother's cheek with her lips. "Thanks, Mom."

"For what?" Ruth laughed, and picked up the empty cups.

Holly smiled and hurried downstairs, feeling more like herself again. Everybody needed a little reminding of goals now and then, she thought as she stopped in confusion.

She had been in a few basements in her life, but none had been like this, with five smaller rooms instead of one large one. Straight ahead of her was the laundry area, kept relatively clean by its constant use. To her right and left were other rooms, varying in size and in cleanliness but all loaded with boxes waiting to be unpacked.

She frowned at the closed doors, feeling as though she were on a game show.

"Which will it be—door number one, door number two or door number three?" a voice behind her said.

Holly started as Zach spoke and turned to find him standing halfway down the stairs. The basement shrank in size as he came the rest of the way down. There was nowhere to stand where Holly wouldn't be practically on top of him, where his breath wouldn't tickle her cheek or send prickles down her spine. There were, however, other ways to put distance between them.

"I thought sneaking up on people died after junior high school."

"What do you want me to do?" he asked. His voice was gentle, only lightly teasing. "Holler, blow a horn, stomp my feet?"

A clever retort ought to be poised on the tip of her tongue, but it wasn't. The annoyance she'd tried to manufacture had been quickly melted by a warm glow in her heart. What had happened to her stern resolve? It was time to retreat. She chose the nearest door and pulled it open.

"Ruth said that your boxes are probably in that big room to the right or the small corner room behind you." Holly turned her glance toward Zach. "She also said you needed some help moving stuff."

"I don't need any help." What she needed was to be alone and recover from the potion her mother must have put in the sandwich.

"Mother knows best," Zach said. "Want to check the big room first?"

Holly grimaced in frustration. He was only too likely to be right. These rooms were all packed with boxes and she wouldn't be able to move most of them.

She slammed the door and went over to the large room. Zach followed her. Not so close as to step on her heels, but close enough that she could hear his breath, imagine that it was ruffling the hairs on the back of her neck. Conversation, that's what she needed. Something to distract her thoughts.

"Was this house ever a jail?" she asked as she opened the door.

"Not that I know of. Why do you ask?"

"It has all these creepy little rooms down here. They're dark and strange."

"This is how they had to build basements in the old days."

"Dark and creepy?"

"No," he said, and laughed as he reached past her to turn on a light. "They didn't have steel support beams in those days, so the interior walls in the basement had to support the structure above. The small rooms resulted from that design need. They didn't start out wanting small rooms in the basement."

The room was filled with boxes. It looked as though a giant's blocks had been crammed into a tiny space. The bare light bulbs sent a crazy quilt of light and shadows across the room, bouncing off the cartons into the corners.

"That doesn't explain why they had to make them dark and creepy," she said, peering around the nearest pile. Hangers and kitchen utensils.

"For the family ghosts, I imagine."

Holly glared at him, but Zach had moved off in another direction to look among the piles of cardboard cartons. "Is that one of your office boxes?" he asked, pointing toward a dark brown cardboard file box.

She nodded.

"Looks like most of your stuff is in that far corner," he said. "We'll have to move a few things to get at them."

"A few things?" Stacks of boxes and miscellaneous pieces of furniture, already covered with dust and cobwebs, thoroughly blocked the way.

He smiled at her. "Don't worry. I said I'd handle the heavy stuff."

"How about the spiders?"

This time he laughed mischievously, and Holly couldn't help but grin back at him. Laughing with him was being neighborly, courteous, since he was helping her get her files. No need for panic or daydreams to follow.

"What do you say we move this table out by the stairs for now and then rearrange the boxes to form an aisle into the corner?" he suggested.

"Whatever you say."

"Oh?" His eyebrows rose in mock surprise, and his gaze took on a deeper glow. "Can I hold you to that?"

Even though he was teasing, with laughter toasting his voice, she felt a tightness in her stomach. A warm hunger tugged at her, but her good sense held her back. "Just move the boxes and stuff, kind sir."

"And if I do?"

"I'll renew your lease for another week."

"Such a slave driver," he muttered, but his words were flavored with a smile and a gentle look. He carried the table out to the stairs.

A box of glassware, two cartons of books and seven boxes of miscellaneous treasures later, they had a narrow aisle made to her files in the corner. She squeezed in and went over to them, checking the notes on the outside of each box to find the one she wanted.

"We ought to just move them all out in the open," Zach noted.

He was a few steps back, blocking the aisle. Her heart felt under siege again but she silently scolded it into behaving. "I suppose you're right, though it may be a while until I have a place at work to keep these."

He came in closer, inching around her to pick up the first box. Holding her breath until he was past, she managed to survive, her heart unaffected.

"Do you work at home a lot?" he asked.

Holly took a second, smaller carton herself. "Only as much as I have to."

He put his box down near the foot of the stairs and turned to face her, his eyes curious. "Have to for business or have to for yourself?"

"Do you really think I'd choose to be away from Jenny more than I have to?" she asked, not giving him time to answer as she dumped her box down next to his. "Auto repair parts is a very competitive industry."

"Not like being a professor."

"I didn't say that."

His smile was soft, tender and sympathetic.

"I have to do well at work. I have a lot of people depending on me," she pointed out.

He nodded and started back for another box of her files. She watched his progress there and back, knowing the ones left were too heavy for her. His generous, nondemanding help ate at her in the silence.

"My mother came to live with me and Jenny soon after my husband died," Holly said suddenly. "She'd had a job as a bookkeeper in a small shipping firm, but they let her go to give the job to the boss's cousin. So she moved in with us and takes care of Jenny and the house. I take care of the bills."

He put down the carton, then looked up at her. His eyes were thoughtful but showed no sympathy. "So when do you have time to watch the Knicks' games?"

"What?" She followed his gaze to her sweatshirt. NEW YORK KNICKS was emblazoned across her chest. "Oh, this. It's just a sweatshirt. I'm not a basketball fan. I know nothing about the sport."

"Then why do you wear it?"

"Because my mother bought it for me." She laughed, a hint of nervousness ringing in the sound. "What's all this? Do you question everybody you see wearing an emblem of a sports team?"

"Everybody who works all hours of the day and night, yes. Why did your mother buy it for you if you aren't a fan?"

"Because she thinks I am." Lord, but the man was pushy. "I sit with her while the games are on and she thinks I'm watching them while I read."

He was silent a long time. His eyes had a strange look about them that she couldn't read. The silence made her uneasy, giving her words extra time to echo through her mind.

"I'd appreciate it if you didn't tell her all that," Holly said carefully. "She enjoys talking about the games, but she wouldn't if she knew I didn't share her interest."

She expected him to agree quickly or to teasingly threaten blackmail. Instead, he leaned against the doorway, arms crossed, a frown on his face.

"Why do you protect everyone around you? Is it part of paying the bills?"

"I don't protect everyone," she snapped.

"All right." He shrugged his acknowledgment. "I can see protecting Jenny, but why your mother? Surely she wouldn't shrivel up and blow away if she knew you don't actually watch the basketball games with her."

Holly knew she should tell him to mind his own business, to leave her alone and only move the boxes, but for some reason she felt it was important that he understand. She wanted him to know that she wasn't a busybody who wanted to run everybody's life. She took a deep breath.

"My parents were divorced when I was ten," she said. "We didn't get much help from my father." Holly knew that was a polite way of saying he gave them nothing, but a way that brought no sympathy, no questions. "It was very hard on Mother. There wasn't much I could do but try to make her smile sometimes."

"And it became a habit?"

His voice was too gentle, too understanding, and she was sorry she'd confided in him. She could deal with anger and with teasing; sympathy made her strike out. But this gentleness made her feel weak. She'd built a careful wall around her life but it suddenly seemed to have chinks. Other secrets wanted to leak out; her heart wanted to have someone to lean on for a change. But even as the weariness of fighting dragons on her own came over her, so did her old habit of being strong.

"Isn't most of what we do habits?" she asked lightly.

"Even watching basketball when you hate it?"

She shook her head, settling the bricks back in place and sealing up the chinks. "I don't hate it. I just don't understand it. I've never had the time to learn what the game is all about."

"I see."

He seemed willing to let things slide, and for that Holly was grateful. He went to get the last two boxes, then replaced the table he'd moved.

"Anything else? Want these upstairs?" he asked.

"No, this is fine." The boxes were up against a wall and out of the way. "I think I'll just leave them here until my office is organized."

"Okay." He glanced at his watch. "Guess I'd better get to those papers my first-year students gave me today. I'll see you at seven."

He was halfway up the stairs before she had a chance to speak. "At seven? What's at seven?"

He turned, grinning down at her. "There's a women's basketball game at the university tonight. We'll take Jenny and I'll give you your first lesson in basketball theory."

"But—"

"Better learn something. One of these days Ruth is going to expect an answer to one of her questions."

He was gone and Holly was left to kick at her files in disgust.

"Can I go down, Mom? Please?"

Children were already running onto the floor for the halftime free-throw shooting contest. Holly smiled down at her daughter's earnest face and nodded.

"Be careful," she called out as Jenny raced down the steps.

"How was her first day at school?" Zach asked.

"Okay. She said the teachers were nice." Jenny really hadn't said much else.

Holly turned slightly, her eyes following Jenny as she chased after a loose basketball. "Do they do this at the boys' games, too?" Holly asked.

"No," Zach said, his gaze on her as if reading all the things in her heart. "There's too much of a crowd."

Panic tightened her stomach at the tenacity of his gaze. "Well, what about those lessons you were supposed to be giving? You know, about basketball," she added, just in case he thought she wanted lessons in something else.

He smiled and turned his attention to the court below. "See that orangy-brown round thing? That's the basketball. And those stringy things hanging from those orange circles are the baskets."

"I knew that already," she pointed out. "I'm not that dumb."

"I never thought you were," he argued. "But you said you knew nothing of the game."

"All right, I don't know some of the finer points."

His eyes met hers again. A flickering that seemed to come from his soul called to her. "Know what a fast break is? That's when the team with the ball comes down the court so fast that the other team can't protect its basket."

Similar to how she'd felt around him lately? Her heartbeat sped, her hands grew hungry for another hand to hold. One larger than hers, stronger, too, that could protect and soothe and also bring laughter. She shoved her hands in her pockets.

"Then there's a steal, when someone's careless in guarding the ball and the other team takes it away."

As she'd been careless in guarding her heart? Except he hadn't managed to steal it away, and now that she was on the alert, he wouldn't ever get it.

"It's Jenny's turn in the free-throw contest," she told him, watching as the official running the contest tossed a ball to Jenny.

"And then there's a time out," Zach said softly. "When the players get a chance to breathe."

Holly refused to look at him. Besides, the quick glance out of the corner of her eye told her he was watching Jenny. The girl made a few baskets but missed most, then trudged back up to her seat and plopped down between them.

"Those other kids are good. I'm going to have to practice." Jenny's face was determined.

"Why?" Holly asked. "Are they giving diamonds for a prize and you want to win next time?"

"There's a fifth and sixth grade girls' basketball team at school," Jenny told her. "The season's already started, but the coach said they could always use another good player."

"I see." So that was the reason for the determination. Making the team would mean acceptance.

"Can you help me practice, Mom?"

"I've never played basketball, honey."

There was only a little break in Jenny's smile, but Holly knew that her daughter was crestfallen. Holly had failed her and it hurt. She had a right not to have played basketball; she'd worked all through high school and college. But the taste in her mouth still said "failure."

"I've already started teaching your mother about the game," Zach said. "I could probably take on another student."

Jenny's face lit up like Times Square. "You will? Oh, boy. Mom, did you hear that?"

Common sense and the desire to make Jenny happy tore at her heart, but common sense won. "We really shouldn't impose on Zach. He does have his own work."

Zach shrugged off her objection. "My hours are flexible and there's a basketball net over the garage. When the weather's good we can practice there. Otherwise there's always a free court around here. All we need is a basketball."

Jenny's eyes pleaded with Holly, her youthful hands clenched in her lap in silent supplication. Holly didn't stand a chance and gave in graciously.

"You mean one of those orangy-brown things?" she asked with a grin. "If you're going to give up your time to help Jenny, the least I can do is get her a basketball."

"This is great," Jenny exclaimed. "Don't you think we ought to have some popcorn to celebrate?"

Holly laughed and gave her some money, watching as the girl flew down the stairs again.

"I guess there won't be any problem with your schedule?"

He shook his head, his eyes following Jenny for a moment, then he turned back to Holly. "If there was, I'd change it. Some of my greatest memories are of my father teaching me basketball," he said.

"I thought you two didn't get along."

"That was later, after my mom died." His voice was different than it usually was. The teasing, laughing note was gone and she knew she was seeing into his soul for the first time. "But when I was in grade school, we were the best of friends. He put a hoop on the side of the barn, and after dinner we'd go out and shoot baskets." The expression in his eyes grew more direct as he blocked the past from his thoughts. "You don't mind, do you? I mean, you aren't thinking I'm trying to take her father's place or anything?"

The chinks in the wall were back but she didn't care. In fact, she was about to make an even larger one. "Her father's place is empty," Holly reminded him. "I'm very grateful that you're willing to take it for a few hours a week."

He smiled at her but she barely noticed, for his eyes seemed to swallow her up at the same time. Her heart was suddenly full of spring, full of the sound of laughter and singing and the sweet smell of life beginning anew. A smile grew on her own lips, just as it grew in her heart.

"You're a very wise lady," he said softly.

She frowned. "I am?"

"You always know what other people need to hear. No wonder everyone leans on you."

The soft intensity in his voice, as well as the intensity of the fire building in her heart, frightened her. Things were moving too fast and she was glad Jenny returned to derail the moment.

"Ah, here's our basketball player," Holly said.

Jenny was holding out a box of popcorn. "Want some?" she offered.

"Sure." Zach's features were relaxed as he took a handful, moving to let the girl sit between them.

"Mom?" Holly was about to shake her head as Jenny went on. "It's got hardly any salt and they use a butter substitute, so there's no cholesterol."

Holly took a small handful. "How do you know all that?"

"I asked before I would buy any," Jenny told her as the teams came back on the floor and began warming up for the second half.

Zach took another handful of popcorn. "I should warn you if you don't know," he said. "But basketball is called the Hoosier madness."

Holly reached for more popcorn out of Jenny's box. "I find it hard to imagine Indianans mad about anything. They don't curse or shoot at crazy drivers. They don't threaten lynching if a person has an extra item in the express lanes at the supermarket. They don't even riot during lingerie sales."

"We save our energy for what's important." His eyes met hers over the top of the popcorn box. The flame in their dark depths told her that closeness and caring were high on his list.

Holly turned back to the basketball court as the whistle blew to start the second half. She would also be a true Hoosier, then, and save her energy for what was important—staying heart-whole.

Chapter Five

Zach took a deep breath of the fresh morning air as he left the front yard. It was a beautiful day even if it was mid-January and winter was barely a month old. As a kid he used to love days like this, when the clean snow fell down, laying a mantel over his world, but lately he hadn't even noticed the little things.

"Good morning, Professor Philips."

Zach looked across the street at Isabel Kuchinski, one of three elderly sisters who lived together in the home they'd been born in. At seventy-five, Isabel was the youngest, and just as Zach feared, she had a snow shovel in her hands. He walked over to join her.

"Isabel, I told you I'd take care of your walk whenever it snows."

"Don't give me any of that nonsense," she scolded like a schoolmarm taking a sassy young lad to task. "You have your own work to take care of."

"I'll clean your walk this afternoon," he ordered. "Now put that shovel down, go into your house and watch nature's beauty from your window."

"I can't just sit around all day. At my age the joints rust up if you don't exercise."

"Then take a walk around the block," Zach said. "Enjoy the beauty of the world around you. Let me take care of the work."

Impish smile lines crisscrossed the wrinkles in her face. "You've got three women to take care of in your own place," she laughed. "I don't think you can handle any more."

"Isabel," Zach said, shaking a finger at her, "you have a naughty mind."

"At my age you have to take what you get." She laughed heartily for a moment. "So how are your ladies liking it here after a couple of weeks?"

"They love it. How else would they feel, living in the same house as me?"

She shook her head as she attacked the front walk. "Professor Philips, you're the naughty one."

Bending, he kissed her on the cheek. "Remember I can finish shoveling your walk this afternoon."

She muttered something under her breath and Zach continued down the block, smiling to himself. The beauty of the snow clinging to evergreen trees, to the glitter of the lane in the cold morning air, to the snowflakes dancing in the air before him, all seemed like presents from the gods to brighten his day. When had he stopped feeling happiness in the world around him? he wondered.

Certainly his world had been a dark and dreary place when he'd come back to "Michiana" after his Dad had suffered his stroke. Things had been colored by worry over his father and, he had to admit to himself, by guilt for staying away so long. For letting those arguments in the past build so high a wall that it took Dad's stroke to knock it down. Recently he should have felt more laughter in the air. Things had begun to look up. The debts from his father's illness were finally getting paid off and the farm wasn't in danger anymore. His sister, Janice, and her husband, Tom, could worry about important things like braces for their oldest, Josh, and whether the nursery should be painted pink or blue.

An all too familiar wistfulness captured Zach's heart, imprisoning him in his cell of gloominess. He stomped the unhappy feeling down as he stomped the snow off his shoes before entering the university gymnasium. Braces and nurseries were hardly cause for depression unless he was supposed to be paying for them. He hurried through the empty lobby and into the locker room. A handful of men were changing into shorts.

"Ready to lose again?" Bill Harrington called out his greeting as he tied his shoes.

Zach tossed his gym bag down with a snicker. "Don't you wish. The history department is going to avenge last week's loss."

"Better arrange a game against the math department, then. You'll never beat us," Chuck Scanlan said with a laugh. "Chemistry reigns over the Friday morning games."

Zach groaned. "I can see why you didn't go into English. Those chemical symbols are probably the closest things to words that you can manage."

"But we don't need words to beat you," Chuck pointed out.

Zach quickly changed into shorts and a T-shirt in the cool air of the locker room, then hurried out onto the basketball court. Three more members of the chemistry department were warming up, taking shots and jogging around the outside of the court, but only Jeff Paunicka and Harry Tatum from history were there.

"Where is everybody?" Zach asked Jeff.

"Snowed in." Jeff shook his head as he grabbed a fleeing ball and tossed it toward the basket. It missed. "Carlton called to say he hadn't even got his driveway shoveled out yet. And O'Malley is waiting for a tow truck to get him back on US 31 and out of the ditch he's parked in."

"Swell. So how do we take on chemistry? Or more important, how do we beat them?"

Harry came over, already sweating and out of breath from his warm-up. "They agreed to three-on-three, unless we can come up with some substitutes."

"Where are we going to find some more players?" Jeff moaned. "The only one around the department this early is Kent Voss, and all he knows about basketball is what the basket is. Think you can teach him how to play in five minutes?"

Zach chuckled and began his stretching routine. He'd given Holly a lesson in about five minutes, but she was more fun to teach than old Voss would be. Maybe he should call and ask Holly to fill in.

Warmth invaded his heart. She'd think he was crazy and would list all the reasons she had to get to work, but just the idea of having her here was fun to contemplate. And the image of her in shorts and a T-shirt wasn't all that unpleasant, either.

The two weeks' time that he'd known Holly hadn't lessened the challenge she presented. She still drew him, like a bee to nectar, but he no longer fooled himself by saying it was from his desire to heal the hurt in her. It was something much more than that. She was water in the desert, a fire in the Arctic, and he couldn't stay away. He was alive with her, alive and full of energy.

"What about Seth Scott?" Jeff suggested. "I know he's more into chess than basketball, but—"

Zach stood up, flexing his arms. "What do we need anybody else for?" he asked. "The way I feel today, we could play three-on-five and still win."

Jeff frowned. "What did you have for breakfast this morning?"

"What a skeptic," Zach said with a laugh, and caught the pass Harry tossed to him. "It's not what's in your stomach that counts but what's in your heart." He dribbled the ball across the court, then went up for a lay-up.

"You can't be serious," Holly protested to her boss that same Friday, even as she grinned in silent delight. "I don't even have a regular office yet. Can't it wait a few weeks?"

"I thought you'd gotten those architectural mistakes ironed out. When's the place supposed to be done?"

Holly made a face at the stack of ceiling panels before her desk and transferred the phone to her other ear. Might be done this week, Slim had said a few days ago, but probably next week. Easily by the week after and surely by the end of the month. How did one explain to a boss their relaxed attitude?

"Soon," was all she said.

"Well, it can't be helped," he told her. "You don't put the *Wall Street Journal* on hold when it comes calling. Just concentrate on presenting yourself and the company well. Our message is simple. Big eastern conglomerate moving out into the heartland. You can play both sides with that. Business opportunity as well as fulfilling our social responsibility bringing jobs to areas that need them. Doing social good is coming back in style."

Holly was used to his flippant talk. "Is it?" she said.

"And bring your family in. The media like their executives with balanced lives these days, especially the women. Your old house might not be a bad angle, either. I read where moving back into old places is a big deal now."

"Well, I'm certainly glad to see how trendy I am."

There was a pause on the line. "Your orneriness quotient seems to have gone up since the move."

"Sorry about that."

"Must be the air in Indiana."

"Must be," she agreed before hanging up.

She took a deep breath and leaned back in her chair, basking in the glow of satisfaction. In spite of her protests about the offices being unready for the interview, she'd let the reporter in today if he showed up.

She'd taken this promotion to prove herself, and she had. Things were going great; a *Wall Street Journal* interview would be icing on her cake. But work wasn't the only place where life was fine. That old castle they'd bought hadn't turned into a real distraction—she hadn't let it—and her heart was back in line after a few early weak moments with Zach. Two weeks in town and she was in control again.

Laughter and the clomping of footsteps outside her door pulled at her thoughts for attention. She knew without looking at her watch that it was four o'clock. The part-timers were coming to add their efforts to the work crew and soon there would be no room for her to move. Time to switch bases and take her work home to finish. She'd take a bunch of files home to work on and let Slim and Shorty have free rein with the place for the next few days.

A little worry bird perched on her shoulder as she hurried out into the snowy parking lot. Today was Jenny's first basketball practice. Holly hoped that it had gone well. Getting Jenny settled in was the last hurdle to be faced. It would be a smooth ride from then on.

Traffic was slow, better than that morning when the roads had been snow covered, but it was not yet back to normal. Holly fiddled with the radio as she waited for a light to change, but all stations were discussing the university's up-coming basketball game—a fierce, no-holds-barred, show-down battle with a rival from Chicago. Apparently half the population of northern Indiana was calling the stations to help coach the game. Beware of fast breaks seemed to be the consensus of opinion.

Holly laughed and turned the radio off. She knew what fast breaks were now. That's what Zach had been doing, making a run at her heart with his charm. He'd succeeded in scoring a few points with his smile, but no more. She'd paid attention during her lesson and knew how to defend against fast breaks now. You never leave your heart unprotected. It might weaken her offense, but it kept her heart safe and that was what counted in the long run.

She put her rental car away, vowing to buy a car over the weekend, and hurried into the house.

"Hello, I'm home." There was no answer. "Jenny. Mom. I'm—"

"Hi, Mom."

Jenny appeared in the doorway, barefoot. Her long brown hair was lying in wet clumps on the shoulders of her robe, and she was carrying a bucket.

"Honey, what's wrong?"

Her daughter silently led her into the kitchen and pointed. A growing despair settled on Holly's shoulders as she watched water dripping from a light fixture in the ceiling.

"Where's Grandma?" Holly asked. "Upstairs?"

"She went to Portage Manor," Jenny said. "It's an old people's home. She's going to be some kind of volunteer lady."

Holly nodded. "But you were going with her after practice, I thought."

"I wanted to come home."

Holly felt her heart sink. Basketball practice hadn't gone well. Jenny liked to be alone when things weren't going right.

"I'm sorry," Jenny said. "This is all my fault."

Drawn by the plaintive note in her daughter's voice, Holly pulled Jenny into a hug. "How can it be your fault, honey? You didn't build this old house."

"I know, but I used the six-headed shower," Jenny explained. "I got tired of using your shower and wanted to try the one in the big bathroom. I thought it would be neat."

"And this is what happened?"

Jenny nodded slightly, her chin almost on her chest. "Yeah. I came down when I was done and there was a big puddle in the middle of the floor and more water falling."

Holly sighed, staring up at the accursed ceiling while still clinging to Jenny. The flow of water appeared to be slowing down, but Holly was sure that was only because the shower was off, not because the leaks were no longer there. She tried to think positively. It might be a geyser of a leak, but it was one with an on-off switch. Wishing wouldn't make the problem go away, so Holly pulled herself into action.

"Let's go upstairs and look at it," Holly said. But after trudging up the stairs and into the white-tiled bathroom, they didn't gain any insight.

They stood for a long moment and stared at the bathtub—regular porcelain with a pale rust-colored drip mark under the faucet. Above the faucet, like spots on a dice, were two rows of three showerheads each. No red Xs had mysteriously appeared anywhere to mark the spot.

"You know anything about plumbing, Mom?"

"Not much."

"Me, neither," Jenny said glumly.

Jenny's miserable tone doubled Holly's despair. "Hey, what's there to know?" she joked. "Water's supposed to be on the inside of the pipe. Any on the outside is the leak."

Jenny didn't exactly laugh, but her gloominess level decreased slightly. "The pipes must be behind this wall," Jenny said, pointing at the faucets, then noticed the cabinet that was built into the space between the end of the tub and the hallway wall. "If we take these drawers out, we might be able to see the pipes."

"Good thinking, honey."

That brought a bit of a grin to Jenny's face and Holly's hug finished the job. "This is kind of fun, isn't it?" Jenny asked. "I mean, we could find that the leak is caused by some treasure hidden away back here."

"Or a giant spider that got thirsty and bit a hole in the pipe."

"Mom." Jenny wasn't afraid of spiders; that was Holly's domain.

"I know, the drawers."

Luckily they hadn't been living in the house long enough for the drawers to have collected an assortment of clutter. Just a few bath towels occupied the top drawer; the rest were empty and easily stacked out in the hallway.

The space left behind after the drawers were all out was far from glamorous. They saw studs and lathing strips with dried plaster oozing through. The inside of the hallway wall was on one side and the inside of Jenny's wall on the other. But the space was big enough for Holly to fit into, once she squeezed between the drawer supports.

"I'll just go—" Holly stopped at the determined look on Jenny's face. If she went to change her clothes now, Jenny would crawl inside there and try to find the leak. Wasn't it bad enough that Holly had taken Jenny from her friends in New York and given her an old wreck to live in? Holly didn't have to compound the unfairness by letting Jenny crawl around inside the wall to find a leaky pipe.

She slipped off her suit jacket and kicked off her shoes. "I'll just play like a snake and slither inside here."

With a grin designed to show how much she was enjoying this adventure, Holly lay on her back and slid under the two bottom drawer supports. She sat up once she was able, then pulled her legs inside and gingerly stood on the plank subflooring.

"You look like you're in jail," Jenny said with a giggle. "Except the bars go across instead of up and down."

"Very funny," Holly said. "Now hand me the flashlight before something comes out of these cracks in the floor and eats me."

"Mom, nothing lives in the cracks in the floor."

"Easy for you to say, standing out there where you can't see the bones of former leak seekers." Holly stooped down, pointing the flashlight at the pipe work crawling up the side of the bathtub and the back of the wall.

"See anything?" Jenny asked anxiously. "Did I break anything?"

"Stop worrying, honey." The pipes looked dry. And felt dry. "Showers are supposed to be able to handle water. You didn't have unreasonable demands."

Holly touched a thin, dark stripe running down the side of one pipe. It was dry and under the light had a greenish tinge. Glue or sealant of some sort. "Maybe you should turn the faucet on."

"The shower?"

"Just the faucet."

But nothing happened. The boards underneath stayed dry, had probably always been dry, if the cobwebs attached to them were any indication. She slumped against the wall, not caring about the century's worth of dust hanging from it.

"Find anything?" Jenny asked, peering into the cubbyhole.

"Cobwebs. Turn the shower on."

Jenny obeyed. Holly still couldn't see anything, but she sure could hear it. Water running onto the subflooring at the far side of the bathtub.

"Anything this time?"

"The pipes under the tub are probably all rotted out." To fix them, the tub would probably have to be removed which would mean wrecking the walls around it. And what if the tub needed to be replaced? How did they get a monstrously heavy thing like that old tub out of the house? Did they make a hole in the wall and shove it out into the yard? Falling from the second floor, it would make a crater in the yard that would have to be fixed.

Holly could feel her lip close to quivering. She wanted to cry. The good humor she pretended for Jenny's sake had worn thin and disappeared. Here she'd thought everything was going great. What a fool she'd been. Nothing about this damned old wreck was great. It was about to fall apart and she'd never be able to sell it. There wasn't another person in the whole world as dumb as she was.

"Jenny. You here?"

Holly barely had time to register shock at the voice before Jenny piped up.

"Zach, we're in the bathroom," she called out the door, then turned back to Holly. "Nobody else was home so I called Zach and left a message on his answering machine." She finished her recitation just as Zach stepped into the doorway.

Wonderful, Holly thought. Just what she needed.

"Hi," he said. "Anything wrong?"

"Wrong?" No, she always stood around in cobwebby cubbyholes, holding flashlights and about to burst into tears. "No, nothing's wrong. We're playing hide-and-seek and Jenny found me."

"The shower's leaking," Jenny said.

"Not now it isn't," Holly insisted. She'd rather board up the bathtub than start depending on Zach again. Her heart had just gotten strong after his few fast breaks earlier in the week, but she didn't need a test to prove it.

"Mom doesn't know anything about plumbing except that the water on the outside is the leak."

"I see," Zach said.

He peered in at Holly, his face a model of serious concern, but she knew he had to be laughing. The only thing funnier than finding her in this cubbyhole would have to be watching her attempt to get out.

"All the water pipes are rotting in this stupid old wreck," she told him, just to point out that Jenny was wrong. She did too know about the plumbing here. "This whole place is going to fall into a heap, but before that happens we're all going to drown."

She took a deep breath that came out in a series of quivers. The urge to cry was back, but she ordered it into remission. She was not going to cry. Not in front of Zach.

"Besides that, everything is just fine," she ended.

"That's good," he said, and looked at the bathtub for a long moment. "But maybe I'll just come in there and take a look for myself."

He kept his serious expression but watched her carefully as he checked out the drawer supports. Holly knew being calm and quiet was probably appropriate behavior when dealing with someone who had gone mad.

"You can't fit in here. The space is only about three feet square," Holly protested even as he lay down and slid under the drawer support.

She was partly right and partly wrong. Technically, he did fit. His body was in the space along with hers, but no room was left for breathing. His right arm pressed against her chest, his right leg against hers.

"Now you're both in jail," Jenny said with a laugh.

Holly forced a smile. She assured herself she wasn't bothered by his closeness. Her heart was racing because she was worried about the leak. Leaking showers always made her heart race. He had a dimple in his chin; she'd never noticed that before.

"Can I have the flashlight?"

Silently she obeyed his request and then gasped for breath when he bent down. His shoulder brushed her leg. Lord, but his hair was thick. What would it be like to run her hands through it?

She crossed her arms, thrusting her hands into safety. "Look all you want," she said. "The pipes are dry."

She watched as the beam of the flashlight caressed the end of the bathtub and followed the pipes into the first-floor wall. Caressed? Where did she dig that word up from? The flashlight moved again and Zach's sweater gently brushed her thigh. It wasn't a caress; none of it was a caress. It was just movement, like what she would do now to get out of his way. Except by melting back into the studs of the hallway wall, she succeeded only in getting her hair caught in some dried plaster.

"The pipes are all dry," he said.

She pulled away from the wall and lost a few strands of hair to the plaster. "That's what I said."

He gave her a curious look, a half smile that said either he thought his closeness was bothering her or else that a spider was climbing up her hair. Since his closeness wasn't bothering her, it had to be a spider. She carefully laid her hand on his chest.

"Is it a spider?" she asked.

Zach just stared at her, his eyes widening slightly.

"Mom," Jenny protested from her perch on the bathroom floor just outside the cubbyhole, "the leak wasn't made by a thirsty spider."

"In my hair?" Holly whispered, trying not to move and shake it onto her shoulder. "Is there a spider in my hair?"

"Oh." Zach's lips twitched just a touch as he moved his head to the side. "No, I don't think so. Just a cobweb or two."

"Oh, gross," Jenny said.

Holly took a deep breath. She was acting like a fool. She had to get away from Zach to where she could think again. Where she couldn't see how long his eyelashes were and how they swept across his cheeks as he blinked. Where she couldn't feel the gentle touch of his breath against her lips. Her cheeks were on fire, but so were her hands, her heart. Breathe, she commanded. Think.

"Are you all right?" he asked.

"Why shouldn't I be?" She nodded toward the pipes. "The pipes under the tub are all rotted, right?"

He shook his head. "Sorry. There aren't any pipes under the tub."

For a moment she forgot all about his nearness. "They're all completely rotted away?" This was worse than she'd expected.

He put his hands on her shoulders; he was a steadying rock that suddenly allayed her worries. "There never were any," he told her. "There would be no reason for pipes to go under the tub. The drainpipe is at this end and there are no drains or faucets in the far wall."

"But I heard it leak over there."

He turned his head. "Jen, put some water in the bucket and pour it in the far corner of the bathtub where the wall meets the tub."

A minute later, the sound of water running onto the subflooring was clearly heard.

"Then what—"

"Grout," he said. "Your grout is cracked and loose, so water got under it and leaked through."

"That's all?"

"Zach, you sure are smart," Jenny said.

And her mother sure was dumb, Holly finished the sentence in her thoughts.

"You would have figured it out," Zach said. "I had to regrout my tub last year. That's how I caught on so fast."

Speaking of catching on fast, her body was noticing how comfortably Zach's hands held her shoulders. How nice it was to feel a man so close to her, to think that if she just swayed forward a fraction she could feel his chest against hers, his strength against her softness.

"Well, I guess I'd better change my clothes," Jenny said. "Can you two get out of there by yourselves?"

"We'll try," Zach promised.

Holly watched as Jenny disappeared, then heard the girl's bedroom door close from down the hall. "I feel unbelievably silly," Holly admitted with a tired sigh. Should she lean forward or back? Should she risk the danger of Zach's charm or the spidery wall?

He made the choice for her, pulling her into his arms. "Why should you feel silly?" he murmured into her hair. "You had a problem and you tried to fix it."

She could hear his heart beating. Her eyes closed and the sound of his heart, his breathing, filled her world. "I thought there were spiders in my hair."

"Want me to check again?"

"No. I should climb out of here before Mother gets home."

"I should, too."

But neither made a move to leave their cubbyhole. Zach's hands did make some sort of movement as they slid across her back, pulling her closer. His sweater was scratchy against her cheek, but wonderfully so. She sighed and slipped her own arms around him. She'd forgotten what bliss a hug could be. To stand in another's arms and be safe, be secure, to have someone else's strength to mix with yours and keep you strong.

"Know what I think?" Zach whispered after a moment.

"Mmm?" She didn't want to ever move again.

"I think I'm going to kiss you."

She should have been shocked; she should have protested and pulled away. But she only looked up, leaning her head into his shoulder and finding his lips with hers.

He was everything she needed and wanted and dreamed about in her secret heart, even as she said she'd closed her life off to dreams. His lips awoke a sweet joy in her that wanted to grow and blossom. Slowly at first, it dared to fight back the shadows in her soul, pushing the past aside in celebration of here and now and Zach. There was nothing to fear and all to be found in his arms.

The sound of a door opening down the hall broke them apart, and the sunshine of his touch dimmed. "I think you'll have to crawl out first," Holly said, surprised at how natural her voice sounded.

"If I remember how." But he did and was standing in the bathroom by the time Jenny came back in.

"You stuck, Mom?" she asked.

"No, just waiting my turn." After an awkward bit of squirming she was out, too, and they were all standing next to the bathtub. Sanity was returning and so was embarrassment.

"Thanks," she finally managed to say.

"No problem. Glad to help."

"When I saw the dry pipes I didn't know what to do. I was sure that everything was all rusted out underneath."

"I thought maybe Pokagon was mad at us," Jenny said a little nervously.

Zach scooped her into a big hug. "Hey, he would never get mad at you, honey."

"I suppose," Jenny said, then made a face. "But you know Mom's always saying how she doesn't believe in him. I just thought he'd finally had enough."

"He's not vindictive," Zach assured her.

"He's not real," Holly said, and walked past them into the hall. The air was less close here; breathing was possible. Until Zach came up behind her and slipped his arm around her shoulders.

"He's got a plan, you know," Zach whispered in her ear. "As the house is healed, so are you."

His touch brought rumblings of a storm in her heart. The peace that had been there before had been chased away by common sense, leaving only fear. "Great. Then when I grout the tub tomorrow, Pokagon will have to find someone else to haunt."

"You think so?"

Holly knew so. She didn't need healing; there was nothing in her life she wanted to change, except to get rid of this house.

The January winds whistled and tore at the building, but that evening found Holly staring at the car before her in the showroom. The hood was up and Zach was reading off a list of statistics about the engine's power. The tension from the afternoon's cubbyhole escapade was over and she'd graciously accepted his offer of help in searching out a car. It wasn't his company she wanted, she had assured herself about every fifteen minutes, but his expertise. After all, he'd grown up in the area; he ought to know what kind of weather she would be facing here.

"Is this what I need?" she asked him.

"No. You don't want all that horsepower or that large a sticker price," he told her. "How about something with four-wheel drive on demand?"

"Did you see that sign, Mom?" Jenny asked. "You get a free pair of cross-country skis if you buy a car this month. If we buy a car, who gets the skis?"

Holly leafed through the brochure she'd picked up at the door. "You can. When would I have time to ski?" Holly found a model that had four-wheel drive.

"I think that model's over there," Zach said, looking over her shoulder.

Holly and Zach walked across the showroom, Jenny trailing along. "Mom, cross-country skiing is one of the best aerobic exercises there is. Maybe you should keep the skis and make time to use them."

"I'll use my exercise bike."

"You got rid of it six months ago."

"Did I?" Holly said absently as she stopped at the station wagon. "What kind of mileage does this one get?"

Zach peered at the sticker listing the features, then at an EPA test paper on another window. "Twenty-five city, forty-five highway."

"That's better than my rental car."

"Rental cars are whipped cream. They go for flash, not substance," Zach said, and opened the driver's side door for her.

Jenny peered into the back of the station wagon. "How come you know so much about different stuff?" she asked Zach.

He shrugged. "I'm just your average, run-of-the-mill genius."

Holly looked up and laughed, loudly and easily. "Boy, fix a leaky shower and right away he thinks he's great."

Jenny came around to their side of the car. "He does know a lot about fixing stuff. He was fixing his car that time him and you got stuck in the garage, Mom."

Holly tensed up slightly, then relaxed as Zach let pass his chance to tease her more about the garage door. He just smiled at her conspiratorially, as if they'd both wanted to get stuck in the garage together even back when they'd first met. A certain fire seemed to flicker to life again in her soul. She turned away, fiddling with the turn signal until her pulse came close to normal again.

"Hey, I not only fixed a shower today," Zach said. "I led my basketball team to victory over the chemistry team."

Jenny opened the back door and slipped into the seat behind Holly. "I thought you were a history teacher."

"I teach history and I play basketball on the history department pickup team," he said. "But before all that I was a farm boy."

"Are farm boys smart?" Jenny asked.

"Jenny," Holly remonstrated her daughter.

Zach laughed. "You have to know a little bit about a lot to make it on a farm. You're too far away from people to always be calling somebody for help."

Jenny digested that data for a split second. "Do you like this color, Mom?"

Holly shifted gears, then tried the side-view mirror adjustment buttons. "The color doesn't matter much to me," she said. "Blue's all right."

"I like red," Jenny said. "Did you have a horse when you lived on the farm?"

Zach nodded. "Yep, my sister, my brother and I rode all the time."

Jenny stretched her legs out, bumping the back of Holly's seat. "I've only ridden a couple of times in my whole life," Jenny said sadly. "And one of the rides was on a little pony."

"If you want to go riding, I can take you up to the farm. My sister and her family live there now."

Jenny abandoned her relaxed pose and leaned forward over the front seat. "Could we, Mom?"

"It's not far," Zach said. "Just under an hour's drive from here."

"Could we, Mom?" Jenny persisted.

Holly got out of the car. "We'll see."

"Great," Jenny exclaimed. "This is really a great car. Are we going to get it?"

A salesman was scurrying toward them. "Well, hello, folks. You like this station wagon here? Perfect car for a young family like yourselves."

While Jenny looked delighted, Holly ignored the salesman's mistake, asking him about servicing and availability. A little part of her, though, deep in her heart, liked the idea of being a family, liked the idea of choosing a car that would cart them off together.

Even as her common sense muscled in, reminding her of hurts and loneliness, of all her responsibilities with Ruth and Jenny and her new job, that smile refused to back into the shadows. And like a single ember amid the charcoal, it flickered, burned and grew, warming at least a corner of her heart against the cold January night.

Chapter Six

Mom," Jenny called from outside the fence. "I'm going to go for a spin around the neighborhood."

Holly looked up from shoveling yet another of Indiana's never-ending parade of snowfalls and saw her daughter maneuvering awkwardly on the short, week-old cross-country skis. "Shouldn't someone go with you?"

"Nope," Jenny said firmly. "Zach says I'm ready to solo."

Solo? Solo where? And who gave Zach the authority to decide when her daughter could solo?

Holly looked around for this authority figure and found him across the street, leaning on a snow shovel while laughing and talking with two of the elderly women who lived there. Should she call him back or go over and ask him who gave him the right to tell Jenny she could solo?

He was becoming a little too much a part of their lives and Holly wasn't sure she liked that. Well, part of her didn't. Most of the time she could handle having him around. During the week their meetings were brief. But weekends were a different story. He always seemed to be nearby, making her heart turn somersaults when she least expected it.

Sensing her mother's indecision, Jenny began moving forward. "Bye, Mom."

Holly took her eyes off Zach in time to see Jenny heading determinedly toward the corner. Ten was supposed to be an age of reaching for independence, but that was easier to accept when your child was two than when she was skiing away from you down a strange street.

"Watch out for traffic," Holly called out.

"Mom." The word used to be a term of endearment; lately it had become a term of exasperation. "This street ain't exactly the Long Island Expressway."

"Isn't, dear."

"Goodbye, Mom."

Holly leaned across the gate, staring after her. Actually, Jenny wasn't tottering all that much. She was getting to be a very competent young lady. Sighing, Holly wondered whether there was only one share of competence handed out per family. She still had her teeth and almost no gray hair, but lately she could feel her daughter's concern. Had people in their thirties seemed like doddering old fogies when she was ten?

"She's quite a little athlete," Zach said, leaning on the other side of the gate.

Holly started. She hadn't noticed him come back across the street. She still wasn't certain that he should have encouraged Jenny to ski alone, so Holly stared after the tiny red figure and did not respond. Damn the man, she thought. Her breath was quickening, and it wasn't in response to her daughter's skiing.

"She learned how to handle the skis and poles in less than an hour," Zach continued.

"I still worry about her skiing in the streets."

"The kids do it all the time around here," he replied. "Don't worry, she'll be fine. Or are you all out of other things to worry about?"

"With this house?" She glanced over her shoulder at the big old place. With the new curtains in the windows, it looked warmer, homier. She frowned. "It's teasing me. Luring me into a false sense of security before something else goes wrong."

"Hey, nothing's broken since last week," Zach reminded her. "You regrouted and the shower works. You've had a whole week of peace since then."

"It's just waiting until I least expect it."

"Boy, that's a cheery attitude. You must be a winter person."

She turned back to him, trying to avoid seeing the glimmer in his eyes or remember the taste of his lips on hers. "What's a winter person? Somebody who likes the cold? It doesn't bother me."

"No, a winter person's someone who likes to look at the cold, dark side of things."

"A pessimist."

"I like my term better."

She shrugged and opened the gate. He moved aside to let her out, but the warmth in his smile kept her from starting to shovel the front walk.

"Actually, I think I'm an optimist," she said. "Would a pessimist have accepted my new job, moved her family to a new part of the country? Would a pessimist give a *Wall Street Journal* reporter an interview in an office filled with workmen and still know it went well? Nope. I knew all this would work out fine, because I always look on the bright side of things."

"Like with the house?" he asked with a chuckle, an annoying response that she chose to ignore.

"That's just being realistic." She brushed the snow from the top of the mailbox.

"What about the spiders?"

"A fear of spiders is neither pessimistic nor optimistic. I suppose you have no fears."

His grin was mischievous. He came a step closer and Holly toyed with the idea of going back on her side of the gate.

"I have lots of fears," Zach told her, trying not to smile. "Mostly I'm afraid of the dark and all the things that go bump in the night."

"Sure."

"And what I need is someone to hold my hand."

Her cheeks flamed, but it was her common sense that answered him. "Right."

"Boy, what a pessimistic attitude that is. I know—come up to my apartment tonight and I'll prove it to you."

"There's a definite difference between being optimistic and being dumb." And dumb was standing out here talking instead of shoveling. Dumb was letting her heart race whenever he was near. Dumb was drowning in his smile and forgetting that her new start did not include a man. She slid her shovel across the sidewalk and cleared a strip.

"You certainly aren't a very sympathetic person," he noted, bending over to shovel next to her. "Does your mother know how unkind you are?"

She would not get involved in his silly conversations. "You don't have to shovel my walk."

"I use it, too."

The walk was not the issue; the state of her heart when he was near was. "I own the sidewalk. Therefore it's my responsibility."

He ignored her and continued shoveling, his strong arms tossing aside the heavy snow with ease. Out of the corner of her eye she watched how his hands gripped the handle, with surety, with strength, with—

For heaven's sake. She caught herself and tackled the next strip of snow with determination. "I told you I'm taking care of it," she said coolly. "Now just leave it alone."

"I enjoy helping people."

"Don't you have some papers to grade or something?"

"The exercise is good for me."

Holly glared at his back. If he wanted to shovel so badly, maybe she should let him and go back in the house herself. But while she frowned at him, she also remembered how broad those shoulders were even with his down jacket and how strong those muscles had felt when she'd rested in his arms last week. Her frown melted into a warm glow.

"Quit standing around and gawking," he said over his shoulder. "I don't mind helping, but I don't want to do the whole thing."

"I didn't ask for your help." Holly scooped up some snow on her shovel and flicked it onto the back of his neck. "So get out of here."

"Hey," he shouted in protest. His shovel fell and he brushed the snow from his head and neck. "Quit fooling around."

"I'm not fooling around. Now get off my sidewalk and leave my snow alone."

He stared at her a long moment. "You look a little hot."

"I'm fine. Just in the mood for some solitary shoveling," she said.

"Can't leave you hot. It's bad for you in this kind of weather." He picked up snow in his shovel and dumped it on her, the light powder scattering over her front, down her pants and into her boots.

"You got snow all over me," she cried.

"What do you think that stuff was that you put down the back of my neck?" He grinned. "Talcum powder?"

Holly threw a shovelful on him. She wasn't going to let him affect her. She would bury him in ten feet of snow and leave him out here, where Pokagon could rescue him if he wanted.

Zach didn't seem to realize the seriousness of the battle and retaliated by dumping more snow on her. She went for her snowbank.

"Children!"

Both of them stopped and looked across the street. All three elderly sisters were out on their front walk.

"You two stop fooling around and get along."

"If you get snow inside your coats, it'll melt and then you'll catch cold."

Holly felt thirty years stripped from her age; the grin on Zach's face was definitely sheepish.

"Yes, ma'am," he called out respectfully.

"Now, Zach, you shovel to the east, and, Holly, you shovel west."

"And stay out of each other's hair."

Holly did as ordered, and from the scraping sound behind her, she knew that Zach was also obeying. They'd been acting silly, she knew, but at least she'd accomplished her wish of getting him farther away from her. Except now she missed him.

She peeked over at him. Did he miss her? Her shoulders slumped, but she continued her shoveling, concentrating on the repetitive actions. Push the shovel across, dump the snow. Push the shovel—

"They're gone," came a whisper from behind her.

She turned to find Zach grinning at her, his eyes dancing with delight. "Your part of the sidewalk isn't done," she pointed out even as she smiled back at him.

"But it's no fun down there by myself."

"Aren't you afraid they'll come out and yell again?"

He shook his head even as he nudged the branch over her head so that snow rained down on her. "The next time they come out, they'll offer us cookies and hot chocolate if we behave." A chunk of snow fell down the back of her neck, and she squirmed to try to avoid its icy fingers. It melted before she could retrieve it. That was it. Zach's goose was cooked.

"You are nasty," she cried, and abandoned her shovel for good. "You don't deserve any cookies, you know."

Grabbing a handful of snow, she hit him soundly on the back of the head as he raced for cover by the tree, and she laughed with delight. The sound somehow surprised her, not because of its free and joyous melody, but because of the song that echoed in her heart.

"I think Grandma has a boyfriend."

Holly blinked rapidly and sat up. The snow shoveling had made her sleepy and that glass of wine with dinner had set her eyelids at half-mast. She'd taken an unintentional break from reading to drift on a cloud of daydreams involving Zach. "I'm sorry, honey. I didn't hear you."

"I said," Jenny repeated, slowly enunciating each word, "I think Grandma has a boyfriend."

"A boyfriend?" Holly's mind was spinning in bewilderment. "Have you seen him?"

"No. She's just acting different. She's wearing makeup."

"Your grandmother's worn makeup before."

"Sure. My mistake in thinking everybody's getting mushy around here." Jenny departed, the words hanging in the air behind her.

Mushy? Holly noticed her book had fallen onto the seat next to her and she put it back in her lap. Who was getting mushy? Holly wondered. Not her; she was a dedicated career woman. Sharing a few laughs with Zach hadn't changed that. And Ruth's only interests were her family and those horror books she crawled into bed with every night. Did she miss having someone, instead of something, to crawl into bed with?

"Hello, dear."

Holly felt a deep warmth fly up her neck and onto her cheeks. "Hello, Mother," she stammered. Ruth wasn't an old woman; it wasn't surprising that she'd want some companionship.

Ruth sat down next to her. An awkward silence fell upon them.

"I hear it's going to be warmer tonight," Ruth said after a moment.

"Yes, I heard that, too. The annual January thaw."

Holly wanted to say something else, something reassuring and accepting, but didn't know the words. Silence stood between them.

"I was hoping to go out with some friends this evening." Ruth cleared her throat. "Well, only one friend really, if that's all right with you."

"Sure. Why wouldn't it be?" Holly put her book down on the end table near her. "What's her name?"

"Her name? Men have names, too, dear."

Holly had known it was a man. Why hadn't she admitted it right out? Was she hurt that her mother wanted someone

besides them? Was she jealous that Ruth had enough lei-
sure time to date? No, she realized. She wasn't that selfish
or petty. But she was afraid, although her fear was absolutely crazy. There was nothing to fear in her mother's having a date.

"Hey, great," Holly said, forcing sunshine into her voice.
"What's his name?"

"Bruno." Ruth's voice grew very bright. "Bruno Bartles. His real name is Bruno Sikorski. Bartles is his stage
name. He used to dance with Broadway touring companies, then he was a choreographer, but he's retired now.
Actually semiretired. He teaches dancing at the nursing
home."

Ruth stopped, her cheeks flushed. Was the color due to
breathlessness, excitement or both?

"He sounds interesting," Holly said. "Where are you
going to go?"

"What are you two talking about?" Jenny asked, sailing
back into the room. "Who's going someplace?"

Holly started, then smiled brightly up at her daughter,
hoping Jenny wouldn't blurt out the wrong thing and spoil
Ruth's excitement about the evening. "Your grandmother
is going out for the evening," Holly said, her tone quiet and
modulated. That was the right tack. Cool dignity.

"Hah!" Jenny shouted in glee. "I told you she had a
boyfriend." She ran over to Ruth and gave her a high five.
"Way to go, Grandma."

Ruth's color deepened, but her smile was pure joy as she
hugged Jenny. Holly slumped back, feeling absurdly left
out.

"When you're hot, you're hot." Jenny's merriment was
interrupted by the doorbell. "I bet it's him," she screamed.

But Holly beat her to the door, opening it to find a portly,
elderly gentleman waiting on the step. His handlebar mustache was dark, but the wild locks that hung down almost
to his shoulders were white as snow.

"Ah, you must be the fair daughter," the man said, then
turned to someone slightly behind him. "She is beautiful,
is she not?"

"Didn't I tell you that?" his partner replied.

Holly's heart broke into a smile. "Zach?"

"Hello, Holly." Zach peered around Bruno. "You don't have your shovel there with you, do you?"

Bruno frowned over his shoulder, then turned back to Holly. "Pray, dear lady, what shovel does this knave ask about?"

Holly grinned at them both, happiness spilling out into her words. "The one I hit him with." She stepped aside to let them in.

"Ah, a lady of intelligence and distinction," Bruno said with a deep bow. "You may have met your match, Zachary, my boy."

"I may have indeed," Zach agreed.

The look Zach gave Holly as he passed brought a hunger to her heart, and to her surprise no fear came to try to wash it away.

Ruth greeted them as she came into the foyer.

"Ah, the fairest of them all," Bruno cried, swooping down on Ruth and kissing her on each cheek.

Laughing, Ruth pushed herself away but let Bruno keep her hand in his as she introduced Bruno to Holly and then to Jenny.

"Three beautiful women, all in one house." Bruno shook his head. "Zach, how do you keep your sanity?"

"Cold showers," Zach said. "Three, four, five times a day."

He was rewarded with hearty laughter from everyone except Holly, for he seemed to be staring into her soul and laughter was impossible, as impossible as breathing. Flames, flickering sparks, licked at her heart, teasing it from warmth into an inferno. She could have used the cold shower herself—or better yet a cold lake so that she could cool and lose herself all at once.

"I have an idea," Bruno said. "Why don't we form a foursome and grace the ice rink with our presence?" His look at Holly and Zach made it obvious who the other couple was supposed to be.

Holly wanted to agree, but habit kept the words from coming easily. "It's rather short notice," she said.

"You have a date already?" Bruno asked.

"No, I—"

"Then would you do me the honor of accompanying me to the skating rink this evening?" Zach asked.

"I haven't skated in years."

"I'm good at holding people up," Zach promised.

"I don't have any skates."

"They rent them at the rink, dear," Ruth told her. "I don't have any, either."

But this was her mother's and Bruno's first date. She couldn't horn in on them. "No, I really couldn't."

"We'd love the company," Ruth assured her. "Maybe then I can hide my pitiful conversational skills a bit longer."

"What pitiful conversational skills?" Holly asked, then spied Jenny grinning at them all. "I couldn't leave Jenny alone."

"She could come with us," Ruth suggested.

Holly nodded. "That's an idea." It would save her from being alone with Zach.

"No," Jenny cried. "Two's company, but three's a crowd. Goes the same for four and five. How about if I go over and visit Isabel and her sisters? They said I could go over anytime I wanted."

"No, Jenny, we really can't impose on—"

"Mom," Jenny pointed out. "They're three old ladies. They probably have a million little chores that they need someone to do for them. Change light bulbs on ceiling lights. Reach behind the washer for lost socks. You wouldn't want Isabel to climb onto a stepladder to change a light bulb, do you?"

"She's just the type to try to do it herself," Zach agreed.

Holly looked around. Four pairs of eyes circled her. There was no escape. "I'll go find something to wear," she said slowly.

The scene at the ice rink looked like the front of a Christmas card. Skaters, dressed as if their bright colors could ward off the cold, whirled and twirled and glided along the glassy ice. The music playing was anything but traditional, though, as rock blasted from the speakers atop the warming house.

"What happened to the 'Skaters' Waltz'?" Holly asked.

"It gets a little tiresome played hour after hour." Zach's arm, which was around her waist, tightened a fraction as a child zipped across in front of them. "Besides, this has a good beat to skate to."

"To fall to, you mean." Holly's feet skidded wildly before she found her balance again. Her ankles ached with the strain.

"You're doing great. You haven't fallen yet."

"I think your arm around my waist might have something to do with it."

"It's hardly doing anything."

That wasn't exactly true. Holly doubted that the fluttering in her stomach, the heat in her cheeks and the way her breath kept escaping were merely from the exertion of skating. But she was grateful its effects were not noticeable. She knew she could protest his closeness, demand a chance to prove her independence, but she didn't say a word. She was independent in every way, yet it was rather nice for a few hours one evening to quite literally lean on someone else.

"Did you skate much as a kid?" Zach asked.

"Roller-skating on the sidewalks."

"That's pretty close to this."

She grinned at him. "Not really. You set your rhythm for four-foot strides to step over the cracks. Here the cracks are everywhere."

"Not to mention little kids." He pulled her to the side of the rink as a little boy, covered almost from head to skate in hockey pads, wove uncertainly by.

They stood for a moment, their backs to the low wall, watching the skaters pass. Bruno and Ruth were arm in arm, like skaters in a Currier and Ives print, their rhythms evenly matched. Even from a distance the glow on Ruth's face was obvious and Holly felt a tremor shake her heart. Was Ruth wanting more from life than she had, more than Holly was able to give her? Holly had thought their life so perfect. Well, maybe not perfect, for what ever was? But balanced certainly. She didn't want to have that balance upset.

"Want some hot chocolate?" Zach asked.

"Wonderful." The rest would give her a chance to re-group, to knock the wobblies from her state of mind. "My ankles are getting tired and they thank you for the chance to sit down."

She soon found out, however, the warming house wasn't the best place for regrouping or any type of thinking. The rainbow-hued benches were littered with skaters' scarves, boots and occasional socks, along with a few weary bodies warming their chattering bones while exercising their lungs. With silent agreement, Holly and Zach took their cups of hot chocolate back outside, skirting the rink to sit on the low retaining wall at the end of the parking lot. The snow-kissed ground beneath them sloped down gently until it spilled into the river, mixing with the dark, glittering diamonds of the water.

"Why were you named Holly?" Zach asked. "Let me guess. You were a Christmas baby."

"The best present Santa ever left."

Zach laughed gently. "That sounds like a father speaking."

"It was," she could admit in the darkness. Usually, the past was as cold as the wind whispering in her hair, but to-night was hot chocolate, strong enough to warm the num-best fingers—or the numbest hearts. "He was the type that liked presents. Not the day-to-day responsibility of them, but the fun and surprise."

"Some people are like that." His words were almost off-hand, but his voice was too warm. She hadn't wanted sympathy.

"Luckily, Mom was a bit more dependable or I might never have gotten my diaper changed."

He laughed and she relaxed, sipping her hot chocolate and letting its sweet warmth touch her. Off to their left, bathed in the streetlights, was a deserted playground.

"There's nothing colder-looking than a playground shut down for the winter," Holly said with a sigh. "Swings down. No more seesaws. And nothing but snow sliding down the slide."

"Who's to say snow's the only thing on the slide?" Zach asked, grinning into his words. "Maybe it's the only thing you can see on the slide, but it's not necessarily the only thing there. Maybe there are beings from other worlds or other times playing there right now."

He ended in a ghostly whisper, moving closer to her so she could feel the warmth of his breath against her cheek. She trembled, wanting his gentleness and his touch to warm her even further.

"Did I scare you?" he teased, and put his arm around her shoulder, hugging her close.

"No, I'm just a little cold," she said, though it wasn't true.

"We can go back in if you like."

"I'm fine. My hot chocolate's still potent enough to keep the chills away." To say nothing of his arm. She took another sip to regain her balance. "Do you really believe all that ghost stuff?"

He didn't say anything for a moment and stared out ahead of him at the river. Streetlights laid a crazy distorted shadow of a bridge across the water and she wondered why she'd asked him such a foolish question.

"I'm not sure what you mean by 'ghost stuff,'" he said. "Spirits dressed in white sheets that go 'Boo!' in the night? No. But I do believe that life is a continuum and goes on. Matter and spirit may change their form, but their essence remains forever."

He turned; she could feel his eyes on her through the darkness. "I guess it really started when I was twelve and my mother died," he went on. "You don't really believe in death until someone you love dies."

She nodded. "I know. The finality of it all is so hard to accept."

His hand found hers. "I couldn't believe how much I missed her. How scary it was to think that I would never see her again. But then this old librarian gave me a book about an Indian who died. The Indians believe that the spirit of the person who died stays with you while you grieve, and the longer you grieve, the longer you keep them from moving on to the happy hunting ground. That death is a part of life and we are a part of all that has gone before us and all that will come after us. Everything I read eased the hurt a little. It took a long time to really heal, but I started to see the world a bit differently. It brought me peace to think of all that had gone before me and all that would follow."

"You were lucky to have people around you who cared enough to help."

When her father had left, she'd felt as if he'd died, but there had always been a lingering hope that one day he'd come back, no matter how angry her thoughts and words. She'd dreamed about him swinging her up into his arms the way he used to when she had been a toddler. She'd imagined seeing him in the crowds when she watched baseball games during the summer. Then when she was fifteen, she'd learned he'd died about a year earlier. The dreams had been impossible. The hope was gone.

The darkness gave her the freedom to speak honestly. The night didn't mock or pry or offer false sympathy. "The worst thing," she said, "is when you don't have a chance to say goodbye. When you've left so many things unsaid." She'd never known why her father had left and never would. That had been the hardest thing to live with.

Zach leaned closer, his lips brushing her ear, teasing the base of her neck. "There's a lesson to be learned, though."

A lethargy began to seep into her blood, taking control of her ability to think clearly. She moved nearer to Zach, closer to his lips and the power of their touch. "What's that?"

"Don't leave things undone. Take advantage of the moment to be happy and give happiness."

"That sounds an awful lot like a line to me," she said, but even as she said it she turned into his arms and found his lips.

In his arms, she wanted to escape the fears that had haunted her for years. He held the key, she knew suddenly, to opening up her heart. For the first time in years she wasn't afraid to laugh, to hunger, to feel. Her mouth moved under his, awakening to the power that his touch had for her, even as his arms closed around her.

This was what life was supposed to hold, she thought in the fleeting brush of sanity's wings. The real magic was in being together, in finding a heart to beat in unison with hers. Her hands moved across his back, wanting to bring some haunting thought to life through her touch. But all she felt was the thickness of down, like a fog that kept her apart and lost from those she needed. Her soul pouted in disappointment, in hunger that would never be met, and then suddenly he was pulling away, leaving her in the dark and the cold without his strength to cling to.

For a wild blink of a moment, she'd felt her destiny in his hands. The source of her happiness in his smile. That was crazy, she assured herself, and slowed her racing heart. She knew better than to trust her happiness to someone else, to the whims of a fate that liked to play with lives the way the wind plays with the snow clinging to bare branches. She felt his eyes on her, burning with a question she couldn't read and wouldn't answer.

"Holly? Zach?" Ruth's voice split the silence.

"Over here, Mom," Holly called back.

Whatever magic had encircled them fled into the dark shadows of her soul as Bruno and Ruth joined them. Zach laughed and talked about where they might all go to eat, but Holly said little. There was an ache in her heart that shouldn't have been there. She should have known that what started with a tiny ember of desire would end only in burning pain.

"That all right with you?" Zach asked her.

"Sure," she said, not having any idea what she was agreeing to but knowing that her heart needed rest and her soul needed time to close the doors again. Close them and lock them tight.

Zach watched Holly out of the corner of his eye as they strolled across the yard to the bird feeder. She'd been like a chameleon all night, changing from bold to shy, from timid to confident, and he wondered what mood she'd take on out here in her own yard. He opened the top of the bird feeder and poured seed in.

"Isn't it kind of strange to fill the feeders now?" she asked. "The birds sleep at night."

He grinned. "I've got them convinced that there's a Santa Claus."

"Some Santa," she said with a laugh. "Where's your beard and red suit?"

"Who needs a red suit?" he murmured, and pulled her close with his free arm. He felt a stirring deep in his soul. The night, the wine and pizza they'd just shared and maybe his presence—everything had worked to make her seem relaxed, ready to enjoy a Saturday night. Ready to enjoy him? "Just tell Santa what you want and I'll get it for you."

He saw the indecision in her eyes, flickering in the pale glow of the streetlight, as she fought within herself. Then she pulled away.

"Two months ago," she said, "if anybody had told me that I would be enjoying the warmth of a twenty-degree night, I would have had them committed."

"There's no wind right now," he pointed out. "No wind, no windchill. Plus, it's a lot warmer than that. It's somewhere in the thirties. Our January thaw."

"And here I thought I was getting tough and used to the freezing cold."

He laughed and closed the bird feeder, starting toward the next one by the huge evergreens in front of the house. She followed.

"Too bad it's cloudy tonight," he said. "Or I could give you a test on the constellations."

"I'd fail," she said with a laugh. "You can't see too many constellations in New York."

"Perhaps, then, what you need is personal instruction."

"And you happen to know somebody who could teach me, right?"

Her eyes invited him, so he leaned over and brushed her cheeks with his lips. "A farm boy who spent many a night in the meadow gazing up at the stars."

"Really?" Her voice was ripe with disbelief. "Didn't this irritate your companion as you lay there gazing up at the stars and ignoring her?"

"Ignoring who?" They reached the other feeder and he emptied the rest of the seed into it. "Are you suggesting I wasn't out in the meadow for the sole purpose of gazing at the stars?"

"I'm suggesting I'm surprised that you even noticed there were stars out at all," she teased.

He grabbed for her hand even as she started to dart away. "I'll have you know that I've never found a woman so engrossing that I wasn't aware of the stars." His arms slid around her, pulling her close. She didn't resist. "Until now," he added softly, his breath kissing her mouth even before his lips did.

He wanted to devour her, to taste that sweetness that the fullness of her lips promised. He wanted to feel her hunger rising to meet his, but he knew her too well to expect miracles. She was like a bird, easily startled and always ready to fly away. He had to teach her to trust before he could teach her to soar with him.

But it was true what he'd told her. He'd never met anyone like her. No other woman had awoken such a hunger in him or such a need to hold and protect. Other women had been easy to laugh with and easy to forget because they'd never needed him the way Holly did. There was so much he wanted to teach her, to give her, to share with her. Time stood still in her presence. The past and future faded into the here and now, the only things that mattered.

His lips, gentle as the night around them, lightly danced across her mouth, promising her wonders and delight but not staying long enough to deliver them. Then he let her go.

She moved slowly back and he could feel her confusion, not over his actions but over her own response. For a moment in his arms, he could have sworn she had forgotten her fears. Now her concerns were returning, but there was nothing he could do to stop that. It would take time to heal all her wounds and fears, and his heart told him to be patient.

"Do you want to sit down or go back inside?" he asked.

"We can sit down."

Zach saw this as a victory for him. Apparently Holly's fears hadn't completely won, after all. He went to the masonry bench and brushed off the snow. "Milady," he said with a deep bow.

"Kind sir." She curtsied with a smile that tore at his heart, then sat down.

"This garden is beautiful beyond compare in the spring and summer."

"Mmm."

"You'll enjoy it," he went on.

"Mmm."

"Don't you think you will?"

"That's a lot of tomorrows from today," she said. "I don't want to think about any tomorrows right now. Not even one."

He responded with silence. The house had been a source of tension for her, but she was starting to accept it as home. He would see that she would be around here in the spring.

"Pokagon's been real quiet lately," he said. "You must be healing very well."

The faintest flicker of tension ran through her body. "He's been dead a long time," she said. "People like that tend to be very quiet."

Zach chuckled and squeezed her shoulder. "Pokagon understands. He'll keep working on you until you're completely healed."

"And how will I know when this wondrous event has occurred?" There was no missing her skepticism. "Is he going to leave a note or will he sit down and have a chat with me?"

"You'll know when you trust your feelings without reservation."

"Well, then." She sprang up from the bench and threw her arms up in the air. "I am healed."

He remained seated, not replying.

"You disbelieve?" she asked.

"I didn't say anything."

"You do disbelieve. Oh, you of little faith. What will Pokagon say?"

He continued looking at her. He could see that even bundled up in her down coat she was beautiful.

"Trust your feelings, you said." She jumped into the silence. "Well, then, here is your proof. I feel like a little kid tonight and we're going to make angels in the snow."

"Angels?"

"Sure. Didn't you ever make them?"

"Yes." What had gotten into her? he wondered. Were her worries making her frantic to keep moving or had she suddenly found peace? No, he decided. It was too soon for that. Miracles took a little longer. "But I haven't made one in years."

"And here I thought you were a fun guy." She lay down in the snow, moving her arms up and down and her legs back and forth, then stood up carefully so her footprints didn't mar the angel she'd made. "I'll have you know I was the champion angel maker in my neighborhood. Whenever it snowed, I'd race to the park the first thing in the morning and make angels."

"And who holds the title now that you've left New York?" he asked as he lay gently down in the snow next to her angel.

"Oh, that was long ago." Her joyous smile suddenly died. "Back when I was a kid. It doesn't feel the same now."

He laughed as his arms and legs pushed the snow into an angelic form. "Nope. The snow is colder than it used to be back then." But he felt like a kid now, here with her.

But she didn't laugh. "This was silly," she said hesitantly. "You don't have to finish."

"Too late for second thoughts. I'm all done." He got to his feet in time to take her hand and keep her from trudging back into the house.

"Look, our wings are touching," he said, pointing to the overlapping indentations in the snow. "Back when I was in school, kids would say you were going together if that happened."

"Neither of us is a kid anymore."

And going together wasn't what he wanted from her. Not by a long shot.

"Besides, if it stays this warm all night, they'll be melted by tomorrow. All gone."

"But isn't it good to experience joy, beauty, even if it's only for a moment?"

She stared at her house across the yard, the light from the kitchen a beacon of warmth, but he knew she was seeing something else. Something from the past that ate at her. Tell me what's wrong, his heart pleaded. Let me carry your hurts for a while.

"I think it's time we went in," she said.

He said nothing. He only took her hand as they walked toward the house. Someday, he decided, the hurts would spill out and he would be there to hold her, to comfort her and make her smile again.

Chapter Seven

Holly made an angel in the snow, the best one ever, but her father refused to look. It had perfect wings and the biggest, widest skirt Holly had ever made. Not a single flake of snow marred the crisp edges. Didn't he care how beautiful it was?

"Daddy," she called out, but his back stayed turned to her.

Maybe if she made another one, an even better one, he would turn around and love her again. So she made another and another, each one larger, better, more desperate than the last. The snow slid down the back of her neck and into her boots, but still she kept making angels until she couldn't find space to make any more.

"Daddy, look," she said, tugging at his sleeve. But when he turned it wasn't him. It was a stranger; her father was back on the other side of the angels, except then that wasn't him, either. Everyone looked like him, but nobody was.

"Daddy," she cried out, but even as she ran from stranger to stranger, the wind changed. It swirled around her, dancing in the air so she couldn't see her father, couldn't see anyone. Her precious angels were getting covered up. They wouldn't be there for her father to see.

She raced over to them, trying to remake them, but as fast as she did, the wind destroyed them. ''Stop,'' she shouted. ''Stop!'' Tears streamed down her cheeks, but she brushed them away. She would save just one angel, but as she tried, hands held her back.

''Let me go,'' she cried, but the hands wouldn't and instead began shaking her.

''Holly. Holly.''

The snowy childhood scene struggled, clutching at her consciousness, but then slipped away. The sun shrank into a bedside lamp and there was no wind.

''Holly,'' Ruth said again, shaking Holly's shoulder one more time. ''Holly, wake up.''

''Mother,'' Holly murmured. She sat up slowly. ''I'm awake now. What's wrong?''

''That's what I wondered,'' Ruth said. ''Were you having a bad dream?''

Holly felt groggy, mired in quicksand, as she tried to think. ''I guess,'' she said, and swung her feet out over the edge of the bed. The cool air shocked her enough to clear some fog from her mind. ''I was dreaming about making angels in the snow.''

''What a strange thing to dream about.''

Holly glanced up at her mother and smiled sheepishly as the evening came back to haunt her. ''Not really. Zach and I made angels out in the yard when we came home.''

Ruth sat on the edge of the bed, looking more concerned than amused. ''*You* made angels in the snow?''

Holly pulled her feet back under the covers as she leaned against the headboard. ''What's so strange about that? I used to make them all the time when I was a kid.''

''You aren't a kid anymore.''

Holly shrugged and looked away. The pool of light from the bedside lamp encircled her bed, but ghosts lurked in the shadowy corners just waiting for the light to dim so they could come rushing back at her.

"I was dreaming about Daddy," she said slowly. "I'd made angels in the snow and wanted him to see them, but he wasn't there."

"Hardly ever was in real life, either."

"No, I guess he wasn't." Holly burrowed under her blankets. She was tired, sleep still clinging like a shroud, but she feared a return to that hazy twilight of dreams. It was raining outside; she could hear the slow steady pit-pat hitting the roof.

"To tell you the truth," Ruth said, "I was a little hesitant to come in here. I heard noises and didn't know... Well, you and Zach seemed to be having such a good time together tonight."

That opened Holly's eyes. "Mother!"

"Don't 'Mother' me like I've said something shocking. I think Zach is one sexy man."

Holly smiled, but more in pain than joy. "I think so, too."

"So what are you doing about it?"

"Staying away from him."

"Holly."

She was tired. The sound of the rain was so soothing. Maybe this time she'd dream she was in the tropics. No past to come jumping out of the shadows in that setting. "I'm not looking for romance, Mother. I tried it once and have moved on to other things."

"Oh, pooh." Ruth moved, bouncing the bed slightly, but Holly refused to open her eyes. "You tried it once and you're scared to try it again."

"Maybe." Holly smothered a huge yawn in the blanket. "I never noticed how soothing rain on the roof can be. I'm ready to go back to sleep."

"What rain?" Ruth asked.

Holly's heart stopped, a reflex action when dealing with this house. No, it couldn't be. Stop panicking. "The rain that's falling outside," Holly said slowly as she sat back up.

Ruth had gotten off the bed and pulled the drape aside from the window. The glass was perfectly dry; there was no distortion of the streetlight Holly could see glowing over the neighbor's garage.

"Oh, no. Not again," Holly said with a moan. "Now what's leaking?"

She wanted to stay in bed, to pull the covers up over her head, but when had life ever allowed her that option? She threw the covers back and trudged into her bathroom. She could hear a steady drip but everything seemed fine. Faucets closed tight, no wet spots in the floor underneath. Shower dry as a bone.

"Holly, over here."

She turned. Her mother was standing by the fireplace in the bedroom. "But there aren't any pipes over there," Holly said. "After that shower fiasco, I figured out where all the water pipes would be and—"

Ruth was staring at the ceiling, and even from the bathroom doorway Holly could see the water streaming down the wall, puddling on the mantel, then dripping onto the brick hearth.

"Oh, great. The roof." Holly groaned. "Damn this house."

"I think we ought to call Zach."

Sighing deeply, Holly looked at her bedside clock. It was ten after three. She was back in her dream, unprotected from the elements, at the mercy of fate. She hadn't been able to keep life perfect to hold on to her father; she couldn't keep this house in shape to shelter her family. She was dejected, and she didn't care who they called.

In about the time that it took for her to put on a pair of loafers and her robe, Zach was downstairs. Old jeans hugged his slim hips and stretched taut across his muscular legs. His feet were thrust into scruffy, untied tennis shoes.

"Look at that," Holly said angrily. "That broken-down roof is leaking like a sieve."

"Sorry," he replied with a soft smile.

Her anger started slipping away, moving to make room for an army of guilt. It wasn't his fault the place was a wreck, but Holly grabbed her irritation and held on tight.

"Now do you see why I hate this stupid old place? It's always leaking somewhere. No, they aren't really leaks," she corrected herself. "This place is so old and sick that it's constantly crying. It's calling out in pain."

Zach's lips curled into that cute, crooked smile that she just hated. "That's very good," he said. "Have you ever thought of going into real estate? You'd be great at writing the copy for the ads. You might not sell many houses, but you'd work up a lot of sympathy for them."

The anger returned, banishing all vestiges of guilt. "It's easy for you to take this so calmly. It's not your roof that's leaking." Suddenly puzzlement marched in, occupying all the corners of her mind. "Is your apartment dry?"

"As the proverbial bone."

"But you're on the third floor and I'm on the second."

He looked up at the ceiling. "I think most of this area above you is attic space," he said. "There must be a half attic on the south side of the house because I haven't got any windows on that side."

Holly slumped back onto the bed. Maybe Pokagon really was mad at her. Zach was on the third floor, yet she was the one with a leaky ceiling.

"Let's go look."

She didn't bother to look up. "What for? It won't make any difference."

"We might be able to fix things temporarily so your ceiling won't suffer any more damage and you could go back to sleep. Got a flashlight?"

She pulled one from a drawer in her bedside table, then followed him up to the third floor. His door was open, but she turned to avoid looking inside his apartment as they passed it. Seeing into his home was like looking into his soul; she didn't want to know those things about him. Knowing led to understanding, and that led to caring—something she'd crossed off her list years ago. When they reached the end of the hallway Zach opened the half door and shone the flashlight in. Its yellow beam struggled feebly to stay alive.

"This thing is almost dead."

"Sorry."

Her voice sounded small, but she didn't care. She couldn't even keep working batteries in her flashlight. Great job she was doing fighting off the elements. No wonder everything was going wrong.

"Watch where you step," he said. "There's no flooring in the attic."

Holly followed the flickering beam, carefully putting one foot on a narrow floor joist before moving on to the next. She kept her balance by holding on to the rafters above her, trying not to think of what creatures were living among the dark, dusty boards. What good was this going to do?

"Ah, I thought so," he muttered.

"What?"

"It's leaking around that fireplace chimney," he said.

"Ruth and Bruno made a fire in the downstairs fireplace when they came home tonight."

"That and the warming trend are what did it," he said. "See, it starts here, follows this rafter and—"

The flashlight died completely. She could hear Zach pounding it with the palm of his hand.

"Damn. It's totally out."

"I'm sorry." Then angry with herself for apologizing all the time, she said brusquely, "I'll call Mother and have her find us another one." But as she turned, her foot slipped and she gasped. His arm was quickly around her waist.

"Are you all right?"

She wondered for a moment how he found her so quickly but then decided that she really didn't want to know. "I'm fine," she said, though any doctor might be alarmed at her rapid heartbeat.

She began calling for Ruth, and after the third shout her mother answered from down the hall. "Where are you guys?"

"In the attic above my room," Holly replied. "We need another flashlight. Zach was showing me something and the one we have died."

"Oh, is that so?"

Holly was sure that she didn't care for the tone in Ruth's voice, but now was not the time to argue. "Get us another flashlight, please."

"Why? Haven't you seen everything you want to yet?"

"We need it to get out of here," Holly explained, ignoring Zach's snicker and the sparks of warmth it ignited in her heart.

The flip-flop of Ruth's slippers echoed in the silence of their attic world. Holly held on to Zach's arm and leaned slightly, just enough to keep her balance, against him. He was so warm, so strong. It felt good, too good. All sorts of dreams danced around her in the darkness, like a child's game, taunting her with promises of things that could never be. Security. An arm to lean on. A heartbeat beside hers in the darkness.

"I'm really all right," she said brusquely. "I don't need to be supported anymore." Her heart laughed at her, but she didn't need support. Not now, not ever again.

"That's okay."

"No, really. I can stand here by myself."

"I don't think it would be wise to go shifting around in the dark. These joists can be treacherous."

Holly felt her body reach out for his. She longed for the comfort of his arms, the sweetness of his touch that could chase all the shadows from her dreams. Joists weren't the only thing that could be treacherous.

"You don't have to show me the leak," she said, still leaning all too comfortably on him. Escape was all she wanted now. Was it? a little voice mocked. "I can't fix it."

"Neither can I. We'll just let Ruth shine the light for us so we can get out of here."

"That would be wise."

"It certainly would."

Was there a tightness in his throat to match hers? The thought that he was wanting her just as much as she wanted him was fuel on the fire in her heart. What had been a smoldering turned into a raging fire. Desire, hunger, love and tenderness all collided in her soul.

"I know some people who specialize in old roofs," he said. "I could give them a call."

"Good idea."

It was getting so hot in the attic that Holly was finding it hard to breathe. The January thaw must have brought temperatures in the eighties.

"I'm going to have to start demanding some payment in return."

"Payment?" Her voice sounded husky. She cleared her throat. "Payment for what?"

"I've been doing you a lot of favors lately."

"What kind of payment?"

"I found one," Ruth shouted from the end of the hall.

"I'll settle for dinner tomorrow for starters."

"Jenny's got a basketball game."

"Not all day."

"Then the school's having a potluck dinner to raise money for new science equipment."

"Monday, then." But before she could open her mouth to protest, he added, "Monday for lunch, when Jenny will be in school and Ruth will have other plans."

His arm tightened around her waist, but that had nothing to do with her agreement. "Okay," she said, caressing his arm lightly. Accepting his date was only polite. He had been doing a lot for them, but lunch would be the start *and* the finish.

"This report doesn't have to be out until the end of next week," Holly's secretary said on Monday morning. "Why don't I work on it now and go over it with you this afternoon?"

Holly pulled the papers away from Maureen's reach. "I just want to look at this last page."

"Don't you have a luncheon meeting today?" her secretary asked. "I thought I saw it penciled in."

"It's nothing." Holly waved her hand. "I'm just getting together with a neighbor."

"It's a date?"

Holly shrugged, trying to keep her eyes concentrating on the figures before her, while Zach's smile was in her mind. She shook her head and the figures reappeared. "I guess some people might call it that."

"Well, for heaven's sake." Maureen snatched the papers from Holly's hand. "Then give me that report. I have two whole sections that I have to do yet. And if you don't leave soon you'll be late."

"I have over half an hour," Holly said, glancing at her watch. "I don't think anything out here is more than half an hour away."

"Then go home and freshen up."

Holly shuffled some other papers around. "Well, I guess I could do that."

Her secretary left the office and Holly sat for a long moment staring at the wall. Slim and Shorty weren't finished yet, but they sure were close. Another week and this place would be humming, just the way a business office should be.

Sighing, she pushed herself away from the desk. She supposed that she could stop off at home, but what for? Picking out another outfit would be more trouble than it was worth. It wasn't a real date, after all, just a thank-you lunch. Maureen gave her a bright smile and a wave as Holly left.

Why had she agreed to this? Holly asked herself as she trudged through the parking lot to her car—the car Zach had helped her pick out. She unlocked the door and climbed inside. Picking out the car was no big deal; he hadn't done more than any salesman.

Holly started the car but made it only to the edge of the parking lot. She noticed the wallpaper store across the street and realized she really ought to be getting some paper for Jenny's room. The walls were faded and colorless, and there would be no time for this type of shopping once the rest of her staff came on board.

She reparked the car and hurried across the street, but after looking through several books, Holly gave up. There were so many patterns to choose from, yet none of them was right.

She slammed the last book closed. Maybe the real problem was that she didn't know her own daughter. She should ask Ruth, since her mother was the one who was actually raising Jenny. Holly left the store with empty hands and a heavy heart. Maybe she should skip lunch so she could leave early and spend some time with her daughter.

But she had promised to meet Zach for lunch. Or rather, her silly heart had promised for her. Grimly, Holly pushed her reluctant feet forward. Regardless of what part of her had made the decision, she had said she'd be there, and she would be. But instead of a full meal they could have a sandwich—or maybe just a drink. She could get back to work more quickly, and she wasn't that hungry, anyway.

Zach had suggested a little country inn just over the border in Michigan, so she circled the university and headed north. What if she was early? Restaurants didn't really know what to do with single women who came early. Maybe she'd take the time to do a little exploring.

She drove up and down some back roads, going from empty fields to sardine-can housing, then back to fields again in the blink of an eye. As her wanderings drew her near the state line, Holly grew more despondent. The houses out here were nice enough, but certainly nothing special. None of the houses, no matter what the price range, had any...any...

She racked her brain for a word. None of the houses had any character. All those houses looked exactly like what they were. Development houses, made in batches and dumped on an unsuspecting landscape that couldn't fight back.

After stopping at a stop sign and looking both ways, Holly floored the accelerator. What did "character" mean for a house? It meant the plumbing was shot, it needed re-wiring and the roof leaked. That was character, and what good did that do a person?

Welcome to Michigan.

"Swell," she muttered to the sign. "Almost there." Though with a little luck, she wouldn't find the restaurant. Why had she agreed to this lunch?

Unfortunately, good luck wasn't with her. The old farm-house with its tasteful black-and-red sign stood out among the cinder-block warehouses and small steel-walled machine shops.

"Hooray," she murmured. "Here I am and not even hungry."

She saw Zach's car over by the doorway and parked at the other end of the lot. After killing the engine, she sat and stared, leaving the key in the ignition. Before the digital clock on the dash had died with the engine, Holly had seen that she was a good fifteen minutes late.

This was ridiculous. She didn't know how to date anymore. There was no vast reservoir of witty conversation to fish from. No flirty flash in her eyes or wealth of time to sit and smile. Dating was for young people, ones with singly focused lives that they wanted to expand. Get your career settled, then squeeze in a relationship. Well, she'd already had a relationship, and now she had a family to claim her time. Why was she trying to pretend she had room for anything else?

Suddenly the wail of an ambulance called for her attention, and she returned to consciousness just in time to see it whizz by in her rearview mirror. The sound was still hanging in the air when she remembered the wail of another ambulance. She hadn't seen that one, but it had come very close to her home. It had stopped outside the little grocery store where Joel had gone to get another half gallon of milk. That was the ambulance that had carried Joel's broken body to the emergency room. He had died before reaching the hospital.

The officers had been very solicitous. 'It was a terrible accident, ma'am,' they'd said. 'Your husband never knew what hit him.' But it happened, especially during the holidays. People were in a hurry and got careless.

The lump in her throat hurt. Holly wondered for a moment if tears would come, but then she knew they wouldn't. The tear well for Joel and their life together had been drained dry. All that was left was a dull, empty ache.

Could she ever live with the risk of that awful pain of loss again? Could she bear a loneliness that was so much more horrible because her life had been full? She carried the emptiness now, but she had grown accustomed to it. It was part of her, like a bad back or farsightedness. She had learned to live with it. What she couldn't live with was filling that void with love and then carrying the fear that it could be taken away in a moment.

She watched as her hand moved forward and started the car. She continued watching as her feet, her hands, all her faculties, cooperated to put her car back on the road.

As she drove down the highway her dark load seemed to dissipate. Things were going to get busier at work. Three more of her new staff were coming on next week and she'd have even less time to spend with Jenny. Holly decided she'd put in a couple of hours' work and pick Jenny up from school. They'd bum around and have a good time with one of Holly's last free days. She didn't need to have a man around to have fun.

Holly stopped at the garage door and paused, her hand over the garage door opener. "Do you have much homework today?" she asked her daughter.

Jenny nodded. "Tons."

Holly's heart sank slightly. "Too much to go to the shopping center and mall around?"

"I've got three pages of math and a whole chapter of science to read."

It didn't sound so bad to Holly, but Jenny's tone said it was a month's worth of work. "Well, maybe some other time."

"Yeah, Mom."

The garage door inched open and Holly drove the car inside. Zach's car was in its spot, but that was no reason to think he was at home. He could have brought it home and then walked back to the university for his afternoon classes.

Jenny took her books and Holly grabbed the groceries, trying to ignore that growing sense of guilt for standing Zach up at lunchtime. It had been for the best. She'd gone back to the office, gotten a lot done and then picked up Jenny from school. They couldn't go shopping as Holly had hoped, but those extra minutes of chatting in the car were worth any price. She didn't want to consider that she might have had her time with Jenny and still had lunch with Zach. Did she have to be rude and leave him in the lurch?

Holly sighed as she opened the front gate. She wished she'd never met Zach. Then she'd be satisfied with work and home and never be tempted to risk something else again. She'd never have had those few moments in his arms to remember how sweet closeness can be.

Jenny followed into the yard, calling out to an imaginary dog, "Here, Duke. Here, Duke. Come on, boy."

"Jenny," Holly said, loading her voice with all the maternal patience she could muster even though she was grateful for the distraction.

"I'm just practicing," Jenny replied with an equal load of a child's innocence. "We do have a big yard, Mom. Just right for a dog."

Holly closed the gate behind them. "We'll get one, honey."

"Every week they publish pictures of poor abandoned dogs in the paper," Jenny said. "Nice dogs that need a family."

"I'm just waiting until we get settled in a permanent home."

"Isn't this one permanent?"

"No," Holly pointed out. "It's liable to collapse any minute." She hoped the defenses around her heart were stronger.

"Mom," Jenny protested, "it's been here more than a hundred years. Zach says it'll be here another hundred."

Zach says. It was always Zach says. Sometimes Holly felt as though she was haunted by him. He was always in her thoughts. She constantly saw his laughing eyes smiling at her. Whose fault was that? her common sense asked her. Jenny had talked about homework, a dog and then Zach. Holly could hardly blame anyone else for treachery that her own heart was guilty of.

"Let's get these things in the house," Holly said. Activity was what she needed to regain her equilibrium.

"Ah, you must be Holly," a man's voice called to her. Holly looked around to find two men grinning at her over the edge of the roof.

She moved forward. "Are you men the roofers?"

"No, ma'am. We're eagles. We're going to build our nest right here on your chimney and raise our young."

Jenny's snicker caused Holly to take her eyes off the men, and by the time she looked back they were rapidly climbing down the ladder.

"Hi, Holly. I'm Joe," said the portly one with a permanent five-o'clock shadow.

The other was a tall, thin man who slouched. His sandy-colored mustache partially obscured a sardonic smile. "Evening, ma'am, I'm Carl."

"You can't be eagles," Jenny said.

Carl looked at Joe. "Little person there says we can't be eagles."

Joe shrugged.

"You can't fly."

"Darn," Carl exclaimed. "I had my heart fixed firm on eagle."

"I guess we gotta be roofers, then." Joe shook his head sadly.

Carl put a painful look on his face. "It's gonna break Momma's heart."

Holly cleared her throat, trying to clear the air, as well. "Could somebody please tell me about my leaky roof?"

Joe said, "It's the chimney, ma'am."

Carl said, "Weren't done right."

"Ice built up."

"Cracked the flashing."

"Gets a little warm."

"Comes leaking into your house."

"We'll clean it out."

"Put in a little patch."

"That'll fix it."

"But only for temporary."

"Might fix it for good later in the week."

"If the weather stays warm."

"But probably sometime next month."

"It'll be done easily by Easter."

"Surely by May."

Back and forth. She went from one to the other. Faster and faster. The Ping-Pong effect was almost making her dizzy. She didn't know who was ahead, but she breathed a sigh of relief when they stopped.

"Thank you," she said, and taking Jenny's arm, hurried away, straight into a broad chest.

"Careful."

Strong arms grabbed her so she wouldn't fall. She looked up and caught her breath. "Oh, hello, Zach."

"Hello." His smile was soft.

Holly had to look away a moment. "I'm sorry about lunch."

"That's okay. I knew what had happened."

Holly pushed herself away. Her apology had been ready, but his calm, easy understanding pushed it back in the deep freezer. He didn't know her as well as he seemed to think he did. "How do you know what happened?"

"Easy." He seemed so sure of himself. "The ice was pretty thick, but the fire last night melted some and a leak was started. You've put on a little patch, but it's only temporary."

She frowned, but it was a mocking one, laughter danced in her eyes. "That was the roof," she pointed out. "I was talking about the date I broke for lunch." She shifted the grocery bag in her arms and started for the door.

"So was I," Zach said softly, and took the bag from her arms. His eyes caught her, pinned her down and refused to let her struggle. "I might get a smile out of you this week. Probably a lunch next week. Easily a dinner this month, and surely I'll win your heart in the end." He went into the house, leaving her amid the echoes of his words.

Chapter Eight

I'll get it," Jenny said that evening, jumping up at the sound of the doorbell.

"That's probably for Grandma," Holly said as she grabbed Jenny's arm. "You just sit down and finish your math homework. That progress report waiting for me when I got home was not the best of surprises."

Her daughter made a face but sat down as Ruth's footsteps echoed on the foyer's marble floor. They heard the front door open, the murmur of her greetings, and then a hearty boom overwhelmed them all.

"I think that might be Bruno," Jenny snickered.

"I'd like you to be polite, please."

"I'm not saying anything bad," Jenny protested. "I like Bruno. He's a real neat guy."

"Good evening, fair ladies. Why the long faces?" Bruno asked as he entered the room.

"Homework." Ruth laughed. She glanced quickly over their shoulders. "To be exact, math homework."

"Ah. The torment of math homework. The memories are enough to freeze my soul in permanent fear."

"Didn't you like math?" Jenny asked.

"Let's just say that we never reached a point of mutual respect and understanding."

"Jenny always did well in math," Holly said. "I don't understand why she's having problems here."

"Indiana math," Bruno replied with a big wink at Jenny.

Jenny grinned. "Yeah. That's it."

"Well, we'd better be going," Ruth said. "We shouldn't be late."

"Where're you going?" Jenny asked.

"Out," Holly answered firmly for them, then tapped the math page in front of Jenny. "And we're staying here to study math, then we're going to look at science."

"We're going to a restaurant downtown to watch the Bulls-Knicks game on their big-screen television," Ruth told her with a hug. "Finish up your homework, honey."

"I will. Bye, Gran. Bye, Bruno. Hope the Knicks knock 'em dead."

Bruno and Ruth left, leaving their goodbyes to dance with their laughter among the crystal in the chandelier above the table. Holly's mind drifted from the scratching of Jenny's pencil on the paper. Resting her chin in her hand, Holly stared off into space.

The house seemed so quiet suddenly. Ruth wasn't a noisy person, not even a hummer or a whistler, so why should her absence seem so obvious? Holly didn't really like to think that knowing Ruth was out on a date made the difference. It made her feel childish and small when she really was happy for Ruth.

Her mother deserved someone who could make her laugh. Holly bit off the next thought before it could barely take root. No, she herself did not need someone to make her laugh. Despite Zach's certainty that she was in need of healing, she was fine. The patch she'd put on her heart this afternoon hadn't been a temporary one. It was permanent, not to be removed.

Jenny's movement beside Holly brought her thoughts back to the present.

"Let's go through this last page and then we'll—" Holly stared at the math work sheet. "You've already finished it."

Jenny nodded. "I did my science, too. Do you want to check it?"

Holly pulled the papers toward her but kept her eyes on Jenny. "I don't understand, Jenny. How can you do the homework so well and still have so much trouble with the tests?"

"I choke under the pressure?"

Holly turned from the earnest face and its shy little smile to concentrate on the papers in front of her. Con artists like Jenny had a harder time conning you, if they couldn't look you in the eye.

"I really don't think your schoolwork is a joking matter," Holly noted as she scanned the papers. They seemed perfect. "And two of your teachers wrote on that progress report that you don't contribute to any class discussions."

"I don't want to right now."

Holly put the papers back together and pushed them toward Jenny. She hadn't been in the new school that long. Maybe once she was acclimated to her classmates she'd speak up more. What was hard to understand was the poor test grades. Jenny had never had that problem.

"I'm doing much better in basketball," Jenny said brightly. "Mrs. Scholl says I'm the most improved player on the team."

"You don't get a grade for basketball," Holly felt compelled to point out.

Her daughter shrugged her shoulders.

"And you can't get a job playing basketball."

"Maybe I'll be a professional basketball player."

"Women don't play professional basketball."

"Why not?"

"I don't know." Tension opened the door for irritation to ride her tongue. "But there just aren't that many professional American teams for women."

"There should be."

"Jenny—" Holly stopped. This was a ridiculous conversation. Jenny needed time to relax, to get over her nervousness about building new friendships, and Holly should be helping her adjust. "Honey, I know things are different here than they were back in New York, but they can still be good. You have to be brave enough to try. Now, do you want some hot chocolate?"

Jenny shook her head. "The caffeine will just make me hyper and I'll have a hard time falling asleep. I'll have a glass of warm milk instead after I take a shower, okay?"

"Sure."

Holly kept up her smile until Jenny had disappeared up the stairs. Darn it. Jenny wasn't dumb; she'd always been a good student. Maybe Holly should go in and talk to her teachers. Together they might gain some insight into Jenny's problems. That also might embarrass Jenny, who seemed not to want Holly to intrude in anything right now.

She got up slowly, her load resting heavily on her shoulders as she made her way into the kitchen. Kids should come with an instruction manual. That way parents would at least have a fighting chance.

She poured the milk for Jenny. Then, as she was returning the container to the refrigerator, another item caught her eye. Cheesecake. Ruth had bought cheesecake. Why had her mother done that? Ruth knew that Holly couldn't resist cheesecake, especially when it was covered with cherries.

Holly shut the door firmly and busied herself warming the milk. Cheesecake was loaded with calories, probably a zillion per ounce. She wondered if Zach liked cheesecake.

Now where did that come from? she asked herself. Why was he always ready to leap into her thoughts? It was a good thing she hadn't had lunch with him. Her overly imaginative heart didn't need any encouragement to give him the starring role in her daydreams.

And just to prove that, Holly took the cheesecake out and cut herself a piece. As she was about to put the rest back in the refrigerator, Jenny walked into the kitchen.

"Oh, my gosh!" Jenny exclaimed. "Who is that for?"

"It's cheesecake, honey. Would you like a piece?"

THE JOKER GOES WILD!

Play
this
card
right!

See
inside!

SILHOUETTE®
WANTS TO <u>GIVE</u> YOU

- 4 free books
- A free digital clock/calendar
- A free mystery gift

IT'S A WILD, WILD, WONDERFUL
FREE OFFER!
HERE'S WHAT YOU GET:

1. *Four New Silhouette Special Edition® Novels—FREE!* Everything comes up hearts and diamonds with four exciting romances—yours FREE from Silhouette Books. Each of these brand-new novels brings you the passion and tenderness of today's greatest love stories.

2. *A Useful, Practical Digital Clock/Calendar—FREE!* As a free gift simply to thank you for accepting four free books we'll send you a stylish digital quartz clock/calendar—a handsome addition to any decor! The changeable, month-at-a-glance calendar pops out, and may be replaced with a favorite photograph.

3. *An Exciting Mystery Bonus—FREE!* You'll go wild over this surprise gift. It will win you compliments and score as a splendid addition to your home.

4. *Money-Saving Home Delivery!* Join Silhouette Books and enjoy the convenience of previewing six new books every month, delivered to your home. Each book is yours for $2.49—26 cents less per book than the retail price. And there is no extra charge for postage and handling! You may cancel at any time, for any reason, and still keep your free books and gifts, just by dropping us a line. Great savings and total convenience are the name of the game at Silhouette Books!

5. *Free Newsletter!* It makes you feel like a partner to the world's most popular authors . . . tells about their upcoming books . . . even gives you their recipes!

6. *More Mystery Gifts Throughout the Year!* No joke! Because home subscribers are our most valued readers, when you subscribe to Silhouette Books, we'll be sending you additional free gifts from time to time—as a token of our appreciation!

GO WILD
WITH SILHOUETTE® TODAY—
JUST COMPLETE, DETACH AND
MAIL YOUR FREE-OFFER CARD!

GET YOUR GIFTS FROM SILHOUETTE®
ABSOLUTELY FREE!

Mail this card today!

Printed in the U.S.A.

PLACE
JOKER
STICKER
HERE

PLAY THIS CARD RIGHT!

YES! Please send me my four Silhouette Special Edition® novels FREE along with my free Digital Clock/Calendar and free mystery gift as explained on the opposite page.

235 CIL R1XM

NAME _____
(PLEASE PRINT)

ADDRESS _____ APT. _____

CITY _____

STATE _____ ZIP CODE _____

Prices subject to change. Offer limited to one per household and not valid to current Special Edition subscribers.

SILHOUETTE BOOKS "NO RISK" GUARANTEE

• There's no obligation to buy—and the free books remain yours to keep.

• Unless you tell us otherwise, every month we'll send you six more books, months before they appear in stores.

• You may end your subscription anytime—just write and let us know, or return the shipment to us—at our cost.

IT'S NO JOKE!

MAIL THE POSTPAID CARD AND GET FREE GIFTS AND $11.00 WORTH OF SILHOUETTE® NOVELS — FREE!

If offer card is missing write to:
Silhouette Books, 901 Fuhrmann Blvd., P.O. Box 1867, Buffalo, NY 14269-1867

BUSINESS REPLY MAIL

FIRST CLASS   PERMIT NO. 717   BUFFALO, NY

POSTAGE WILL BE PAID BY ADDRESSEE

SILHOUETTE BOOKS

901 Fuhrmann Blvd.
P.O. Box 1867
Buffalo, NY 14240-9952

NO POSTAGE
NECESSARY
IF MAILED
IN THE
UNITED STATES

"Are you going to eat all that, Mom? I mean, like, it's loaded with cholesterol. Your arteries are going to be clogged tight after the first bite."

"Since you don't have the courtesy to answer, I take it you don't want any." Holly put the cheesecake back in the refrigerator and shut the door.

"I'll just have my glass of warm milk, thank you."

Holly sat at the kitchen table and ate her cake in silence, staring across from her at the dancing green coffeepots on the wallpaper. Why was it that the ugly wallpaper in this house stayed firmly in place while the roof fell apart? Didn't Pokagon have a sense of order about what should go wrong? In spite of the green coffeepots the kitchen looked homey. Ruth's cookbooks were lined up along the back of one counter, and the refrigerator was already covered with notes and lists.

Jenny finished her glass of milk and, after wiping off her milk mustache, stared at Holly. "You only eat cheesecake when you're depressed," Jenny said. "What are you depressed about?"

Holly frowned at her. "I eat cheesecake whenever I have a taste for it."

"Which is when you're upset," Jenny insisted. "Is it because of the roof?"

"No, it's not because of the roof," Holly said, then hurried on. "It's not because of anything except that I had a taste for it."

"Is it because of Zach?" Jenny asked.

Holly stopped, fork poised above the cheesecake. "Because of Zach?" Was it so obvious that he haunted her thoughts?

"Because Bruno asked Grandma out tonight and Zach didn't ask you out."

"No," Holly said, and ate another bite. The cheesecake had somehow lost some of its appeal. "Your grandmother and Bruno are dating. Zach and I aren't."

"But don't you want to?"

"Jenny, honey," Holly said with a sigh. She put her fork down and reached across the corner of the table for Jenny's hand. "I like Zach. He's a nice person, but I don't want to date him. I don't want to date anyone."

"Because of me?" Jenny leaned back on her stool, balancing on the back two legs as she frowned at the tabletop. Her finger traced a scratch that had been left behind after jack-o'-lantern carving one year. "Hey, I know that single mothers have a harder time dating because lots of guys don't want a kid around. I didn't want to be causing you problems."

"Jen, don't ever think something like that!" Holly swept the girl up into her arms, the hurt in Jenny's voice stabbing at Holly's heart. "It has nothing to do with you."

"Sure."

Holly shook her slightly, as if to wake up Jenny's good sense, which must have been misplaced in the move. "It's because I loved your father so much," Holly told her. "And when he died, I thought I would die, too. I just decided I'm not going to love a man that way again."

Jenny snuggled a little closer, resting her head against Holly's chest. "How can you decide something like that?" she asked. "I thought love was something that just happened."

"No."

Holly's fingers slid through Jenny's wet hair, taking Holly back to a day long ago when she'd given Jenny a bath and was combing her hair afterward. Jenny had been perched on the arm of the sofa, singing "Old MacDonald Had a Farm" as loudly as she could, and every time she came to an animal sound Joel had chimed in, but always making the wrong noise. Jenny had laughed so hard she'd fallen into Holly's lap. Holly's arms now slid around Jenny, hugging her even tighter. Would there ever be days of pure happiness like that again?

Jenny squirmed slightly. "So if love doesn't happen, how does it work?"

Holly let go of Jenny and of the memory. "It grows. You meet someone nice and spend time with him and you might fall in love. If you don't want to fall in love, you don't spend time with the nice guys." She frowned. "Not that you should spend time with the rotten guys, either."

"You know what, Mom?" Jenny pulled away enough to look Holly right in the eye. "It sounds to me like you're afraid."

"I am not—"

"And a very wise person once told me that even though something is different it can still be good. You just have to be brave enough to try."

"A very wise person?"

Jenny grinned and threw her arms around Holly's neck. "G'night, Mom."

Holly hugged her back, a little tighter and a little longer than usual before letting her go. "Good night, sugar. Thanks for the advice."

"What advice?" Jenny stopped at the foot of the servants' stairs. "That was an order, Mom. A homework assignment for you. I want you to find a date for next weekend."

"Jen—" But the girl was gone, clattering up the stairs to her room. Holly sank back onto her stool, staring at the empty plate of cheesecake. Swell. Now she had ten zillion calories to work off before she went to bed, plus a homework assignment for next weekend. All she needed was for something else to go wrong with the house.

"Just kidding, Pokagon, sir," she called out quickly. Not that she believed in him, but there was no sense taking any chances.

Zach yawned and reached for the ceiling, stretching every muscle that he could notify. Then he sank back into his chair and contemplated the far wall, smiling grimly. He'd just finished writing a paper on the dig in southern Indiana he'd been on last summer. The artifacts they'd found proved that there was real communication between the tribes in the area. Written communication. He sighed.

Communication. He and Holly weren't communicating. Every time he tried to move closer, she backed away until they ended up farther apart than when they started. It was the most frustrating dance he'd ever tried. He knew she needed time; he accepted that. But just how much time was she going to need? Maybe if he saw some progress, no matter how slow, he wouldn't be getting so pushy. This afternoon's broken date was the final straw.

Yawning, he rolled his head and rubbed the back of his neck. The yawns indicated he was ready for bed, but the tightness across his neck and shoulders said no way.

Standing, Zach paced the room, again stretching his muscles. Should he try to force the issue with Holly? Confront her with the fact that she kept running away from him? Or should he go back to being kindly, patient Dr. Philips, a pose he was getting decidedly tired of? He stopped at a window and let his eyes savor the beauties of a winter night's scene. It had been relatively warm that afternoon and was overcast now; the temperature would be pleasant.

Zach threw open the window and breathed deeply. It was just what he'd expected. Crisp but pleasant, in a wintry sort of way. Like Holly had been. Wiggling his nose, he breathed a little more carefully this time. He could smell snow in the air. Did that mean a storm front was moving into her heart, also? Maybe—

Zach stopped, his thoughts sidetracked by a strange thumping from outside. He listened, still as the night—or still as the night usually was—and the noise came again. A couple of dull thumps, then a ringing sound, sort of like . . . like someone shooting baskets?

A quick glance at the clock told him it was just past eleven. He slipped into his boots, then pulled his coat on as he hurried down the stairs. Just what Holly needed—some neighborhood kid appropriating their basketball hoop in the middle of the night and waking her up.

He slipped out the door as the basketball thudded against the garage roof. The kid was a lousy shot, whoever he was. Maybe Zach should tell him to come back and practice during the day; Zach doubted Holly would mind. He walked down the path toward the alley. Over the fence he saw another ball wang against the garage roof. He reached the gate in time to see the kid retrieving the ball from under the evergreens on the far side of the alley.

"Hey," Zach called out. "Isn't it—"

The kid started at the sound of his voice, bumping against the evergreen and losing his stocking cap. Only it was soft, curly brown hair that shone in the light from the street lamp.

"Holly?"

She slowly straightened up, brushing snow and evergreen needles off her hat. "Hello, Zach." Her voice was tentative as she picked up the basketball and tucked it under one arm, then the other. Finally, as if deciding there was no way to hide it, she held it in both hands. "What are you doing out this late?"

"Chasing away some kid playing basketball," he told her, expecting a laugh in return.

"I'm sorry," she said.

No smile, just an apology. Couldn't she see the humor in this?

"Was I keeping you up?" she asked. "I had no idea you could hear the noise in the house."

He smiled. "It was the fact you kept missing that was bothering me. You're a lousy shot and I came out to give you some lessons."

"I made a few baskets," she retorted. Her voice had crept a bit closer to her normal feistiness.

"A few?" he teased. "Does hitting the roof count as coming close?"

"Hey, I'm not trying out for the pros, just looking for a little exercise." Apology over, she tossed the ball in the direction of the basket. It landed with a plop in a bank of snow next to the fence. "And it's not easy shooting baskets when you're wearing a winter coat."

He retrieved the ball and took a shot himself. It missed, too, but at least it bounced off the rim first. "So why are you looking for outdoor exercise at eleven o'clock on a Monday night in January? You should be curled up in bed. Or was your conscience bothering you about standing me up today?"

She got the ball and wiped some snow off one side. "I told you I was sorry about that."

"I was just teasing." He moved away from the fence to lean against the garage, his hands shoved deep into his pockets. He sensed a vulnerability about Holly tonight. Some fragile piece of herself seemed exposed, and he knew to tread carefully for fear of shattering it.

"Jenny's having some trouble in school," she said, tossing the basketball as she spoke. It hit the backboard and dropped near him. He tossed it back. "She wants to do well on the basketball team and I want to help her practice."

"Isn't that kind of to be expected? A new school is bound to be different, and then to come in in the middle of the school year, she'll need even more time to adjust."

"But she was a top student back in New York. Here she's just skimming by."

"She's a bright kid. Just give her time."

"It's obvious you don't have any children."

"Guilty as charged." He caught her next miss and tossed the ball back again. "Shoot more up instead of out. You need more height on your shots."

Her next shot went in. "Wow! Look out, Knicks, here I come!" she said with a laugh that died suddenly. "I'd better watch what I say. I just told Jenny tonight she had to concentrate on her schoolwork because she wasn't going to be a professional basketball player. If she heard what I just said, I'd be in for a lecture."

He bounced the ball, or tried to. The snow deadened its impact and he had to reach down to get it. "I can't believe Jenny lectures you."

"Well, I was in for one tonight."

He tossed the ball into the basket and she came over to catch it as it dropped.

"About what?"

The silence seemed to last halfway until dawn as she took another shot. It bounced off the back of the rim. "About not wanting to date you," she said, her back turned as she chased down the ball.

"I see." It wasn't what he expected. "I'd hoped we could improve our communication, but I guess I was hoping to hear something other than that. So Jenny thinks I'm nice and you don't."

She just laughed, the sound of tiny bells at Christmastime, and hope still flourished in his heart. "I think you're nice, too. I just don't want to date, and that's what the lecture was about."

Not great, he thought, but certainly better than it had first sounded. "She told you to start dating?"

"She told me to get a date for this weekend."

"I'm available," Zach said.

"Thanks. I'll keep that in mind." She tossed the ball, and after it rolled around the rim to clear off any lingering snow, it fell through. "Wow. Two baskets in one evening. Am I good or what?"

"I thought you said you'd made a few before I came out here."

"I lied." She darted for the ball, but he got it first and spun around her for a lay-up.

"Show-off," was all she muttered as she grabbed the ball back, but the silver threads of her laughter gleamed in the streetlight and he smiled back. Maybe he should be a little bit pushy, he decided.

"Tell me about Joel," he said softly.

He knew she had heard him because suddenly the basketball needed careful studying. "What do you want to know?" she asked after a while. "He was a nice guy, a good accountant, and liked to restore antiques as a hobby. He broke his wrist the day before our wedding when he tripped over a throw rug while ironing the brand-new shirt he planned to wear to the ceremony, all because he wanted everything to be perfect for me. He couldn't sing to save his life, was allergic to coconut and died too young."

Zach's heart grew leaden at the river of love flowing through her voice. "You have good memories of him."

"We had a good marriage. We had a good friendship."

"You were lucky." He was out of luck. How could he win her heart when it already belonged to another? Ghosts were damn hard to go one-on-one with.

She tossed the ball lightly in her hands, then looked up at him. Her face in the glow of the streetlight was thoughtful. "That's not what you really wanted to know though, was it?"

He shrugged. "Maybe the answers weren't what I wanted to hear."

She laughed abruptly. "You didn't want to know he was an accountant?"

Her mood was strange, unsteady, like the night and the approaching storm front. "I didn't want to know that you're still in love with him."

"I didn't say that."

"You didn't have to."

She pursed her lips, rolling the ball between her hands. "Were you ever in love? I mean, really, truly in love with someone so that you wanted to spend the rest of your life with them?"

"No," he said, though he had the uneasy feeling he was heading in that direction.

She stopped playing with the ball, walked over to the garage and leaned next to him. Close but not touching. An invisible wall stood between them. "When that happens," she said, "that love changes you. It makes you into someone new, and even if the love ends, you can't go back to who you were before."

"I can buy that." Even here in the shadows, clutching a basketball, he could feel her beauty, her power over him. Why did she have to be so tied to the past?

"Because my love for Joel changed me, made me into a person able to share his life, that love will always be a part of me. Just as the things he taught me about antiques are a part of me and I can't pretend I don't know them."

"And you shouldn't."

"You don't see the difference, though, do you?"

"What difference?"

"That my loving Joel now isn't the same as being in love with him. Did you stop loving your mother because she died?"

"No, but that's not the same." Dreams were starting to dance again and he was afraid to let them.

"Not exactly, but close." She turned to face him. "You see, it's not that fact that a part of me will always love Joel that keeps me from loving someone else, it's the fact that I was once in love with him. I know what real love is and what real loss is. It's not that I can't love another. It's that I won't."

"I see." Silly for his heart to leap for joy at such a statement, but it did. At least there was no ghost to challenge. "You're afraid to love again because you're afraid to lose again."

"Yes."

He let her answer hang in the air for the winter winds to whip at and blow away. "Are you happy?"

"Of course I am. I have Jenny and my mother—"

"But Jenny is growing up and will soon have a life of her own and your mother seems quite fond of Bruno."

"Everyone goes away eventually."

"Maybe it's not the leaving you should concentrate on but the part before then. The things that make up the happy memories."

"I wish I could."

"Let me help you."

"Zach—"

He put his hands on her shoulders and felt a surge of desire course through him. He longed to pull her closer into his arms, to let this hunger for her direct his hands into building a matching hunger in her. He wanted to teach her that the here and now could be so wonderful that the future faded from sight.

"Let's relax together and have fun. No strings. No plans for the future. Just good times between good friends. I won't expect any more from you than you're willing to give."

She didn't pull away, but she cradled the basketball in her arms. "Maybe I'm afraid that I'll end up giving more than I planned."

"Hey, we're not kids who believe in love at first sight. Emotions can be controlled. Friendship—that's all I'm asking for."

She grinned and nodded. "You're right. Friendship."

But then he was pulling the ball out of her hands and taking her into his arms. "Shall we celebrate our newfound friendship?"

"We really ought to."

Their lips found each other easily. They felt so right together; she fit so perfectly in his arms that he wondered how they had ever lived apart. How had he found air to breathe and reasons to smile before he'd met her? Life could hold no more delight than seeing the laughter in her eyes, feel her hunger at his touch. He wanted to pull her closer to him, to keep her forever safe in his embrace, but life didn't give gifts like that. Just little miracles to savor for the moment, and the way she was pulling away told him that this moment was over. He let her go with a gentle smile, knowing there would be more moments like this in the future. Many more.

"So what are you doing tomorrow night? Want to take in a concert at the university?" he asked.

"Sure. Maybe it'll even fulfill my homework assignment."

"Nope, that was for a date over the weekend. But don't worry. We'll find a way to make sure you don't miss any assignments."

Chapter Nine

Wow, Mom, you look gorgeous.'' Jenny was perched on the end of Holly's bed. Her voice held such awe that Holly wondered just how bad she'd looked at other times.

"I've had this dress forever," Holly pointed out.

"It's not the dress. It's you."

Holly frowned at herself in the full-length mirror. Was Jenny making a big deal out of a casual date or was Holly? Either way, Holly had to admit that she felt a glow about her. Nervousness, she tried to tell herself. She hadn't been on a date for years.

"Holly, Zach's here," Ruth called up the stairs.

"Okay." But a clutch of panic in the pit of her stomach asked if she was indeed okay. Why was she doing this?

"You're going to have a great time," Jenny assured her as she ushered her mother down the stairs.

"Are my doubts so visible?"

"You look like I felt on the first day of school here," Jenny said with a giggle. "And that wasn't so bad, so smile."

"You're a little demon," Holly said with a smile that she carried down the stairs with her.

The smile dimmed slightly, though, at the sight of Zach waiting at the bottom of the stairs. His dark suit and tie made him look different, more distant and forbidding. And made it seem more like a real date.

"You look lovely," he said, and held out her coat for her.

"Thank you." Holly turned to slip her arms into the sleeves and caught sight of Jenny's wild gesture to smile. Holly grimaced at her daughter but was smiling by the time she faced Zach again. "This should be fun."

"Of course it will, Holly. What a thing to say," Ruth said, almost pushing them both out the door. "Now, have a good time and stay out as late as you want."

The door closed and the night embraced them. "She never said that to me when I was younger," Holly said.

"Maybe she and Jenny are planning a wild party this evening," Zach teased as he offered Holly his arm.

"Could be." She walked carefully at his side to the garage, wincing as he pushed the button to open the garage door, but he said nothing and helped her into the car.

He got in and the car seemed to shrink in size. She could hardly move without touching him. When he started the motor and shifted gears she found he couldn't move without touching her, either.

"Do you like organ music?" he asked her. He shifted into reverse, his gloved hand brushing against her leg—or rather her coat, which covered her dress, which covered her stockings, which covered her leg. The touch burned.

"Why?"

He looked startled, stopping the car to stare at her. "That's what this concert is. Organ music."

"Oh, right. Sure." He was still staring at her. "Yes, organ music is great. Is it the big pipe organ in the church?"

He relaxed, obviously relieved that she was at least coherent, and continued backing the car out. "Yes, that's the one."

"Should be fascinating." She kept her eyes away from him, watching as they navigated the narrow alley, passing between fences with gossiping evergreens leaning way over and garages built in the days when one car was a luxury. The car felt even smaller and she didn't breathe until they reached the street.

"Nervous?" Zach asked.

"Is it that obvious?"

"No, just figured you were feeling the same way I was."

She laughed. "You're lying, but I thank you for it. Yes, I'm nervous. It's been ages since I've been on a date."

"No need to fear. I'm harmless."

Her eyes raked over his profile, seeing that gaze that could delve into her soul, seeing those lips that tasted of sweetness and hunger. He was anything but harmless. "I'll remember that," she said.

"You don't sound relieved."

"I don't remember enough about dating to be relieved. I'm not good at small talk."

He smiled at her in the passing glow of a streetlight. "I see you're in need of a refresher course and—"

"You happen to know the perfect teacher," she teased.

"As a matter of fact, I do. Now, we won't consider this a real date. It'll be an internship. I'll instruct you as we go along."

"All right."

"You sound dubious."

"Cautious," she corrected him. "I may have forgotten how to be a student."

"Don't worry. I'm an excellent teacher."

She groaned with laughter as he pulled into the parking lot and was still chuckling by the time he came around to her door. "Now what, excellent teacher?" she asked.

He took her hand, helping her from the car. "Respect, first of all."

"For your venerable years?"

"For my wisdom," he said, and slid his arm around her shoulders. "Though I'm questioning it myself just now. Why did I want to take you out?"

"My wit and charm?" She leaned into him as they walked from the car.

"I take it you're not independently wealthy?"

"Depends on the level of independence you're talking about."

They walked arm in arm through the campus. The wind buffeted them, pushing them along, together and apart, but they just laughed. The campus was lovely, blanketed in the new snow that had fallen last night, and she was sure the stars had never looked so bright. She felt as if they'd been polished just for her. Students hurried by, a few heading in the same direction as they were, but Holly felt as if she and Zach were alone with the night. Her nervousness was a faint memory.

"What's the next step in my instruction?" Holly asked as they neared the church.

"This is the easy part," he said. "You just sit by my side, listen to the music and smile at me occasionally."

They climbed up the worn steps of the church. "To show how I'm enjoying the music?"

"To show how in awe of me you are."

Holly shoved him lightly, a playful push, when her heart wanted to hold him closer. She was having a good time; dating wasn't so hard. She was feeling young and free and ready for laughter. She took his arm, holding it a bit closer than necessary, and they went into the church.

The crowd was relatively small, but the music proved to be marvelous. The baroque pieces were intricate and conflicting, rather than light and carefree, but they fit her mood. The organ music filled the small church, echoing faintly amid the high ceilings and coming back to encircle her.

With its contrasting effects, the music echoed her soul. How long had she hidden away from life, afraid to be hurt, while she was, in fact, hurting even more? She'd been missing so much by staying within the narrow walls she'd defined for herself. Like the alley, her path was growing all the more narrow each day, overgrown with old worries and fears that were habits rather than choices. Maybe it was time to try new paths, strike out in new directions. If South Bend was to be a new start for Jenny and Ruth, it should be a new start for her, also. This could be her time to throw off old fears and embrace life once again.

The music was centuries old, just as the church seemed, and she felt wonderfully secure. What worries could she have that were so great as to last as long as this music had? Her nervousness about being with Zach seemed ridiculous.

With a wild crescendo, the concert ended, as if it had been waiting for her decision. The applause followed, then the murmur of voices as everyone filed out of the church and back into the night.

"Now, you make a polite comment about how you enjoyed the music, regardless of your true feelings," Zach whispered as they descended the steps.

"I don't have to make something up. I enjoyed it a great deal," she said. She peered at him through the darkness. "Why? Didn't you like it?"

"I guess baroque isn't my style," he admitted. "I'm more into country and western."

"Then why did you invite me to this?"

He took her arm and grinned. "It was the only thing I knew of that was going on this evening. If I came up with something later in the week, I figured it would give you too much time to change your mind."

Holly shook her head. "So you sat through a concert you didn't enjoy because it was the first thing you thought of to ask me to?"

They walked slowly through the campus. "I didn't say I didn't enjoy it," he pointed out. "I enjoyed it quite thoroughly because I had a gorgeous lady sitting next to me whom I was able to watch for almost two hours."

"Why, you—"

She burst into laughter, then was somehow in his arms. Her laughter died as something stronger, deeper, took over. She couldn't see his face for the crazy shadows of the bare trees in the moonlight that fell across them, but she could feel his gaze. It was hard and strong and reached into her heart. He was asking her to trust him, to let the feelings build that were growing untamed even now. She trembled slightly, her fears coming to the surface, but for once the need to be held was stronger than the worries.

She wanted to kiss him, to fold herself within his arms and lie in his touch where the shadows couldn't reach her, but a group of students huddled deep in their winter coats hurried past and broke the spell. Zach smiled at her and took her arm, walking her back toward the car.

"Now, this is where you express your undying gratitude for my taking you out this evening and promise to do anything I'd like to show your appreciation to me."

She laughed in relief but also in surprise that her heart was still strong enough to smile. "And this is where the professor finds out that his student isn't quite that gullible."

He shook his head. "This whole evening has been wasted. You haven't learned a thing about dating, have you? Well, I'm willing to try again tomorrow night."

"You shouldn't be here." Holly sniffed and shuffled back to her bed on the sofa. "You'll catch my cold."

"I never catch cold." Zach closed the door and followed her into the living room. "You promised to spend the evening with me and I'm here to make sure you keep your promise."

"Zach." But it was a faint and distant protest. It had been a week since their concert date, a week spent laughing and touching and getting to know each other. As January had progressed into February, they'd progressed from internship dates to the real thing. For Holly, seeing Zach was better than two aspirins and a hot toddy, even though she was feeling lousy.

He put a small grocery bag down on the end table. "When are Jenny and your mom due back?"

Holly shrugged and tried to stay sitting up. Lying on the sofa in a shapeless gray sweat suit, clutching a box of tissues, was not a femme fatale pose. "They're stopping for some hamburgers after Jenny's game. So it should be a couple of hours at least." Her head swam and she gave up, lying back down and resting her head on the arm of the sofa. "You don't have to stay. I'll be awful company."

"A chance to see the inner you," he teased, and felt the back of her neck. His hand felt so cool, so soothing, she was sure any doctor would prescribe that hand as a remedy for her fever.

"You don't feel feverish," he noted.

Little did he know her fever had nothing to do with her cold.

"Dr. Philips will take care of what ails you," he murmured, and after planting a kiss on her forehead went into the kitchen.

More than just a cold ailed her, she admitted to herself as she snuggled down farther in the sofa and stared at the game show on television. Jenny had chosen the channel for her, obviously believing that cold germs could be bored to death. The cold wasn't the problem, however. It was her rapidly intensifying obsession with the good Dr. Philips that was so worrisome. She hadn't been looking for romance, so why had her heart pounded when he'd come down this evening?

It didn't make sense, Holly scolded silently. Zach was a wanderer. A confessed, dyed-in-the-wool nomad who was planning on raking leaves in Paris, not Michiana. Why, then, was her heart turning cartwheels at the sight of him? She was a fool. She knew that he was leaving; she knew when he was leaving.

She stopped, her lips smiling along with her heart for once. Of course she knew when he was leaving, and that was why he was perfect for her. She wouldn't have to lie awake fearing he'd go. He would; there was no doubt about it. So she could just relax and enjoy his company. She couldn't lose what she would never really have.

"Here we go," Zach said, coming back into the living room. He was carrying a tray with a steaming bowl on it.

"What's this?" she asked.

"Dinner. Chicken soup, just like my mother used to make."

Holly got herself into a sitting position in time for Zach to lay the tray on her lap. The scent of the soup wrapped around her body and chased all the aches into the back of her mind. "You made this from scratch?"

"I didn't say that." He sat down on the chair next to her and handed her a spoon. "I said it was just like my mother used to make. Same brand and everything."

She laughed and started in on her soup. The steam soothed her tired lungs, the hot liquid warmed everything down to her toes, and Zach's smile took care of her heart. "It's good," she said, not certain what she was referring to.

"No, it's me. A miracle cure."

His smile was gentle enough to build a lifetime of—no, erase that—a few months of dreams on. She grinned at him and went back to her soup, spooning up the last few drops from the bottom.

"You really ought to let the medical world in on your curative powers," she said. "Think of all the good you'd be doing for mankind."

"I hate to tell you this, but I'm more interested in womankind. One woman in particular. Let the rest of them find their own cures."

When she was finished, he took the tray, carried it back into the kitchen and left her trying to smooth her hair into some semblance of its normal style. She'd hardly slept at all last night and had collapsed into a sneezing heap after work today. Now, she must look like something that escaped from the swamp. Zach was either blind or very brave to see her and still stay. No, he was gentlemanly. Chivalrous. His mother had taught him it was rude to take one look at a disease-ridden date and flee, so he'd stay and feed her chicken soup until she felt better. Then he'd make a break for it and she'd never see him again.

"Your second course, madam," Zach said, handing her a mug with a slight bow.

She took the cup in her hands. It was warm but not unpleasantly so. "What's this? Another miracle cure?"

"Tea spiced with rum, and you weren't really paying attention before. *I'm* the miracle cure, not the food I bring."

He sat back in his chair, close enough to curl her toes inside her thick old sweat socks. She had a sudden urge to crawl into his lap, to have him put his arms around her and to snuggle down into the warmth of his embrace.

"I guess I wasn't paying attention." She actually had been, but she sipped at the tea rather than pursue her reactions.

"So how's it taste?"

"Like drinking fire."

"Too much rum?"

"No, it's wonderful." The heated liquid seeped into every corner of her body, easing the aches away. Her heart was busy delighting in Zach's presence, and her mind had tossed away its worries about the spell he seemed to cast over her. She stretched out her body on the sofa. She took another sip, then another. No more weary joints, no more nagging cough. "I must remember to renew your lease. I need your secrets to get through an Indiana winter."

"You needed your boots when we went to the movies on Saturday."

"How was I supposed to know it would snow while we were inside?"

"It's winter. It always snows in the winter."

She smiled at him. He was trying to look so stern, his dark eyes frowning at her. Except that she could see a smile twinkling far back in the shadows. A smile just for her. The fire in her spread out to her toes. Maybe the warmth wasn't from the rum at all.

"I'll be more careful next time."

"I hope so."

His hand was so close to hers that her fingers wanted to touch the hairs that curled on the back of it. No, she wanted that hand to fight back the fever again. Wasn't that what doctors prescribed? Two of Zach's hands and then a call in the morning?

"Then again," she went on, "maybe I won't be more careful if I can get this kind of treatment when I'm sick. Nobody's fussed like this over me since I had chicken pox when I was five."

"Are you sure there wasn't too much rum in that drink?" he asked, and reached over to take the mug.

"I'm not done," she argued, and moved it away from his reach. "It's my medicine and my cold, so I get to say when I'm done."

"Is that so?"

He got up, obviously to steal her tea away, so she drank the rest of it quickly. It went down like molten lava. Cold was definitely the wrong word for the virus she had. He took the mug from her hand and put it on the table.

"What's next, Dr. Philips?" she asked.

"Bed."

"Aha! Just as I thought. A nefarious scheme to seduce me." She got to her feet and found that the room was wobbling. Stupid old house, she thought.

Zach pushed her gently back onto the sofa. "Maybe you should just stretch out here."

It seemed the only way to stop the wobbling, so she laid her head back down on the sofa pillows. "It's not that I have any strong objections to seduction, mind you."

He was lifting her feet so they were on the sofa, too. "Glad to hear that."

"I would just prefer that you do it when I'm not holding a box of tissues."

"You're a sexy lady with or without them." He pulled her afghan over her. "But since they provide you with a weapon to bop me over the head with, I'll wait until you put them down."

"Good."

Zach changed the channel to a basketball game and she stared for a while at the gigantic men loping from one end of the court to the other.

"Who's playing?" she finally asked.

He grinned at her. "The Knicks. Don't you recognize them?"

"Very funny." She went back to the game. "Ha, that was a fast break. See what a fan I am?"

"Who was the player?"

But her eyes had somehow closed and her brain could move only in slow motion. "Mighty Mouse," she said.

"Mighty Mouse? You're not paying attention, are you?"

"Yes, I am." It was just a matter of what she was paying attention to. Right now she could hear Zach's breathing. In and out. In and out. So soothing, so peaceful. With her eyes closed, it was almost like lying beside him in the night, which was a most appealing thought. Suddenly she felt as if the world was opening up to her. She had found someone perfect, someone safe, who wouldn't break her heart in the end.

Zach stirred slightly, and even without looking she could see him cross his legs, see those thighs so tight with muscles. What would it be like to touch them? To run her hands along their surface? There didn't seem to be an ounce of fat on him. How did he stay in shape? Did he go jogging when the weather was warmer?

Suddenly they were outside in the sunshine, both jogging. Except that Holly wasn't very good at it and Zach kept getting ahead of her. He'd stop to wait, but she never seemed to catch up to him. Her feet were running but weren't getting anywhere even as Zach ran farther and farther ahead.

She heard a scratching noise next to her and opened her eyes. Zach was writing something. His shirtsleeves were rolled up and a cup was on the table beside him. The television was off.

"What are you doing?" she asked.

"Ah, Sleeping Beauty awakens. I'm correcting papers."

"I wasn't sleeping. You seem to be making a lot of marks on that paper. Is that good or bad?"

"In this case, it's bad. Mr. Tyler seems to have missed the point entirely."

There was more scratching of his pen on the paper as Holly watched Zach's frown grow deeper. "How do you think I would do in one of your courses?" she asked.

"Just fine as long as you did your homework."

She rolled over onto her back and stared up at the ceiling. "I always did my homework when I was in school."

"And if you were having trouble, I'd be available for extra help and private tutoring."

She twisted her neck to look over at him. His eyes still held that warm invitation that made her cold disappear into a memory. "Do you do that for all your students?"

"Provide extra help? If they need it. But I had a different type of tutoring in mind for you. A different type of course, actually."

"Oh?" The fire of the rum should have worn off, but it was back, only this time it was not at all relaxing. It wove a tension through her blood and teased her heart into longing.

"Something in interpersonal studies," he said softly.

She smiled back. "I've always believed in furthering one's knowledge." But what she really wanted to know was how she could feel so good when she felt so miserable.

Holly knocked at the door twice before Zach opened it.

"I guess I'm late, aren't I?" he said, stepping aside to let her in.

"A little. Doesn't matter, though. I doubt that the bowling alleys will be all filled up." Holly frowned at him, not because of the half hour she'd been waiting downstairs but because he didn't look himself. He was smiling, but that laughter didn't seem to reach his eyes. If it hadn't been for his assertion last week that he never caught colds, she would have thought he was coming down with hers now that she was done with it.

"What's the matter?" she asked.

He reached over for his jacket, slipping it on as he flicked the switch to turn off the lights in the hallway. "Who said anything's the matter?"

"Me."

The phone rang as he turned to usher her out and he went to answer it. Rather, he limped over to it, favoring his left leg. What was wrong? she wondered as her protective juices started flowing full strength. She closed his door, flicking the lights back on.

The phone call was brief, but she was sitting down by the time he turned around. "What happened?"

He glanced toward the phone with a shrug. "I was supposed to meet tomorrow with this new teaching assistant for my Native American class, but he—"

"I mean your ankle," Holly said. "You were limping."

His next shrug was eloquent in its unconcern as he sat down on the arm of the sofa. "I twisted my ankle a little in our basketball game today."

A little? That probably meant it was close to a fracture. "So why are we going bowling?"

"Why not? I'm fine."

"You can't bowl with a twisted ankle."

He got to his feet. "I hardly feel it at all."

"It's numb, then."

"It's fine." He walked over to the door, a stiff, dignified walk that might have fooled her if he'd been eighty-five years old.

"It's not fine." She crossed her arms and stretched out her legs, refusing to budge. "We're staying here tonight."

"Holly."

She stared ahead at the night sky visible through the window over his stereo. "There's no reason to go bowling when you've hurt your ankle."

"Holly."

She closed her eyes and lay back. "I hate bowling anyway."

"Holly."

She kicked her shoes off. "My all-time high score is a twelve."

He sank onto the sofa next to her, laughing. "Holly, Holly, Holly."

"What? What? What?" She opened her eyes and snuggled up next to him, running her hand over his chest. Why was he so stubborn, so needing her care? "Are we staying here tonight?"

"Can't take you bowling if you hate it," Zach said with a sigh, then caught her hand and brought it to his lips. "You are one stubborn lady."

She pulled her hand away slowly, replacing it with her lips. Their kiss was sweet and slow, the makings of magic.

It certainly beat out bowling hands down. "So what really happened to your ankle?"

"Just what I told you." He leaned forward, shrugging out of his coat, then helping her out of hers. "I went up for a lay-up and came down to my downfall."

"My, how poetic!" She tossed their coats onto the chair across from her and came back to his arms.

"I was definitely poetic when it happened."

"Did you miss much of the game?"

"No, just the last couple of minutes."

She pulled slightly back to look him in the eye. "Then what's the real reason for the glum face?"

His frown was teasing. "Isn't an incapacitating injury reason enough?"

"Not to keep you from teasing me about bowling a twelve."

He touched the collar of her blouse, a gentle touch that smoothed and soothed and could go on forever. "Maybe I was being kind."

But she wasn't fooled or distracted. "Maybe something else is bothering you."

He sighed and leaned back on the sofa, resting his hands behind his head and staring up at the ceiling. "We played the math department today and lost."

"You never lost before?"

"Not to the math department." He sat up, his eyes reflecting the unbelievability of the whole thing. "Nobody loses to the math department. Until now, at any rate."

"So what happened? Your injury lose the game?"

He shook his head. His shoulders slumped; defeat was in his face. "It was lost way before then. They got a new guy on their team. A young kid. Well, he's not a kid. He's old enough to be an assistant professor, but he looks like a kid."

"And plays like a kid."

Zach nodded.

"And now you feel old," Holly finished for him, suddenly understanding and wanting to cuddle him forever—or at least until he smiled again.

"Silly, huh?"

"No. But it's not necessary." She sat away from him so she could face him, so she could brush that piece of hair back from his face and remove the shadows from his eyes. "Name one thing a young kid can do that you can't do better."

"Play basketball." He sounded serious but his eyes were laughing.

"One important thing," she corrected. "And don't say basketball. It's hardly a matter of life and death. Or even good health. There are other ways to stay in shape. I know because I've avoided them all."

He took her hand, spreading the fingers out against his, then curling his own to clasp hers tightly. "I used to be a very good basketball player."

She smiled, dragging her free fingers with whisperlike softness against his jaw. Such strength she felt there. Such stubbornness. "I bet there are other things you're very good at."

A flicker of light gleamed in his eye as he looked at her. "As a matter of fact, there are."

"Things that you probably could do in spite of the grave injury to your ankle."

"Yes, even with my injured ankle, which is feeling stronger by the moment." He freed her hand to slide his own hands up to her shoulders. They roamed and touched, explored and devastated.

She swayed into him, lying lightly across his chest to meet the hunger of his lips. Those frowns of worry were still shadowing his heart and she needed to bring back his sun. She didn't ask herself why; it was what he needed from her and something she wanted to do for him. The touch of his lips was sweet, moonlight kissing the night, but the heat that started warming her was too strong for moonlight, too bright for the night. But then the heat cooled slightly as he pulled away from her.

"First of all," he said, "I'm going to get my guest some tea."

She didn't want him to move, and when he did, her heart pouted. "What if your guest doesn't want any tea?"

"Then I'll get her coffee."

"Zach."

He turned, and even from across the room his gaze captured her eyes, holding them prisoner. She felt that he could see into her soul, read all her fears and joys, and there was no way she could stop him. She wanted him to know her, to feel her happiness as well as her worries. Her heart began to beat faster in a rhythm that was echoed by her breath. What did he want from her? Silly question, she thought, but knew the answer wasn't so simple. A night of passion was easy; his eyes were asking hard questions and expecting impossible answers. Then the intensity died and his gentle smile bade her relax.

"Tea or coffee?" he asked.

"Tea," she replied weakly.

Once he'd left the room, she got up and wandered aimlessly about. From the window she could see down into the garden, where winter's shroud still covered the yard. Did she want to stay? Did she want what staying would bring?

"How about the grand tour?" Zach was back in the room; hunger was back in her heart. "You've never officially been up here before."

"No, somehow I haven't had the honor yet." She stared at him, not moving. Surely that wasn't his heart she could hear from here. No, it was her own, telling her to cross over to where he stood, to fall into his arms like a child jumping from her first tree climb. He'd catch her; he'd keep her safe.

But her mind was giving louder orders, shouting them over the pounding of her heart. Look at the chair, it said. Look at the rich brown velvet with six buttons across the back. No, eight buttons; she'd missed the two in the corner nearest her. Wasn't that interesting? Ask him where he got it and what other colors it came in so you can get some for the library downstairs. Or check out the end table with its disheveled pile of magazines. Was that top one a farming journal? Discuss with him the relative merits of those fat red tomatoes and those anemic-looking yellow ones. Farm boys, even ex-farm boys, should know those things and it wouldn't hurt her to learn a bit about them, too. You never know when you'll have to know something about yellow tomatoes. Oh, wait. That arrowhead collection.

"What's this?" she asked, and moved over to the framed display near the kitchen door.

"Arrowheads." He was right behind her, his breath tickling her neck, tingling her senses and stoking the flame that was licking at her soul so she couldn't think. "I collected them as a kid."

Holly knew that if she stepped back just a half step, she'd feel his strength along her softness. She'd discover then if his heart was as hungry as hers, if his arms needed to hold her as much as her embrace ached for him. But she kept her feet steady and her eyes ahead.

"You mean you found all of these? Where?"

"A lot on the farm. The rest in this general area. We're in Indian country, remember?"

She chanced a turn then. His eyes were steady, deep as the ocean. The look in them rocked her soul. "Ah, yes. Pokagon. Haven't heard much from the old boy in a while, have we?"

"No need."

"I'm healed?" she teased.

"Maybe we both are." His voice was as soft as the first rays of sunshine in the early morning. His came out to hold her, as if they couldn't stay away any longer.

She wanted to lean into, to sway into, his strength but was content with his touch and those eyes. "Were you in need of healing?"

His smile was slight. "My ankle, remember."

His answer was unexpected, a splash of pure joy. She couldn't help but laugh, and even as she did, the bonds holding her back were loosed and she was in his arms. His lips came down on hers, possessing every thought, every breath she would ever take. It was sweet heaven. The fire exploded within, consuming her reason, her common sense, and saving only her heart and her hunger.

Her arms slipped around him. She needed him close, needed to feel bound to him with bonds of need and hunger and the night. Again and again he kissed her. He kissed her lips and trailed gentle bits of sunlight along her throat. The night was alive and radiant, the magic in their hands to explore. She found his lips again, missing them in that brief blink of an eye while they had caressed her neck.

What about your fears? her mind kept trying to ask her. What about his leaving soon? What about the tour? She pulled back gently, needing time to think, to quiet the racing of her heart, or else time to quiet the warning bells going off in her mind.

"So, what happened to our tour?" she asked. Her voice wobbled, a pitiful attempt at control. "Or isn't your bed made and you want to distract me from it?" Lord, why had she chosen an unmade bed as an example of bad housekeeping?

His eyes danced with laughter. "Is that what I'm doing?"

"Dishes," she said quickly. "Your dishes aren't washed. You have a week's worth of dirty dishes sitting in your sink."

She didn't wait for his reaction but walked past him to the kitchen doorway. Away from him, she could breathe. She could think. Except that everything in the small, cozy kitchen spoke of him. There were no dirty dishes, but she could picture him using the mugs hanging above the stove for his coffee in the morning. Or sitting at the breakfast bar and reading the newspaper. A sweatshirt was draped over the back of a chair, the sweatshirt he'd been wearing the night the roof leaked, when he'd taken her up in the attic and Pokagon had maneuvered her into his arms. The air got thin again.

"Want to discuss redecorating?" he whispered into her ear.

His breath tickled her neck, sent shivers down her spine. "What?" she asked vaguely.

"The room." He nodded behind her. "As my landlady, I was sure you'd want to modernize my kitchen. You know, make things more pleasant up here."

How could he be so coherent? How could he joke when her stomach was knotted. "It looks wonderful to me. Marvelous even.'' She was looking at his lips, remembering their feel against her skin.

Somehow she dragged her gaze away and dragged her feet back into the living room. What was wrong with her? Why had her will turned into jelly, her backbone into marshmallow?

''Oh, what's this?'' she cried, and stopped in front of a glass bookcase filled with Indian pottery.

''Indian pottery,'' Zach said.

He was still in the doorway, watching her. His eyes burned holes in her back, weakening her backbone even more. He was a wanderer, a nomad. She couldn't let him love her. Her feet kept moving.

''Now, this is interesting.'' It was a sculpture; a weirdly modern piece that looked somewhat familiar lay on his desk. Its main appeal was the respite it provided from his gaze.

''That's the filter from my humidifier.''

''I knew that,'' she insisted, but when she moved this time he was there, his arms waiting to hold her. It was time to decide, to weigh passion and joy against the cold hard light of dawn.

A ghostly rattling of metallic bones split the silence and she started. It was the radiator, she told herself, but then the jeering hiss of steam escaping made her jump and she was in Zach's arms.

''Thank you, Pokagon,'' Zach murmured into her lips.

Holly didn't try to fight any longer. Some things were meant to be. There was no fighting the rising of the sun, the glow of the fire or her hunger for Zach. Her mouth met his in a blaze of passion, a rocking of the stars in the heavens. She tasted him, melted in his fire and felt the flames of her heart strain higher. The night suddenly held such promise, such wonder.

''Holly.'' His voice was harsh, strained.

Passion was meant for action, not words, but she pulled back from his arms. ''What?''

''Maybe we ought to go bowling, after all.''

His lips were wonderful, their wizardry beyond belief. Why then did his words make no sense? "Why would I want to go bowling? You're injured, you know." Her heart stopped, then raced ahead. "You probably ought to be in bed."

His eyes whispered promises of delight, of hungers and sweet mornings after. "But I promised to spend the evening with you."

"Maybe we can find a compromise." The toying and teasing was over. She was back in the embrace of his gaze as if she'd never left.

"Oh, Holly. Do you know what you are to me?"

She took his hand. "Maybe it's time for the rest of the tour."

They skipped his office and entered the haven of his bedroom. Warm, earth colors welcomed her, then Zach was all she knew. His lips spoke of pleasures and delights as they roamed her neck over and over, teasing her heart into ecstasy, until she wanted to cry out with the fire raging in her. His hands opened her blouse, button by button. His touch went lower. His lips found the valley of her breasts and sang a silent song of wonder into her heart.

She sighed closer into his arms, closer to the touch that was all things to her. Everywhere his lips touched she burned. Her hands touched him as if by their very desire they could pull him to her. Their mouths met again in splendor and promise, speaking unheard words of joy.

His shirt was quick work, then his pants were off and he slid her skirt onto the floor. Zippers, buttons, ties, nothing could stand in the way of his needs. Then they were on the bed, lost in the soft depths of a fiery red bedspread that echoed the fire in her heart. Zach's hands roamed freely, enjoying the smoothness of her skin as his lips caressed her breasts, sending rockets of flame through her soul.

When his hands and lips roamed lower, stroking her thighs and the fire between them, there was no time. Their needs were ready to explode, demanding fulfillment. Zach entered her then, as if returning home. Bodies intertwined, they moved in an ageless rhythm of love. Holly closed her eyes, seeing Zach's face within her heart and her mind. It felt as if they had always belonged to each other. As if they'd been parted to soar through time and space, only to be reunited in this embrace.

They clung together in the dreams they'd woven, climbing higher and higher into the sun, until they were lost in a blinding flash of magic. Then slowly, the sunlight dimmed and moonlight returned, the darkness of the night come to guide them safely back to the hidden smiles in their hearts.

Chapter Ten

"Good morning, Mother," Holly sang out as she floated into the kitchen and over to the refrigerator. Life was starting to be wonderful again. Friendship was a marvelous thing to have. "Good morning, Jen—"

She stopped dead in her tracks, her nose quivering like a scared deer. It was Friday, which usually meant cereal and bananas for breakfast, but the kitchen was filled with more smells than Aunt Ellie's Pancake House. "What kind of cereal are you eating, Jenny?"

"Knicks won last night, Holly," Ruth said. "That makes them 21-23 for the season so far."

"They ever have that good a record before the All-Star break before?" Zach asked.

Holly started and spun around. Words were poised on the tip of her tongue ready to come tumbling out, but she held them back until she could organize her thoughts.

"Good morning," Zach said.

He sat there, a soft smile on his lips, fork poised, his brown eyes gleaming in anticipation. Holly continued staring. What was she supposed to say? What did one say to one's lover the morning after, when one's mother and daughter were there watching?

"Holly," Ruth scolded. "It's not polite to stare. Say good morning to Zach."

"Good morning, Zach."

At least that sounded like her own voice! Zach was here for breakfast. He was here in their very own kitchen. Those hands that had worked such magic in her heart last night were calmly buttering a piece of toast.

"The eggs are delicious," he said, waving his fork slightly. "You should have some."

"Grandma makes real good scrambled eggs," Jenny said. "It's more nutritious than those cereals."

Slowly, painfully, Holly's mind began returning to reality.

"What are you doing here?"

"My goodness, Holly," Ruth said in a shocked voice. "Where are your manners? Besides, it's very obvious what he's doing here. Zach's eating breakfast."

"Your mother invited me," Zach hastened to explain.

Holly turned to Ruth, who shrugged nonchalantly. "He was down here first thing in the morning. I thought the two of you had some sort of... understanding."

"I came down to see how you were," Zach noted.

How she was? How *was* she? She turned to her mother. "What kind of understanding?" she asked. Did they all know how she'd spent last evening?

But Ruth ignored her. "Would you like more coffee, Zach?"

"Thank you."

"What kind of understanding, Mother?"

"To be friends." Ruth shook her head. "For heaven's sake. What other kinds of understanding are there?"

Good Lord, they did all know. Over the table, Zach's eyes danced at her. She wanted to join them, to waltz around in perfect happiness, except that single mothers who also lived with their own mothers didn't do such things.

"Grandma, I have to be at school early for a study session," Jenny called from the stairway.

"Okay, honey," Ruth replied. Then she turned and took Holly by the arm. "Holly, get Zach his coffee, please. I have to take Jenny to school."

"I can take her," Holly said. She wasn't sure she was ready to be here with Zach. "I can get a bite on the way to work."

Her mother shook her head. "Get Zach his coffee, please. He's our guest."

Then she quickly exited the kitchen. Holly pursed her lips, sending silent pleas after her mother's back, but to no avail. Holly was left alone with Zach.

"I don't want to bother you," Zach said. "I can get my own coffee."

He doesn't want to bother me? she thought. Holly wanted to laugh hysterically. It was a little late for that. If he hadn't wanted to bother her, then why had he brought her such joy last night? Joy that haunted her dreams and still had her heart racing?

"My mother said you're a guest." Holly hoped to bury her true feelings in brusqueness. "So sit there and be quiet. I'll get it."

"Yes, ma'am."

She quietly refilled his cup and poured a cup for herself. After returning the pot to its place on the counter she sat down across from Zach. To come down here and find him waiting wasn't fair. He'd been prepared to see her; she hadn't the faintest idea how to react to him. She wrapped her fingers around the cup, feeling the silence.

Zach cleared his throat. "Do you get many guests for breakfast?"

"No," she said, without looking up.

"I can see why," he murmured.

He was laughing at her. Holly looked up and shot her fiercest glare straight into his eyes. Unfortunately her fire died, drowned in the soft tenderness. Her anger never had a chance. She could feel a sensation rumble up from her stomach, and her lips began to quiver.

"If I laugh, you die," she threatened.

"Your smile is more than worth the price."

A comfortable, soft warmth filled her whole body, reaching out to the tips of her fingers and toes. A smile tried to force its way onto her lips, but she held it back. It was enough to know that such feelings still lived in her soul; she didn't need to exercise them right now. In fact, it was time to dispel that kind of mood before things got out of control again.

"Look, Zach, about last night—"

"You're sorry it happened. It'll never happen again," he finished for her.

She stared at him. "It won't?"

His look was gentle, tinged with sadness. "Isn't that what you were going to say?"

She frowned and picked up her coffee cup. "I don't know."

He leaned forward, closer to her, and her body warmed to the thought. "It was wonderful, wasn't it?"

"Yes." But, damn it, where did they go from here? Where do you want to go? a little voice asked. And that was the problem. She didn't know. After all, no one else was home. They could go back upstairs right now. The thought was too tempting and she forced it under a mound of guilt over the work awaiting her. She finished her coffee, then stood up.

"Well, I have to be going," she said, looking at her watch.

"Is that all you're having for breakfast?"

"Yes." Then realizing that her tone was hesitant and defensive, Holly cleared her throat. "I don't usually have much for breakfast. I can get something at work if I'm hungry."

"A sweet roll or a doughnut."

The warmth stayed, but it was becoming fueled by irritation again. Why couldn't they reach a happy medium? She was either irritated with him or she was—

"You're not my mother," she grumbled.

"I can't be anybody's mother," he said. "I thought you noticed that last night. Anyway, don't change the subject.

A mass of dough all covered with gunk is not exactly a balanced meal.''

"You're starting to sound like Jenny." She took her cup over to the dishwasher.

"She's a smart little kid," he said, following her. "Sit down."

"I'm due at work."

"You're the boss. You can be late."

"I have a big sales meeting today. I don't have time for games."

"I realize that, but you do have time for breakfast."

"That's my decision," she said, slowly and carefully.

"Sit down."

"Zach, just in case you have any problem with it, I run my own life."

"Sure." His smile was large, his eyes gentle and his arms strong as he gently pushed her back into the chair. "But I'm in charge of breakfast today."

"Hooray for you."

Holly knew that she should straighten him out, but this had been enough of a mixed-up morning already. There was no need to waste more time. She watched him break two eggs into a frying pan and continued watching him, sternly, as he adjusted the heat on the stove. It just wasn't worth it to argue. He took a plate from the cupboard.

"Over easy or hard?"

"Over easy, please."

"Your wish is my command," he said with a quick bow and slid her eggs onto her plate.

"Don't I wish."

Oh, damn. The words were out and they could mean anything. The look on Zach's face clearly indicated what meaning he gave them. He stood looking at her, his eyes glowing as he put the plate down before her.

"Go ahead," he said. "Make a wish."

Holly chose to put her head down and eat. Stuffing her mouth with food would keep her quiet and maybe safe.

He turned and poured her a glass of orange juice. "If I was more familiar with things in here I would have made you bacon or sausage."

She almost told him he didn't need to be any more familiar with anything. The words were poised, foot soldiers ready for the assault, waiting for the command. Holly beat them back with a forkful of food. Her words had not been serving her well today. Besides, she really didn't have time for any kind of discussion.

Zach refilled his cup with more coffee and sat across from her, smiling. His gentle eyes caressed hers and it took every last ounce of her power to concentrate on her food. She needed to finish breakfast and get out of here. She had some decisions to make about this friendship.

Holly kicked off her shoes and dropped back onto her bed, wiggling her feet in a semiecstatic relief. The sales meeting had gone on and on. They'd finally ordered sandwiches in. Good thing she'd suggested it, or they would have gone out to eat and then the session would have dragged on to midnight or worse.

Dark spots on the ceiling reminded her that all the rooms needed painting. Holly rolled over onto her stomach. She didn't want anything to hassle her mind any more today.

She had wanted to see Jenny, but her daughter had a hand-lettered Do Not Disturb sign on her bedroom door. Ruth had said that Jenny had a lot of homework to do and had gone straight to her room after dinner. Holly smiled. Her daughter was starting to put things together. She'd go in later and they would share a hot chocolate and conversation about the day.

Holly put her hands under her chin for support. Maybe she should go up and visit Zach. A smile started on her lips but its warmth quickly spread through the rest of her body. She had done a lot of thinking today about him. About the two of them. She hadn't come up with any answers, but mulling over his body had certainly been fun. She rolled over and laughed to herself, her cheeks fiery with the power of her thoughts. Goodness, friendship was great.

There was a knock at her bedroom door and Jenny came in. A subdued-looking Jenny. Some of Holly's sunshine dimmed.

"Hi, Mom."

Holly sat up. "Hi, honey. How was your day?"

"Okay." Jenny shrugged and brought a paper from behind her back. "I'm supposed to have you sign this."

The rest of the sunshine fled, dread filling Holly's heart. "What's this?" she asked.

"A math test."

Holly took the paper that had been so reluctantly offered and looked at it. A D. "When was the test?"

"Today," Jenny said. She clenched her hands behind her back and rubbed her toe across the bare floor. She was a forlorn little figure if there ever was one.

Holly's heart was torn by love; she wanted to do nothing but hug Jenny tight, but instead she forced her gaze to the paper. There were red marks everywhere, even over the simplest answers. Six hundred and eighty rounded to the nearest hundred was five hundred? She looked up. "Jenny, did you study for this?"

"Yes." But her eyes were on the floor, not able to meet Holly's.

"Did you ask me to review with you?"

The silence was almost long enough for the snow to melt and the trees to leaf out. "No."

"Why not? You know that I'm more than happy to help you."

"You were going out with Zach and I didn't want to bother you."

"Bother me? Jenny, you wouldn't have been bothering me. I didn't go out until later in the evening. I had time to help you study."

"You were relaxing and getting ready to go out. And you had worked all day. You shouldn't have to do everything."

"I don't do everything. But some things are more important than others, and your doing well in school is one of the most important."

"I'm doing okay."

"A D is not okay."

"I won't get a D again."

Holly had been about to scold her daughter, but she stopped and sighed. There were ways to make sure this didn't happen again, but not all of them relied solely on Jenny. Holly reached for a pen and signed her name next to the grade. "Tell me when you've got another test coming up. I don't care what you think I'm doing. You tell me."

"All right." Jenny took the paper and trudged from the room, her shoulders slumped under the burden she was carrying.

Holly sat for a moment, gathering her thoughts. There was no denying it; this was partly her fault. She'd known Jenny was having problems, but she'd let herself get distracted. She didn't want to give up her friendship with Zach, but she had other needs to consider besides her own. Setting her jaw firmly, she went upstairs.

Fortunately, Zach was home. "Hi," he said, pulling her in and closing the door after her. His eyes danced with a happy surprise that she couldn't reflect, even though her heart wanted to remind her of the joys they'd shared here last night.

"Hi," she said, and went to a window seat. Cold breaths of winter seeped through the window and kept Zach's warmth from melting her resolve.

Zach followed her. "What brings you up here?"

She shook her head. His voice, his eyes, tempted her so she turned to stare out the window. The January thaw was over; a new dusting of snow was on the yard. Large, thick flakes were falling even now. A brief thaw didn't mean winter was over; a night of passion didn't mean an end to other responsibilities.

"Anything wrong?" Zach asked. His voice was cautious now, the joy in it having been rudely shouldered aside.

"Jenny's having some more problems with her studies."

"I'm sure they're temporary. She's a smart kid."

His voice was so confident, so filled the sureness of a nonparent, that it angered her. He'd said what she wanted to believe, but it wasn't his risk.

"I really don't know," Holly snapped. "But I can't take a chance."

"I understand."

"She didn't ask to move out here. She didn't ask for a single parent. She didn't ask for any of it." Her voice had been rising with each word.

"Hey, I said I understand."

The voice was soft and close, and Holly turned around, straight into the safe harbor of his arms. She'd been holding her breath and she let it out in a sigh. Was it wrong to hold him, to lean on his strength and for the moment to let her worries wait?

She closed her eyes as his hands traced tenderness across her back. The tension and fears drained from her mind, the chill from her heart. Her days needed his sunshine; her nights needed his dreams. She wouldn't let last night be just a passing smile, never again to work its magic on her. There had to be a way to be both lover and mother.

Holly pulled slowly from his arms, where thought was impossible. "I really have to spend more time with Jenny on school nights. She needs my help."

He let her go, but not very far. His hand reached out to gently stroke the hair from her face. "That's the way it should be."

Did he understand or wouldn't he miss her as she'd miss him? "That'll mean less time for us."

He rubbed her neck. The tension had tried to return but wasn't any match for his touch. "We'll have weekends," he said.

"True."

His lips came to meet hers, to erase the last of the shadows, and in their place a flame flickered and grew. Winter hadn't really returned. Not everywhere, not in her heart or in his arms. It was spring there, the world about to be reborn in sunshine.

"You're very understanding," she murmured.

"Hey," he whispered. "We're friends, and friends help each other."

Friends. Holly snuggled farther into Zach's arms. She was a mature woman with responsibilities, and a friend was exactly what she needed right now.

"My, aren't we chipper for a Monday morning?"

Zach tried to give the department secretary a dignified glance but quickly gave up and went back to shuffling through his mail. "Lucille, I'm always in a good mood."

"I agree that you're not a grump." He didn't have to look up; Lucille's voice clearly painted the aristocratic smirk that he knew she now wore on her face. "But whistling and humming to yourself? Come now, Dr. Philips. The next thing I know, you'll be dancing in the halls and telling me your physician prescribes it for exercise."

A momentary frown danced across his face. Whistling? Had he been whistling? "It's a beautiful day," he said.

"They're forecasting more snow."

"Hey, you keep forgetting I'm just an old Michigan farm boy. I love the snow."

Lucille raised an eyebrow. "Of course you do. And you're going to build a snowman this afternoon."

"A snowman?"

Zach was about to snort but stopped short. A broad smile came to his face and he kissed Lucille on the cheek. "Lucille, I love you," he said loudly.

The secretary's cheeks were blazing red, complementing her green sweater and white hair very nicely. "Good heavens, Professor Philips. Control yourself."

"Oh, Lucille," he laughed. "If only I could."

She looked around the area quickly, then stared at Zach, shock forcing her mouth open and all dignity to flee. Zach went quickly into his office and closed the door behind him.

He picked up the telephone and dialed, chuckling as he waited for Holly to answer. The weekend had been magic, pure and simple. They'd attended Jenny's basketball game and gone cross-country skiing. He'd broiled some steaks for dinner Saturday night. On Sunday night he took them out for pizza, then they played Trivial Pursuit. All the ingredients of a wild, exotic weekend. He had loved every minute of it.

"Holly Carpenter speaking."

"Hi, lover."

A longish pause. "How are you?"

"Aren't you going to ask me how you can help me? I thought they taught you telephone etiquette in a customer-relations course."

"I'd rather not get into that at the moment."

The words were stiff and formal—someone must be with her—but Zach would bet the farm that all the ice had melted off any telephone lines between them.

"I'd like to get together for lunch," he said.

"We discussed my availability last week. I told you then that weekdays were impossible."

He smiled to himself. "I'd like you to meet somebody."

"Business?"

"Not directly," Zach replied. "But he is something of a community fixture. He's usually around town this time of year."

She sighed in resignation. "All right. For lunch, but I really can't spare much more than an hour. I have to be back by one-thirty."

"That's fine," he said. "I'll pick you up at twelve-fifteen and have you back in time."

"You are a humbug."

Zach caught the scrap of bread Holly threw at him and tossed it to the geese wandering nearby. Then he bit deeply into a hamburger covered with cheese, tomatoes, lettuce and mustard. "Boy, I love these burgers. Flame broiled. There's nothing like them."

"You are a charlatan and a sham."

"Did you say cute?" he asked.

"I did not. Why would I say that?"

"I don't know, but that's what all my other girlfriends always said."

"Not only are you dishonest, but you are also conceited."

Zach smiled smugly. "I am indeed blessed."

He watched out of the corner of his eye as Holly tried to turn a dirty look into a full-fledged glare. Suddenly she fell into his arms, and they both laughed heartily. His heart leaped for joy as they held their hamburgers out of the way and their lips met. It was a wonderful touch, tasting of catsup and pickles but feeling of love and togetherness. If only they weren't in the park.

After reaching the edges of their hungers, she leaned against his chest. "You really are awful, you know."

"Eat your burger," he said. "It'll get cold quickly out here."

She stayed where she was, leaning against him and causing his heart to race, slowly eating her hamburger. "You don't appear the least bit ashamed of yourself," she said around a mouthful.

"Ashamed? For what?"

She reached over to sip at her cup of hot tea. "Have lunch with a community leader." She rolled her eyes at the small snowman across the bicycle path from them.

"I said community fixture."

"I thought you meant community leader."

"Not my fault. Anyway, what's wrong with Frosty?"

"He's a shrimp," she muttered without looking up.

"I didn't have much time," he protested. He finished eating and wiped his hands on a paper napkin. "Don't you like short people?"

"I have nothing against short people, but Frosty's not exactly flesh and blood."

"It's not Frosty's fault. We all have to play the cards life deals us."

She didn't reply to that bit of philosophy, and Zach leaned back against the tree, wrapping his arms around her as she ate in silence. When she was done, she gathered the cup and used napkins into the bag he'd brought them in.

"Care for any dessert?"

She shook her head and leaned back against him, gazing out at the scene in front of them. "It's real pretty out here," she said.

Zach's gaze followed hers as they took in the white blanket of snow over the ground. The dark trees were charcoal drawings against the snow, and the river glittered in the sunlight as it meandered by. Even the houses on the bluff across the river seemed put there for their enjoyment.

"It must be nice here in the summer," she said.

"Each season has its own beauty, although you can't beat January and February for privacy."

She laughed with him and slouched farther into the depths of his embrace.

"Cold?" he asked.

She shook her head. "Just comfortable."

Her hands were thrust deep in her coat pockets, so Zach put his hands in there, too, enabling them to hold hands. Geese wandered over the riverbank, and the water murmured as it passed. He wished he could make this moment last forever.

"That's a nice hill over there," she said. "Do kids sled on it?"

"We sure do."

She didn't look at him, but she smiled. "I should bring Jenny here."

"True." He pulled her closer. "You know, weekends don't have to be the only time we have. Jenny or Ruth can't possibly need you at lunchtime."

She turned to smile up at him. "Maybe my office does."

"You have to eat."

The temptation was too great and he bent down to touch her lips. They clung for a moment, suspended in time. There was no one but the two of them, no hungers but their own. But then the moment ended and she returned to staring across the river.

She stood up. "Time for me to get back to work."

He knew the world would call them, but it didn't mean he liked it. "And I have an afternoon class today."

They walked, hand in hand, along the winding trail out of the park. At her car, he took her in his arms and brushed her lips with his. His heart told him to sweep her away and bring laughter and joy to her eyes. Touch her, love her and chase away any shadows still in her heart. But he just kissed her again. Lightly. Promising with his lips the joys that the night would bring.

"Frosty wants to know if he'll see you again," he said.

She snuggled farther into his arms. "Sure. I enjoyed his company."

"Another lunch soon?"

"I'd like that."

He kissed her again. And no one would call it light.

Chapter Eleven

Holly's head snapped up a couple of days later and she stared wide-eyed as Zach marched into her office. Pushing some papers aside, he laid a package in front of her.

"Cold submarine sandwich, Italian bean soup and hot coffee. And for dessert, a small box of chocolates from the Philadelphia Candy Company."

She stared dumbly at him, her heart bursting into song. "You went to Philadelphia for candy?" she asked, before the incongruity of it all and especially her own stupidity struck her. "Strike that. I didn't say anything."

She buried her face in her hands for a long moment without saying another word, pretending Zach's unexpected arrival hadn't destroyed her ability to think. When sanity began to surface again, she slowly peered up at him. "What are you doing here?"

"I brought you your lunch."

Things were getting fuzzy again. Holly shook her head hard, really hard, but it didn't help. Was she going crazy or did his presence make her forget the simplest things? Maybe she'd picked up some sort of February virus. "You called this morning and asked me to go out to lunch," she said slowly, comparing her notes to his. "But I said I was busy."

"Right."

"Then what are you doing here?"

"Like I said before, I brought your lunch."

Was it his smile that confused her so or was it the twinkle in his eyes? "I didn't order lunch," she pointed out carefully.

"Your secretary did."

Now she knew she was insane. "Maureen ordered lunch from you?"

"Not exactly."

Holly sent a deep, hearty sigh through her bones and stared at the wall over his head. "I'm not sure what I should do right now," she said.

He smiled and sat on the edge of her desk. "I called Maureen to check your calendar, to see if you had any free time this afternoon."

"Should I kill you?"

"And she said the only time you didn't have an appointment was at lunch."

"Or should I let you live?"

"She also said that you had told her to order in lunch, so anything I brought was fine."

Holly let her gaze lower slightly to rest on his smile. "Live or die? That's the question."

The smile vanished. "What kind of question is that? Don't you like submarines?"

"I love them."

"How about Italian bean soup?"

"That's fine, too."

"And I know you'll love the chocolates," he said as he pulled a chair over to her desk and sat down. "So let's eat."

"You're incorrigible."

"Hungry, too." He laughed, opening his sack.

Holly slowly opened her package, pulling out the sandwich and cup of soup as she tried not to laugh herself. Life was so good lately, mostly sunshine and smiles. Ruth and

Bruno were becoming an item, and Holly felt only joy for them. Jenny seemed to be applying herself more at school, and Zach... Well, Zach was always there when she needed him. Bringing a smile, a laugh or lunch.

"How is the sandwich?" he asked.

"Delicious."

Everything seemed to be more fun with him around, every problem more solvable. How had she managed before he'd pushed his way into her life?

"You know," he said, putting his sandwich down, "I've been thinking about Jenny."

"Oh?"

"She's such a smart kid," he went on. "I'm just wondering if she might not be going the way she's planned."

Holly stared at him, clutching the remains of her sandwich. "Going the way she's planned?"

"Sure." He wiped his mouth with a napkin and leaned back in the chair. "Doing it on purpose."

"On purpose?" Holly couldn't believe he was serious. "That's ridiculous. Why in the world would she do poorly in her schoolwork on purpose?"

"It's not as bizarre as it sounds," he assured her. "Kids will do all sorts of strange things because they think it will make them more popular. When I was in second grade, I wore an old cape to school for weeks because I wanted everyone to think I was Superman's son."

Holly laughed. "Did it work?"

"Nope. My brother kept telling everyone the only thing super about me was my stupidity. He was not very understanding of my need to feel accepted," Zach said. "But as boys get older, a lot of them concentrate on athletics and let their academics slide because they think no one likes a bookworm. Teenage girls will pretend that they don't know anything about sports."

Holly took another bite of her sandwich. "And you think Jenny might be faking ineptitude in order to be accepted by her classmates? I guess it's possible."

The more Holly thought about it, the more sense it made. Jenny was playing down her academic strengths because she didn't want her classmates to resent her. "I'll talk to her and see," she said.

"I have a better idea," he said. He reached for their coffee cups, carefully prying up the plastic lids. "Why not invite some of her friends over? She gets along well with the other girls on the basketball team. Invite some of them to go roller-skating or out for pizza. I'd be glad to help."

"No, a slumber party," Holly said. "That's what girls this age really love."

Zach made a face. "That's a bit out of my realm, I'm afraid."

"A bit out of mine, too, but it's a wonderful idea to have some girls over. Mom will be able to advise me." She reached for her coffee, blowing at it lightly to cool it off. "The more I think about it, the more I think you may be right about Jenny doing this on purpose. Mom thought Jenny needed more time to adjust and I thought the work was somehow much harder here, but I think you've hit the nail on the head. I'm forever in your debt."

He leaned forward just a touch, his eyes taking on a hungry gleam. "Shall we speak of ways to repay that debt?"

She sipped her coffee, ignoring the answering gleam in her heart. "Once Jenny feels accepted, she'll probably move back up to her normal academic level."

"And depending on how nicely you repay that debt, I may be willing to use my academic standing to bribe the admissions officer of the college Jenny chooses to attend so they won't look at her grade-school performance."

Holly laughed, her eyes promising full repayment of all debts, and reached for the chocolates. "These are delicious," she said, biting into an orange cream.

"Handmade, too, just this morning, so they're fresh."

She took another, a chocolate-covered caramel that was soft enough to melt in her mouth. "I'd hate to see them get stale."

Zach took one, also, as he gathered up the empty food wrappers. "So aren't you glad I brought your lunch today?" he asked.

"Eternally grateful." She leaned forward to meet him, their lips meeting over her desk. "In fact, there's no way I can ever repay all that I owe you, so I won't insult you by even trying."

"Try. I'm impervious to insult."

She just laughed and, coming around to the front of her desk, pushed him gently toward the door. "Get back to the university. Your students are crying for learning."

"I'm crying for another chocolate," he said, reaching around her to snatch another. "Or should I just take the whole box with me?"

"Don't you dare." She slapped his hand away with a laugh, then put on a mocking, simpering sigh. "They're all I have to remember you by this afternoon."

"I could stay."

Her heart was in favor of the idea, but she shook her head. She had appointments all afternoon. "Goodbye, Dr. Philips." Once he was gone, it seemed his presence lingered, making it harder to concentrate on anything but the memory of his smile.

"It's snowing again," Jenny said, as if she was announcing the return of the Ice Age.

Holly came over to the window and stood next to her daughter, sharing the winter's view of the late Saturday afternoon snowfall as they waited for Jenny's guests to arrive. Holly put an arm around Jenny's shoulders.

"The flakes are really big," Holly said.

"That's lake-effect snow. It means that it's probably not snowing on the west side of the lake at all."

"So it's clear in Chicago."

"Maybe." Jenny hedged her pronouncement. "Or maybe it's a big blizzard heading our way."

Holly just laughed. "Stop worrying. It's not going to snow much. See, it's slowing down already."

"That's just the squall effect." Jenny sounded determined to be glum.

They watched the falling snow in silence for a few more minutes, then Jenny's mood slipped another notch lower.

"The lady on the radio said the forecast is for four to six inches. Maybe they aren't coming. You and Zach should just go out and celebrate Valentine's Day."

Holly squeezed her shoulders. "This is just how I want to spend my Valentine's Day," she assured her. "And besides, this isn't New York. People around here aren't bothered until they have a foot or more of snow."

"I guess."

Her own shoulders slumped to match Jenny's. Wasn't she ever going to get this parent stuff right? She had thought her words would cheer Jenny up; instead they made her more mournful. Apparently her daughter was figuring that the kids weren't going to come anyway, so she was hoping for a good excuse, like too much snow to drive in.

Holly looked at her watch. It was five after six. Jenny's basketball game had ended at five. The girls had said they'd be here around six, after they showered, dressed and packed. That never happened in a hurry, especially not with ten-year-old girls.

Holly felt the gloom radiating from her daughter's body and sighed. The reasons for the girls' not being here yet were easy to see, but would Jenny buy them? Would she agree that it was hard corralling four ten-year-old girls? Besides, they really weren't late. Especially not on Indiana time.

Holly felt her own spirits sag in spite of her pep talk. She wished the kids would get here soon. She was well on her way to talking herself into a blue funk. Then she and Jenny could be a matched pair, modeling mother-daughter blue funks.

"There they are," Jenny cried with sudden happiness as a beige minivan pulled up outside the gate. "Sara's mother brought them all."

While Jenny ran to the front door, Holly hung back and stared out the window as four girls with overnight satchels and sleeping bags tumbled out of the van.

Momentary tightness gripped her stomach, but she took a deep breath and made it go away. She had never managed a sleep-over party for Jenny before. In fact, she'd never run any kind of party for Jenny. Ruth had always done that, but this time Holly had insisted that Ruth keep her date with Bruno. Zach had offered to help, but Holly had politely refused. This was her daughter and this was her daughter's party, she had told him, declaring it a mother's responsibility. But now she had to take another deep breath before the icy dread within her could establish a beachhead. Maybe she'd been too hasty in turning him down. No, how much trouble could five young girls cause?

Holly moved quickly to the door. She didn't know and she wasn't planning on finding out. The girls and the mother were clustered at the gate.

"Come on in," Jenny called, racing down to meet them.

"It says Beware of Dog," one girl said.

Holly had been thinking she ought to remove that sign but had never gotten around to it. There was always something to do with this house.

"We don't have a dog," Jenny said. "Yet."

Holly gave Jenny a look that was returned in the sweetest smile any mother could wish for, then Jenny opened the gate and the girls streamed into the yard. Holly walked down to meet the woman waiting at the sidewalk.

"Hi, Holly," the woman said. "I'm Bess Turner. Going to need any help tonight?"

"No. Thank you for your offer, but everything's under control."

Had she always been able to lie like that? Holly's voice sounded so positive that she almost believed herself.

"Okay," Bess replied. "Give us a call if you need anything." Then she shouted after the girls, "You guys behave now, you hear?"

They didn't bother to reply, but Bess left anyway. Holly hurried after them, stepping on their conversation.

"This is a neat house, Jenny. It looks real spooky."

"It is," Jenny said. "And we have our own ghost."

"Jenny, there are no such things as ghosts," Holly pointed out.

"My mother doesn't believe in ghosts."

Four pairs of eyes glanced briefly at Holly and then went back to Jenny.

"Anyway," Jenny continued, "his name is Pokagon, just like the street, and he likes apples and rum for a snack."

"Oh, wow."

"Hey, neato."

"Super neato."

Holly lined the words all up in her mind, logical, rational arguments that would return Pokagon to where he belonged, to the world of make-believe, but Holly couldn't say them. What difference did it make if Jenny told a few tall tales? The girls were all laughing and giggling. It was all in fun and no one was taking it seriously.

"And my room doesn't have any corners at all."

The girls moved even more quickly, running up the stairs to gaze upon this eighth wonder of the world, while Holly just shook her head and pulled herself up the stairs after them. She hoped she would last through the night. Even just watching all that energy and enthusiasm was draining her.

Suddenly she halted on the stairs, a frown building on her forehead. What was all this nonsense about apples and rum for Pokagon? Holly had never heard that before. Then a squeal of giggles came floating down the stairs toward her and she decided Pokagon would have to wait. It appeared the party had started.

"Hello, lover." Zach stepped aside to let her into his apartment.

Holly straightened up from the wall that had been keeping her vertical. Somehow, waiting horizontally for someone to open his door seemed likely to be one of Miss Manners's no-no's. "Hi, Zach. Happy Valentine's Day." She handed him the miniature Black Forest torte she'd gotten for them to share. The shaved chocolate on top was laid in the shape of a heart.

"This looks delicious," he said, his eyes widening, but he was looking at her lips and bent to taste them. "Where are Jenny and her friends?"

"Not with me," she assured him. "Mother came home with some gosh-awful videos for them to watch and told me

I could be excused. Since New York was being eaten by giant grasshoppers, I didn't put up a fuss.''

"And you thought you were having problems with this house. I haven't seen one grasshopper.''

"Yet.'' Holly shuddered as she sank onto his sofa. The cool leather surface eased relaxation into her bones. "Jenny thought the movie was great. She was pointing out all the places of interest she's seen. I think the girls were convinced we lived in the World Trade Center.''

Zach chuckled. "What can I get you to go with this sinful dessert?''

"Tea would be wonderful,'' she told him as he went into the kitchen. He was back in a few minutes with two steaming mugs and slices of torte on plates.

"There you go,'' he said, putting her mug on the coffee table in front of her. Then he sat next to her on the sofa, slipping an arm around her shoulders to pull her close.

"Oh, this is heaven,'' she said with a sigh as she tasted the torte, then lay back against him. She kicked off her shoes and put her feet up on the edge of the coffee table. His heart beat behind her. No. She closed her eyes. His heart beat all around her. Up, down, inside and outside. Everywhere.

"Happy Valentine's Day to you, too,'' he said softly, and she opened her eyes to find him holding out a small silver-and-red gift.

"Zach, you weren't supposed to get me something,'' she protested as she slowly took the gift.

"What was that you gave me?''

"Something for both of us to share.''

"So we'll share this, too.''

She unwrapped the gift to find a small portrait of an Indian, an old portrait. "Don't tell me,'' she said with a grin. "Pokagon.''

"Who else? I thought you could hang him up downstairs someplace.''

"I'll do that,'' she agreed. "The old boy's been behaving lately, so I'll put him up. Thank you, kind sir.'' She kissed Zach lightly, then returned to her torte.

"You look a little wan," he said after a moment. "The kids wear you out?"

"I suppose a little."

They were silent for a moment, finishing their torte, then Holly burst out laughing, shaking her head. "You should have seen dinner. That was a horror show in itself."

"Why?"

"They had hot dogs and shoestring potatoes."

"Sounds normal."

"Only to an adult." She put her tea down and lay back against him again. "Well, I put out catsup, which some kids used for their potatoes."

"Still sounds normal."

Holly gave Zach a quick over-the-shoulder frown, which he kissed back into a smile. Her toes wiggled in reply. A little bit of strength was finding its way back into her.

"Anyway," she went on, "that wasn't enough for the little gourmets. One of them wanted barbecue sauce."

"Sort of like catsup."

"Then another wanted applesauce."

"Creative," Zach replied.

"Then they were all trying a little of everything."

"They just wanted to experience life."

"Right." They both laughed, then let the curtain of companionable silence fall again.

Maybe that was what she was doing with Zach. Experiencing life. Everything was certainly more exciting with him around, more wonderful. But it didn't feel as though she was experiencing life so much as finally being alive. It was different being with Zach than it had been with Joel. She'd loved Joel with her whole heart and they'd had a good life, but somehow with Zach she seemed to be laughing more, singing more, seeing more of the beauty all around her.

Maybe it was like almost drowning. Being without air for a few minutes made you breathe all the more deeply. Being without love for those years made her love all the stronger.

"So then what happened?" Zach prodded.

Holly started, lost in the shock of her revelation and somehow muddled her way back to their conversation.

"Oh, one of them found some kind of chicken sauce from a fast-food restaurant, but I threw it away."

"Why?"

"The girl found the little packets in her coat pocket but couldn't remember when she'd gotten them. Sometime before Thanksgiving, she thought."

Zach laughed and made a face.

"Right," Holly agreed. "'Super yucko gucko,' as my little buddies downstairs would say."

They returned to silence again and Holly groped her way back to her shock. Why had she used the word love in her thoughts? She didn't love Zach. Or did she? What was love if it wasn't feeling whole in the other's arms? If his smile didn't light up her world and if her shoulders couldn't help carry his sorrow?

"So was it really a bad evening?" Zach asked.

Holly shook her head, relieved to be drawn from her thoughts. "No, actually it was fun."

"Then why do I sense something's wrong?"

Maybe because something was. Friends—that's all they were supposed to be. That was all she'd wanted. Friends who could say goodbye with a smile when it came time for him to leave. But the whole idea was too new, too shocking, to talk about, so she latched on to her other nagging worry.

"They played Trivial Pursuit after dinner," Holly said.

"That does sound bad," Zach mocked.

"You should have seen Jenny. She was a whiz at answering her questions, yet if I had called it a science test, I bet she wouldn't have answered even one."

"How did the other girls react to Jenny's answering?"

"They all wanted her on their team."

He hugged her a little closer. "Sounds like the prognosis is promising."

"Yes, it does." But what was the prognosis for her heart?

"Can I get you more tea?" he asked.

"No, this was enough." She put her cup down, leaning forward, away from him, as she did so. She felt cold without his arms around her. Winter's winds seemed to be blustering all about. But she stood up, arms wrapped around her chest to convince herself that warmth was a state of mind and could be achieved by oneself.

"Have to get right back?"

She shook her head. "Only if I don't want to miss the grasshoppers snacking on the Statue of Liberty. Otherwise I've got a couple of hours off. More than that, actually. Mom brought the grasshopper movie and its sequel."

"What do the grasshoppers do in the sequel?"

She stopped in front of his collection of arrowheads, staring at their unevenly chipped surfaces from so long ago. "You mean, what's left after New York? Maybe South Bend. That's the route I took, after all."

He got to his feet, grinning. "If it's good enough for Holly Carpenter, it's good enough for the grasshoppers, is that it?"

"Sure. Why not?"

"But was it good enough for Holly Carpenter?" he murmured, coming close enough to take her in his arms, except that he didn't.

"What does that mean?"

"I mean, was it a good move for you? Are you happy here?"

She shrugged, wishing his eyes weren't piercing hers with such intensity. Wishing his lips weren't so tempting and his hands didn't have such power over her soul. Wishing he would just take her in his arms and forget all this silly talk.

"Yes. I'm happy here, but I'll be happier when Jenny's more settled."

He stirred slightly, but only to shift his weight, not to end her torment of missing him. "What about the house?"

"I guess I'm used to it."

"You wouldn't have been happy in your bland suburban split-level, you know." He reached for her then, pulling her into his arms, into her heaven.

"I wouldn't?"

"You're not a suburban split-level person," he said, smiling down into her eyes. "You've done your best to make yourself bland over the last few years, but you aren't. You're like this house."

"A hundred years old and falling apart?"

He touched the tip of her nose in teasing. Then, as if he couldn't help himself, his hand slid over her cheek to run through her hair. "Deep and solid. Filled with beautiful little surprises. A treasure to cherish over the years. You have a history and that makes you even more special."

"Thank you," she said, not knowing what to say and laughing from embarrassment, uneasiness. "I've never been compared to a beaten-up, decrepit house in such nice terms before."

He laughed. "What shall I compare you to next? A tree? A fish?"

"Let's stop while we're ahead, shall we?"

His laughter faded; his eyes grew serious. "Are we ahead?" he murmured.

"Seems like it to me."

There wasn't any time or need for words as his lips came down on hers. The silence of the night grew, enveloping them in its sweet embrace. At the first taste of his lips, she knew that she did indeed love him. All her speeches to the contrary had been just bravado. Fear had held her prisoner, and Zach had set her free.

His hands lit a fire in her soul, raging against the moment to come alive. She touched him, stoking the fire in his heart until their hands and their hearts were everything. The night had ceased to exist, just as time stood still. Nothing mattered but his lips on hers and the caress of his hands on her hunger. Love cried out to him and he swept her up in his arms, carrying her off to his bedroom.

The first time they'd made love it had been a sweet dance of sunlight and moonlight. Now it was a raging fire that needed to consume. Her love for him drove her higher, wider and deeper as they stripped each other of their clothes.

She needed to feel his power over her, her majesty over him. Lips and love, hands and hunger. The world spun out of control as she clung to him.

Finally he came to her and together they felt the flames of love engulf them. She gave everything to him, her heart, her soul, her very life, for nothing else mattered but him and the moment. They soared into the flames, then found peace, floating back to reality wrapped in each other's arms.

Chapter Twelve

Hamburger Hut," Holly exclaimed, and clapped her hands. "Now, this is a special place for lunch."

Zach pulled his car into a parking place on the far side of the lot. "Boy," he grumbled. "You certainly have a mean streak in you."

"What are you talking about?"

"I told you I was taking you out for a real business lunch and you get sarcastic on me."

Holly stared at him for several moments. "That building over there is a Hamburger Hut," she said, pointing toward the trademark building with the bright red roof. "Right?"

"Right."

"And this," she said, pointing downward, "is a Hamburger Hut parking lot, right?"

"Absolutely," he agreed.

"Then I can logically assume that you are taking me to the Hamburger Hut for lunch."

"Not necessarily."

She looked at him sharply, but he didn't flinch. "Is this another one of those Indiana laws? You know, like the Indiana math that Bruno tells Jenny about? Or how about the Indiana time that the tradespeople use—the 'might,' 'probably,' 'easily,' 'surely' stuff they're always giving out when you ask them how long a job will take?"

Zach shook his head as he got out of the car to come around to her side. "You have a very definite attitude problem," he said as he shut the door after her. "But I'm willing to work with you." He took her in his arms, kissing her under her right ear.

"That tickles," she giggled.

"And I'll stay on the job until your gentler side is fully developed." He kissed her under the left ear.

"I told you that tickles," she said, snuggling into his arms. "And I'm not going to turn into a wimp."

He let her out of his arms but kept her hand in his as they started walking toward the fast-food restaurant. "Ah, New York women," he said with a deep sigh.

"What's the matter with New York women?"

"You are lovely beyond belief," he said. "But you capture men's hearts in an unbreakable trap."

"You better believe it," she replied.

It was late February and the mixture of rain, sleet and snow beating on their heads was anything but pleasant. Yet Holly felt as if she were walking on clouds, with bright sunshine warming every last inch of her body and soul. So what if she loved Zach? So what if he was a wanderer, waiting to explore the next port his ship stopped at? It was still a relief that she didn't have to worry that he might leave. She still knew he would go, but it would have nothing to do with her. She could enjoy her love without fearing each new day.

Zach led her right past the fast-food restaurant.

"Where are we going?"

"Lunch."

They crossed the street at midblock and Zach hurried her into a ten-story building, one of the tall structures in downtown South Bend.

"Here we are." He guided her to their left and into a tiny coffee shop, past the blackboard at the door indicating the specials. "Ah, good," Zach said. "They have bean soup today. That's my very favorite."

Misti's Mug and Muffin had one short counter that seated three people and nine tables, but it had smiles and good cheer enough to fill a room four times its size. All the patrons took time to nod and smile a welcome to them.

"Hi, stranger." The blue eyes of a black-haired young woman sparkled brightly with good humor.

"Hi, Misti." Zach and Misti traded hugs. "Stop trying to lay a guilt trip on me. I've been busy."

"I can see that," Misti said, turning her smile onto Holly.

"Misti, meet my landlady."

Misti laughed. "Whatever you say, Zach."

"Her name is Holly."

"Hi, Holly." Then Misti turned to the sole waitress. "Sylvia, let's put Zach and Holly—he says she's his landlady—over in that corner booth." Holly's introduction to Sylvia was delivered with an elaborate wink, then she and Zach were led to the only empty table in the room. Sylvia picked up a coffeepot on the way.

The waitress poured Zach a cup, raising her eyebrows to Holly as she gestured with the pot. Holly nodded and her mug was also filled, then they gave their orders. Holly was ready to relax in the warm friendliness.

"So how's Jenny doing these days?" Zach asked.

"She seems to be doing fine. At least, I haven't had to sign any almost failing tests." Holly sipped her coffee.

"Maybe the party helped."

"I think so. It's only been a week and a half, but she seems to be relaxing."

"Are you?"

Holly smiled. "I'm trying." Her smile suddenly took a dive into uneasiness and disappeared. "I'm very grateful that you shared your opinion with me. If you hadn't, I might still be ready to lynch her past teachers for not teaching her anything." She stared into her cup as if it held the voices that had been haunting her the past few nights. "I should have seen it myself."

His hand came over to cover hers. "It's not a crime to need help in parenting. No parent can do it alone. It really takes a community to raise a kid right."

How did he always know how to silence those voices? She smiled at him. "Did the horses and cows help raise you?"

"Hey," he scolded. "I said I was a farm boy, not a hermit."

"Sorry."

He stared out the window and Holly listened to the minutes tick by, worrying that her teasing might have hurt his feelings. The waitress brought their soup and sandwiches and Zach began eating.

"A farm is also part of a community," Zach said. "We went to school, to church, shopping, participated in sports. Everything a city kid does. The only difference is we had a longer walk to our neighbors."

"I didn't mean to put country people down."

His smile cleared the clouds from her world. "I'm sorry," he said. "I wasn't taking anything you said badly. I was just remembering all the people who helped keep me on the straight and narrow."

Holly bit into her sandwich, savoring the meat and tastefully seasoned sauce. "Were you a problem child?"

His face took on such a sweet kind of sadness that Holly wanted to pull his head to her heart and spill comfort over him until he smiled again.

"Not to the community," he said. "Only to my father."

She ate in silence. Zach was usually so carefree, but not now. Sadness had softened the edges of his eyes, and he wore a cloak of seriousness.

"Things were nice, normal, until Mom died." He took another bite of his sandwich and shrugged. "Dad and I were both hurt by the loss. It's just that Dad and I took it differently."

She nodded in understanding. "Everyone grieves in their own way."

"But our ways just happened to rub each other the wrong way. He got quiet and withdrew into himself. I got all hyper and became the world's greatest comedian. I had a joke, a smart remark, a foolish saying, every minute. After a while it got on Dad's nerves." He sipped his soup. "Actually, we got on each other's nerves."

Holly hesitated. They were in the private corners of Zach's soul. He looked comfortable, but she'd never been this way before. "Did that difficult period last long?"

"Too long." Now sadness alone captured his face. "Much too long."

Finished with his food, he pushed his plate aside. "It got progressively worse for a year or two, then through the intervention of teachers, our minister and just plain friends we reached a state of armed truce."

Her sympathy turned almost to envy. It was more than she and her father had ever reached.

"I stuck it out that last summer after high school, but once I went away to college I was gone. I came back for a few of the holidays. Darn few."

Her envy grew deeper. Few was better than none.

"Money was a little tight for me, so most of the time I worked during my holidays rather than came home and my summer jobs were always near school. Janice was home on the farm and she was more than enough help."

There hadn't been anybody when her father left. Just Holly and her mother.

"I didn't really forgive the old man until he got sick." Zach shook his head. "Both of us were damn fools. One thing I learned was that grudges are really heavy. It takes two to carry them for any length of time."

Her father hadn't even done his share in carrying the grudge. Like everything else, she'd had to do it alone. But it had made her strong. Maybe too strong. Was that why she didn't need anybody now? Or was it she didn't want anybody?

"Say, how about you and Jenny going up to the farm with me this Sunday? Meet Janice and Tom and the kids." Zach's voice was louder than normal, a show of strength to chase his demons away, then an easy smile returned to his face.

"Sounds like fun." Holly forced a smile. It required a bit more effort than she had hoped as she faced her own demons. They'd been with her a long, long time. They came second only to her family, but here with Zach they were almost gone.

"Here, honey. Try these on," Zach's sister said to Jenny as she gave the girl a pair of tall black boots. "They should keep your feet nice and dry."

Janice's hair was lighter than Zach's, but her jaw had the same stubborn line and her eyes were the same brown. Her voice, however, was firm, brooking no nonsense. On their drive up to the farm, Zach had said his sister filled in whenever the archangel Gabriel was busy, but Holly could see the woman radiated love.

The boots came up almost to Jenny's knees, but the girl smiled politely. "They're fine. Thank you, ma'am."

"Don't you 'ma'am' me, sweetheart." Jenny was enveloped in a fierce hug. Zach had also said that his sister spread love the way she used to play basketball, aggressively and unmindful of any bruises that might occur. "You just call me Janice. Zach brought you, so you're as near to kin as the law allows."

Jenny grinned and tried to return the hug but couldn't quite get her arms around Janice's thick waist. Both broke into giggles.

"You come back after the first of May," Janice told her. "Once I have the baby I'll be skinny as a rail again. Plus, Josh and Tessa will be home then, so you'll have someone to play with."

Janice punctuated her speech with a dark look aimed at Zach and he launched them into a replay of their earlier debate.

"Hey, I said I was sorry. A thousand times I said I was sorry. How was I to know that their grandparents were going to take them to some old winter carnival?"

"You could have called."

"I did."

"You called last night. I meant earlier."

Zach's face emphasized its stubborn lines. "I'm not going to apologize anymore."

Holly couldn't help herself and started laughing. She could picture Zach as a child, always arguing with his sister as she followed him around, trying to show him the "right" way to do things. "You two must have driven your parents crazy," Holly said.

"Well, Zach certainly did," Janice admitted.

Zach's glare was one of sorely tried patience, then he turned to Holly. "I'll get my coat and we can go out back."

Holly nodded and took a deep breath, inhaling the kitchen's homey smells. Cherry pies, pot roasts, Thanksgiving turkeys—years of scents danced and played in every corner. The house literally breathed love. It must have been a good place to grow up.

"Don't let him take you around back of the barn," Janice warned. "It's too muddy out there in late February and early March. That's where he always led me around this time of year when we were kids, hoping I'd get stuck in the mud."

"And did you?" Jenny asked.

"Only once, and I yelled so much my dad came out and got me." Janice grinned. "Zach never took me back there again."

Jenny giggled, then giggled even more as Zach came back into the room, zipping up his coat.

He took one look at Jenny, then shook his head. "Whatever she said, it was a lie. She was always lying and getting me in trouble."

"As if you needed my help." Janice shooed them out the back door.

As they climbed down the wide wooden stairs, a taffy colored dog raced up to them, dancing around them all then butting Jenny's hand with his head. His long tail wagged against Holly's legs.

"Look, Mom, he likes me," Jenny cried.

"Fred likes everybody," Zach says. "But mostly pretty little girls who don't believe Janice's lies."

Jenny looked up at him, her eyes wide and solemn. A sure sign devilment was coming, but did Zach know that?

"I didn't believe any of her lies," Jenny told him.

Zach smiled. "Good."

"'Cause she only told the truth." Jenny's giggles spilled out into the wind as she and Fred raced ahead.

"Whose side is she on?" Zach muttered. Then he eyed Holly and pulled her arm through his. "Whose side are *you* on?"

"Must there be sides?" she asked in her best mother voice.

He laughed and tucked his hand into hers.

The wind was brisk, racing across the open fields, and Holly pulled her collar up around her ears. In the distance she could see the next farm, but a person would have to be one good shouter for it to be considered within shouting distance. The place should feel desolate, she thought, but was surprised that it didn't.

"Mom, can I come here in the summer?"

Holly was startled out of her reverie. "I guess so, if it's all right with Janice and Tom."

"There's no doubt there," Zach said. "The whole family would love having her."

"Janice said I could go swimming and horseback riding every day. And the only time I'd have to wear shoes was when we went to church on Sunday."

"Sounds great," Holly laughed. "I wonder if I can come, too."

"I'll ask Janice," Jenny said. "Maybe we can all come."

Holly imagined how the meadow would look once the snow disappeared and it became filled with wildflowers. She could see herself running barefoot, her feet flying over the soft, cushiony surface. It was a wonderful feeling to be so free and alive.

"Oh, look, Mommy. Aren't those lambs cute?" Jenny cried, running over to the fence to look at the animals feeding.

"Those are sheep," Zach pointed out. "Lambs are the babies."

"So what? I got the genus, specie or whatever right."

Holly reached through the fence to scratch the sheep. "Their coats are all scratchy and oily," she said. "I thought sheep were soft and cuddly."

"Another myth of farm life down the drain." Zach moved them on to the pen where the cows were. The animals rhythmically moved their jaws as they gazed at the three of them.

"They look like they're chewing gum," Jenny said.

"That's called chewing their cud," Zach said. "They stuff one of their stomachs, which is like a holding tank, with food, then bring it up later and chew it properly."

"Yucko. Can we see the horses now?"

"Sure," Zach replied. "They're in that barn over there."

Jenny skipped ahead, Fred racing around with her as Holly and Zach followed along more slowly.

"What was it like growing up on a farm?" Holly asked.

"Myth or truth?"

"Truth."

"A lot of work. Isolation from your friends, school, the library. Never-ending dependence of the animals on you. The stereotype of a Tom Sawyer type of life, going barefoot and fishing in the creek, is just that—a stereotype. But there were good things, too. A sense of accomplishment and worth. I hated cleaning the chicken house, but the chickens were my responsibility and I was proud of that. I learned to value my free time and never complained there was nothing to do."

They came to the barn and Zach pulled open a smaller side door. "Watch your step," he said, pointing to the high threshold. The inside was warm and shadowy, the damp air filled with animal smells.

"Man," Jenny exclaimed, "this is really a huge barn."

"The horses are kept in stalls down there," Zach said, then with a sweep of his arm he indicated the upper floor and the space stretching up to the ceiling far over thei heads. "During the summer the hay is put up there, then fed to the horses during the winter."

Jenny and Holly craned their necks to look up at the huge piles of hay.

"It also helps keep the barn warm during the coldest months. By the time summer comes the hay is all gone and the high roof helps keep the barn cool. Roger and I used to hide up there," Zach said.

"From who?" Jenny asked. "From your mother and father?"

"Most of the time we hid from Janice."

"That was mean," Holly said.

"We had to," Zach protested. "It was the only way for us to preserve our sanity. She was always following us around."

"She loved you," Holly said. "She admired her older brothers."

"No, she didn't. She just wanted to irritate us."

"Don't listen to him, Jenny," Holly told her daughter.

"She was a pest."

"Zach."

"She probably still is," Zach grumbled as they walked along the stalls. "I mean, she was really awful." By now Jenny was ignoring him and gazing up in rapture at the horses.

"This is Flicka," Zach said, indicating a light brown horse with a blaze of white down its face.

Jenny waved. "Hi, Flicka."

"Flicka?" Holly muttered in disbelief.

Zach shrugged. "That's what Janice wanted." Then he went up to the animal and scratched its ears. The horse returned the favor by butting him in the chest.

"How come she's hitting you?" Jenny asked.

"Because she knows I have this." Zach whipped a carrot from his coat pocket. "She loves carrots." Flicka strained toward it. "Would you like to feed her?"

Jenny nodded her head vigorously and climbed onto the crossbar gate in front of the stall.

Holly noted the animal's big teeth and released a motherly caution. "Careful, honey."

But Flicka was as gentle as a kitten and Jenny's face glowed. "Her lips are so soft," she whispered.

"Flicka's going to be a mother about the same time as Janice," Zach said.

"Could we come and see the colt when it's born?" Jenny pleaded. "Could we, Mom? I'll clean my room every day. I'll apply myself and do better in school. Much better."

"We'll try to."

Jenny's face lit up like the sun. "Did you hear that, Flicka? We'll come and see you and your baby." The horse began playfully butting Jenny now, when suddenly they heard the clanging of a bell.

"Dinner," Jenny cried, and gave Flicka a last kiss on her wet nose. "Janice said when she rings the bell we should get our butts in gear and head for the house."

Jenny ran ahead with Fred, while Zach and Holly followed more slowly. Loving Zach made Holly want to savor every moment they had together.

"You really don't have to help with this," Janice protested. "There isn't that much that doesn't go into the dishwasher."

"If I stay in the living room I'll get forced into a game of Scrabble, and I always lose." Holly spooned the leftover carrots into a plastic container.

"I don't remember Zach ever being that cutthroat at games."

"It's Jenny," Holly admitted with a laugh. "She always seems to get the high-point letters and use them on the bonus squares while I get nothing but vowels."

"Tom's like that, too. Probably best if we stay out of their way and let the two of them slug it out."

Holly closed up the container and put the empty bowl by the dishwasher. "The question is, should we warn Zach or let him learn the hard way?"

Janice chuckled as she scraped the plates into the garbage. "Zach can take care of himself."

"That's true." Laughter floated in from the other room, and Holly stood still for a moment, letting the warmth o the sound bring a smile to her face. She heard Zach's voice, the sound of it but not the words, and another wave of laughter. "Was Zach always like this?" she asked Janice. "Never taking anything seriously?"

"Oh, there's a lot he takes seriously. It's just his way to make jokes." Janice stopped. "When our mother died he was about twelve. That's when he really got into humor."

"To hide his grief?" Holly asked as she packed up the slices of leftover roast, stacking them on a piece of aluminum foil.

"No, just to keep us all sane, I think. It really started when Mom got sick. She lived about a year longer than the doctors expected, but not very well. Zach would get really silly trying to distract her from her pain. And distract the rest of us, too."

Holly nodded. "He has a way of making you forget what's bothering you, even for just a few minutes."

"The one he used to tease the most was Roger because he was so solemn." Janice started loading the dishwasher, lining up the plates in the bottom rack. "Being the eldest, Roger could sometimes be a bit much, but Zach always knew how to bring him back down to earth with his Roger impersonation. Mom used to laugh so hard."

Holly wrapped up the leftover roast and put it in the refrigerator. "He told me that his troubles with your father started over his jokes."

"I guess they did in a way." Janice loaded some cups and glasses into the top rack of the dishwasher, then went on. "Dad never really got over Mom's death and used to be irritated by Zach's clowning around, but I think it was more than that. Mom died when Roger was a sophomore in high school and starting to talk about college and careers. Roger couldn't wait to see the world and never gave a thought to staying on the farm. It really hurt Dad. He wanted one of us kids to love the place the way he did, so he focused all his hopes on Zach."

"But Zach turned out to be as much of a wanderer as Roger," Holly said.

"Not really." Janice closed up the dishwasher and pushed a few buttons. A quiet whirring filled the room as she started in on the pots piled in the sink. "For all Zach's teasing, he idolized Roger and thought everything Roger did or said was wonderful. Since Roger wanted to travel, Zach decided he did, too, especially since Dad was making the home situation so unpleasant for him. Dad never asked Zach to stay, never even said he hoped he would stay. He'd just pick holes in all his ideas and mock all his hopes, which of course was as good as telling him to go."

"So Zach did," Holly said, picking up a dish towel as Janice started to wash the pots.

"Only for a time. He came back."

"Because your father was sick."

"That's what he said, but I think he came back because he belongs here. Dad died almost a year ago and Zach's still here. I think he left in anger, stayed away out of habit but came back because it was home."

"He doesn't seem to be putting down roots." Holly didn't think Janice knew Zach as well as she thought.

"You just can't see them."

Holly wasn't so sure of that.

"There's a lot here he cares about. Us. His work. This farm even. The place was mortgaged to the roof after Dad died and Zach helped Tom and me pay off the bills."

"He didn't tell me that," Holly said, frowning at the pot she was drying. Though his staying to pay off the debts was only proof that she was right. He stayed for a reason, not for roots.

"No, he wouldn't tell something like that."

"All he told me about the farm was that cleaning out the chicken house convinced him he wasn't a farmer."

Janice wrinkled her nose even as she grinned. "That is the world's worst job, believe me. It's Josh's now and he hates it. The complaining he does, you'd think we were asking him to do something against his religion."

"Zach says it builds character."

"Obviously an adult perspective." Janice rinsed off a pot and stacked it in the drainer. "Where did you grow up?"

"New York City."

"The farm must seem really strange to you."

"Strange and wonderful. Like an ideal way to grow up."

"I doubt there is such a place." Janice scrubbed some knives, then a spatula. "You can be happy anywhere or miserable everywhere, if that's what you want."

"True. But sometimes the happiness or misery isn't your choice."

"But the way you react to things is your choice."

"Lies, lies, lies," Zach cried, coming into the kitchen to put his arms around Holly from behind. He kissed the back of her neck. "Everything she's been telling you about me is a lie."

"How do you know it wasn't good stuff?" Holly asked with a laugh.

"Because I know my sister."

Janice gave him a look. "How do you know we were even talking about you?"

"Because I know you couldn't pass up this chance to rescue Holly from my clutches."

Holly turned enough to give him a quick kiss on his cheek before picking up the last pan to dry. "Well, I'll have you know she didn't succeed. I heard all about what a rotten brother you are, but I have decided to reform you."

"Uh-oh, you're in for it now," Janice said with a laugh. "So how's the Scrabble game going?"

"It's not, as far as I'm concerned. Those two are too vicious for me. I quit." He peered into a cookie jar and pulled out something large and covered with chocolate chips. "I think Tom was trying to bribe me into saying it was time to leave so Jenny would have to forfeit."

"But you refused to be party to such underhandedness?" Holly asked.

"The bribe wasn't big enough," Zach said, and bit into the cookie. "I figured your mother's pride would force you to make a counteroffer that would be a better deal."

"How about if I let you stay in your apartment another week?" Holly asked.

"Ouch." Zach pretended to be wounded by her words. "Maybe I'll look into Tom's offer after all."

Janice chuckled as he left the room, then grew serious. "He cares for you a great deal. And Jenny, too."

Holly turned back to Janice. "What makes you say that?"

"The way he watches you. The way he teases you. The fact he even brought you here at all."

"I think it was Jenny he brought to the farm. I just tagged along."

Janice shook her head. The dishes done, she leaned back against the counter, her arms crossed and her eyes glowing with little-sister righteousness. "He's dated a lot of women but he's never brought one here for us to meet."

"Maybe because it was kind of far to bring someone for a Sunday dinner when he was living in London."

Janice grimaced. "I know him and I know that he brought you here to let you see who he really is, his roots."

"And to let Jenny see the horses." Holly didn't know whether she wanted Janice to be right or not. Falling in love hadn't been in her plans, but she was coping with it. Zach in love with her was a complication she hadn't thought about and wasn't going to.

"You're as bad as he is," Janice said with a laugh.

"Who's as bad as who is?" Jenny asked, skipping into the room. "Can I have one of those cookies Zach was eating, please?"

"Jenny, you just had dinner."

Janice clucked like a mother hen as she held open the cookie jar for Jenny. "Oh, there's always room for chocolate chip, isn't there, honey?"

"Just what I always say," Jenny agreed around a mouthful of cookie.

Holly shook her head. "So how's the game going?"

"It's over," Jenny said. "I won."

"You did not," a voice from the living room cried.

Jenny called out, "I did, too. Zach's your relative. So you have to lose."

"What does Zach have to do with it?" Holly asked.

"He knocked the board over, so I claimed the old 'guest wins' rule. Can I have another cookie, please?"

Janice gave her the jar back. "So Zach succumbed to bribery after all, eh?"

Jenny looked startled and Holly rushed in to protect the girl's childlike illusions. "It probably was an accident."

Jenny shook her head. "No, I offered him a cookie to do it. But how'd you know?" she asked Janice.

Janice laughed, even harder once she caught sight of Holly's chagrined look. "Sisters know these things. Here, take a couple more cookies."

Ever obedient, Jenny took a handful and scampered back into the living room.

"What did I tell you?" Janice murmured with a pleased grin. "I told you he cares about you and Jenny. Tom would have offered him a half interest in the farm to help him win and he chose a cookie from your daughter. Now, if that isn't love, what is?"

Maybe love, but only for chocolate chip cookies, not for her.

Chapter Thirteen

I'm leaving now, Professor Philips.''

Zach was leaning back in his chair, hands locked behind his head, feet on the desk, studying the cracks in the ceiling. A good occupation for a Friday afternoon in mid-March. He rolled his eyes toward Lucille. "Okay by me, but I didn't think you needed my permission."

"I most certainly do not need your permission." The department secretary was only five foot one, but looking down her nose she appeared ten feet tall. "But I want to go home and I always lock up."

He shrugged. "That's also okay by me." Before the last word had passed his lips, Zach had his feet on the floor and was hastening to explain. "I don't mean to imply that I'm giving you permission. I just mean that you should pretend I'm not here."

"But you are here." The tone was accusing. "This is the first time I've seen you around so late."

"I'm sorry," Zach said. "I have things to think about."

"Very well." Lucille pursed her lips a moment. "I will lock up now and take my leave for the evening. I will lock up all the files and you are responsible for whatever is left out on your desk."

"Okay."

"And I will set the lock on the door. All you have to do is pull it shut after yourself. Do you have any problems with that?"

"No, ma'am."

"Very well. Good night, then."

"Good night, Lucille."

He went back to studying the cracks in the ceiling. A ceiling without cracks was like a man without wrinkles. Totally lacking in character. He heard Lucille bustling about outside his office, then silence when she left for the night.

Yawning, Zach turned his chair toward the window. The little bits of snow left on the ground were cowering under bushes and next to buildings; the ends of the tree branches looked swollen. It was just about spring, another few days on the calendar and another few degrees on the thermometer, but it had been spring in his heart for months now. Two months and seventeen days, to be exact. Ever since Holly Carpenter climbed into the Luigi's Pizza car and into his heart. His gaze found the letter lying on his desk. There was no choice to be made after all. Once spring had come there was no stopping it.

Zach cleared his desk and his mind of worries, then left the office, humming. Once outside, he took a deep, deep breath, stretching his lungs to their farthest point. It was a beautiful evening, cool and crisp with the smell of spring in the air. Zach set his feet to home, his senses to appreciation and his mind to pondering. He touched the letter in his pocket to focus his thoughts.

He had waited, eagerly looking forward to receiving this letter, for months. Yet, now that it was here, it didn't bring him the elated joy he had expected. Instead it brought him an examination of who he was and what he really wanted out of life.

His brother had traveled to the far corners of the earth—Saudi Arabia, Indonesia, Nigeria, Venezuela and all points in between. As a boy, Roger had always talked about roaming the world, so he majored in geology and took employment with the major oil companies. Roger was doing what he wanted with his life.

Zach stopped in his tracks. *Doing what he wanted with his life.* Couldn't Zach say the same? He'd traveled a good bit himself, but it hadn't given him the same kick it gave Roger.

He continued on his walk home. In truth, he and his brother were both quite lucky. Each was doing exactly what he wanted. There was no single ideal that a person needed to conform to. Happiness came from finding your niche and putting yourself there.

And that was exactly what Zach had done. He'd always loved studying the past and seeing how it influenced people in the present.

His life was more than he had ever hoped for. It gave him the time he wanted to study the things that interested him and the time to talk and write about those very same interesting things.

And back in October he'd still had the feeling that something was missing in his life. He'd been ripe when he'd picked up that faculty journal; his application had been in the mail the following morning. Then in the beginning of January, his life had turned perfect, right after Ruth had asked him to drive out to the airport and he'd picked up her daughter and granddaughter.

Zach's feet turned him into the alley behind his home, and his mind brought him to the present. No, his life wasn't perfect yet. Almost but not quite. There was another step that would give him everything a man could want out of life. He stopped at the back gate, and looking at the formidable brick hulk before him, he smiled. Home, in the total sense of the word. It was four walls and a roof. But it was also the warmth of people he cared for and who cared for him.

Zach smiled. He'd plan out a weekend to end all weekends with his little family, ending with that one special question for Holly. He pulled the letter from his pocket and threw it toward the trash can. Maybe *he* was the one Pokagon had healed.

"How come they call it Rum Village?" Jenny asked as they drove south through South Bend the next day. "That's a funny name for a park."

Zach looked over his shoulder at the frowning girl who'd become part of the sunshine in his life. "There used to be a trading post there, back in the early days when the only people around were Indians and French traders."

"Is any of the village still left?" Jenny asked.

"Just a few empty bottles," Zach said.

Holly burst out laughing and Jenny looked from one to the other. "I don't get it," she said.

"Rum is a drink, like wine," Holly said.

"Yeah," Jenny said.

"And it comes in bottles."

"Yeah?"

"Well, Zach's saying that the only thing left from Rum Village is a few empty bottles."

Her daughter stared at her.

"Those bottles would be over two hundred years old," Holly said, her words trailing off lamely.

So many question marks flooded into Jenny's eyes that her forehead wrinkled with the load. "Wouldn't someone have cleaned them up by now? And what's so funny about junk left lying around for two hundred years? You're always saying it's not right to litter."

Zach tried not to laugh; the glare he was getting from Holly made it all the harder. "I'm sorry," he said. "I was just trying to make a joke."

"You guys think it's funny for bottles to lie around for two hundred years, but I can't let anything lie around my room for even two hundred seconds."

"Sorry. You're right. It's not funny," Zach agreed. Holly gave him a look that said she knew he was only teasing. He had never been happier, as his plans for this weekend would show. Plans that would keep their lives in smiles and laughter. And this unexpected snowfall from last night gave him the perfect first course for his day.

He turned at a stoplight. "They have some great sledding hills at the park."

"Better than your jokes?"

"Jenny," Holly exclaimed. "That's rude."

"No, no." Zach laughed. "She's right. My joke was a weak attempt at humor."

"That's no reason to—"

"I'm sorry," Jenny interrupted.

"No problem," Zach assured her. "There's the park."

Holly and Jenny stared out the window at the high hills visible from the parking lot. Although it was only mid-morning, there were already a fair number of sledders.

"Well, what do you think of the hills?" he asked.

"Not bad," Jenny said.

"Not bad?" Zach repeated. "Give me a break, kid."

"Sure," Jenny said with a wide grin. "Stick out your arm."

Zach feigned shock and rolled his eyes at Holly.

"Don't look at me," she said. "You're the one who's always teaching her those so-called witticisms."

"I suppose you had better hills in New York."

"No," Jenny said. "We had to slide down the sides of buildings."

"Give me a break."

Jenny grinned broadly. "Sure. Stick out your leg."

"This conversation is getting boring," Holly said.

Zach laughed; he hadn't had such fun in years. It wasn't from the joking, however, but from the sense of belonging. That was what he'd been missing all these years, missing it but not even aware of the longings until now. He got the sleds out of the car—the small one Holly had bought for Jenny and the larger one he'd borrowed from the Schmidts down the block—and carried them over to the hills.

"Mom, I'll race you down," Jenny shouted when they had reached the top of the hill.

"All right," Holly said. "If Zach will lend me his sled."

He and Holly carried it toward one of the inclines before them.

"Mom," Jenny hissed after her, "that's the little kids' hill. We're supposed to go down this one." The long hill, with wild twists and turns, stretched out before Jenny.

Holly frowned at Zach. "Is there some kind of law that governs who goes on what hill?"

"No," he said. "But I'm sure you'd want to go where there was the greatest challenge."

"Of course," Holly said through clenched teeth.

"Come on, Mom. Time's a-wasting."

"Don't be so pushy, young lady."

Jenny stood poised, sled in hand, ready to take a running start down the hill. Holly gingerly sat down on her sled.

"I don't think I've ever been sledding before."

"It's easy. Just stay on the sled," he advised.

"Very funny," she said, then visibly gathered her courage. "All right. Would you give me a push, please?"

"My pleasure, ma'am," he said, and gave her a good head start on Jenny's self-start, then stood back with a smile and watched his two girls slide down the hill.

Holly shrieked with a mixture of terror and delight as she careened down the hill. Jenny passed her about halfway down, but Zach doubted that Holly even noticed, the way she was clinging to the sides of the sled. Jenny met her at the bottom, and laughingly they climbed back up together.

"So how was it?" Zach asked.

"Great," Jenny cried.

"A little like falling off a cliff," Holly noted.

"Really?" He took the sled from her hands and slipped his arm around her shoulders. "And how many times have you fallen off a cliff?"

She laughed, her cheeks bright from the chill air, her eyes dancing with laughter and happiness. He couldn't resist bending over to lightly taste her lips.

"Geez, are we sledding or getting mushy?" Jenny asked, but her voice was teasing. "Last one down's a rotten egg."

She threw herself onto her sled. Zach got Holly onto the front of his, then jumped on behind her once they got up some speed.

"Are you sure you want me in front?" Holly screamed, trying to turn her face into his chest.

"Sure. I trust you not to lead me wrong?"

"You'll be sorry," Holly cried as they plowed into a snowbank. The sled tipped over and they went rolling in the snow, laughing like kids.

"That'll teach you," Holly said, sitting up, snow covering her hair and shoulders.

"Let's do it again." He loved to see her smile, to hear her laughter in the air, and pulled her to her feet to climb back up.

Jenny soon found some children her own age, leaving Holly and Zach to sled alone together. They would sit together like kids and go zooming down the hill. The faster he took the turns, the tighter she'd cling to him. He felt like a teenager with his first love. Come to think of it, he mused, Holly *was* his first love. The first woman he'd ever really loved.

The morning sped into the afternoon, and Zach could see Holly's jeans were getting damp and her gloves were wet. "Maybe it's about time we called it a day," he suggested. "We should go get some lunch. How about one last ride all together?"

Holly called Jenny over for the last big ride. "Let's do a triple-decker," he said, lying down on the sled. "Holly, you lie down on me and then Jenny will lie on your back."

Holly did as she was ordered and Zach groaned as if he had trouble breathing. "Cut that out," she ordered. "Or I'll give you something to groan about."

She was such fun to tease. "It wasn't really a groan. I was moaning in ecstasy."

"Behave yourself, sir. There are children about."

He ignored her words. "This sled has some interesting possibilities."

"Hey," Jenny shouted. "Are we going to slide or do mush-mush?"

"Get on," Zach called. "And we'll slide."

Jenny ran alongside pushing them, then jumped on. Zach could feel Holly's grip tighten. Jenny must have given them a little faster start than Holly would have preferred. The little devil in him whispered a suggestion to his hands as they steered the sled.

"Zach," Holly shouted in his ear as he turned the sled toward the steeper side of the hill. "Zach! We're going to crash. Can't you stop this thing?"

Then they went headfirst into a snowbank, rolling over and over, covering all of them with snow. Holly looked suspicious and Zach could barely sit up for laughing so hard.

"You did that on purpose," Holly cried, and sprang up, throwing snow at the two of them, for Jenny was laughing as hard as he was. Unfortunately for Holly's revenge, the snow was light and powdery, great for sledding but no good at all for snowballs.

Zach jumped up and slipped his arms around her. "Now, wasn't that great?" he asked.

"I thought we were going to go off a cliff," she said with a grin. "I should have known you were planning something rotten."

"That's me. Rotten to the core."

They carried the sleds up to the car, then drove to the Hamburger Hut for lunch.

"You know, this food is loaded with fat and salt," Jenny warned as they carried their trays to their table.

"Ah, but sledding works off all those bad things in advance," Zach assured her.

"You learn fast," Holly said quietly, leaning over closer to him.

His heart told him to take her in his arms, then and there, to ask her now to share his life with him, but his brain said this wasn't the time or place. This evening, after dinner, he'd ask her to go for a walk with him. He had his whole speech planned.

"So what do you say we go over to the university for some swimming this afternoon?" he suggested as they finished eating. "You've never seen the pool there yet."

Jenny's eyes lit up, but Holly shook her head. "I'm afraid we've got a house to clean and Jenny's got two tests to study for."

He was disappointed, not wanting to lose them for a minute, but he just nodded. "How about dinner, then? I make a mean bowl of spaghetti."

"Sounds wonderful."

On the way home they sang "A Hundred Bottles of Beer on the Wall," reaching the house by bottle number sixty-seven. The three of them walked hand in hand from the garage, then Zach kissed them both at the door.

"Dinner about six?" he asked.

"Fine," Holly said with a smile. The day had been perfect so far, and she couldn't wait for six o'clock to arrive. "That'll give Jenny a chance to clean her room."

Jenny shook her head. "See, what did I tell you? Right away, I have to clean my room."

"Make sure you pick up all the empty bottles," Zach teased.

"I still don't get it," Jenny said with a sigh and went inside, leaving their gentle laughter out in the cold.

Holly kissed him, then followed Jenny inside. For Holly, Zach could make March seem like July, the dreariest day magic with sunshine. She missed him already.

Jenny hung up her coat and hurried up to her room as Holly moved more slowly, more leisurely. She took off her coat and boots, then went upstairs to shower and get into something dry. Maybe she should make some dessert for Zach's dinner. She hadn't done much baking lately, but if Ruth came home from her shopping date with Bruno, Holly could ask her advice about a simple, foolproof recipe. Holly showered quickly, anxious to look through the cookbooks even without Ruth's guidance, but when she stepped out of the shower she found Jenny sitting on her bed. Her daughter was close to tears.

"Honey, what's wrong?"

Jenny didn't answer. She just held a paper toward Holly, a letter on an ornately designed letterhead from a foreign university.

"Jenny," Holly said. "We shouldn't look at other people's—"

The words died in her throat. The letter was to Zach, confirming his appointment to some university in Paris. They were expecting him to begin in June. Her heart sank down to the pit of her stomach. He was going, just as she'd known he would.

"I didn't mean to be nosy," Jenny said quietly. "I was emptying the wastebaskets and found that on the ground by the garbage can. I picked it up because I thought it was from a king or something with that little shield painted on it."

"I know, honey. It's all right." But how would she explain to a child that love is never meant to last? How would she explain that to her own heart?

Holly patched her heart back together with slow, careful stitches, locked it away, then walked upstairs to Zach's apartment.

"Well, hello," he said with a grin that wanted to light up her soul when he opened the door. "Just couldn't stay away, is that it?"

She forced a smile. Her heart had ceased to feel. She had known this moment would come; she had known and had prepared for it. It would hurt for a time, then she would be fine. Well, maybe not fine, but she would survive.

"I wanted to talk to you," Holly said slowly. "If you've got a minute. Jenny's pretty upset."

His smile died away; his eyes turned dark with worry as he waved Holly into his living room. "What's the matter?"

Holly held up the letter. "She found this next to the garbage can."

He took the letter, wet and smudged from the snow, from her hand. "I was aiming for the garbage can," he said with a half laugh. "Looks like I need more practice. What does that have to do with Jenny, though?"

"She had no idea you were leaving."

He shook his head. "I'm not. I turned down the offer."

His words should have brought joy, but Holly allowed nothing to touch her. It was Jenny she was worried about, Jenny whose tears she wanted to stop. Holly sat carefully on the edge of his sofa.

"I blame myself, if I'm really honest," she said. "I knew you would be leaving one of these days but I didn't warn her. I guess I never thought about it, but she's taking it pretty hard. I thought maybe you could promise to write to her or something like that. Not often. Mind you, I'm not asking for a full-time pen pal, but once in a while. She's very fond of you."

Zach frowned at her. "Didn't you hear me? I said I turned down the offer." As if to reiterate, he crumpled up the letter and tossed it across the room to land in a corner.

"I heard you. I was speaking about the future." Holly clasped her hands lightly around her crossed knees, proud of the way she was handling things.

Zach came over to sit next to her. Too close. The patches on her heart weren't strong enough to withstand his nearness, but her feet wouldn't let her move. Be strong, she whispered to her heart even as he took her hand.

"This isn't the way I'd planned it," he said. His voice tried to weaken her, to loosen those stitches and rip the patches apart. "There was supposed to be a fine dinner and candlelight, wine and soft music, then a walk under the stars. But I never counted on any of you finding the letter." He took a deep breath. "Holly, I love you. Will you marry me?"

"Marry you?" It wasn't what she expected. It wasn't what she wanted. She jumped to her feet, grabbing her hand back from him as if his touch suddenly scalded. "Marry you?"

He was on his feet, also, startled, confused and slightly angry. The room was alive with tensions—living, breathing emotions trying to ensnare her.

"Yes, marry me," Zach cried. "Is that such a strange idea?"

"You're a wanderer, a nomad. You told me that yourself."

Some of his anger faded from his eyes and a softer light took its place. She backed away from him a step. The less angry he was, the more dangerous.

"I know I did," he said. "Because that's what I thought, but I was wrong. I realized that when I got the chance to leave. For years I was running in anger, then from the memory of those arguments. Even when I came back here I wasn't happy. I was lonely, lost. Until I met you. Once you moved in here, I knew I was home."

"How nice!" she mocked. It was her only protection against such words. "But I'm not that foolish."

"Holly."

He tried to take her hand, but she wouldn't let him. She didn't care how silly she looked as she put her hands behind her back, then stepped behind the coffee table. It was her sanity, her ability to breathe, that was at stake here.

"Come on, Zach," she said. "Let's be honest. We both knew how this would end."

He stared at her, confusion written on his face, in those eyes she loved so much. No, that was the wrong way to think, the weak way.

"End?" he repeated. "Why are you talking end when I want to talk beginning? I love you. I want to start a new life together."

"For how long? A year? Two years? Until that wandering bug strikes again or until we get boring. Then you'll be gone."

He sighed, a deep, weary sigh that she could see pass over him. "Holly, come sit down." His voice was soft and pleading, worming its way to her heart. "You're afraid. I should have seen that this would happen."

No, her heart cried out. Don't let him come close again. Don't let his words caress and his eyes delight.

"How dare you always presume you know what I'm feeling?" she cried. Anger sucked her into its whirlpool, pulling her down into its depths. She accepted the drowning with joy. It would make her strong. "You don't know anything about what's inside me."

"You're afraid that I'll die and leave, just as Joel did," he said. "I thought those hurts had healed. I thought our love was strong enough that you'd be willing to take a chance, but—"

"I'm not as stupid as you think," she snapped.

"Holly!" No more pleading in his voice, but anger.

"I don't blame Joel for dying. Maybe I did at first. It's part of the grieving process. Enough magazine articles told me that. I know that death is a part of life."

"Then what the hell are you afraid of?"

"Nothing! Nothing at all!" She could match his anger shout for shout, hurt for hurt. Knife thrust for knife thrust. "I knew when I started to date you that you would be leaving. I knew that and it was fine with me. I liked a relationship where I knew where I stood. Jenny's the one I'm worried about. She's the one hurting now."

"She's not the only one." But his anger seemed gone and he sank onto the sofa, running his fingers through his hair. "Holly, I don't understand. I know you love me. I've felt it in your touch. Every time you kiss me. Every time you look at me. Deny it if you can."

"Why should I?"

That startled him. She could see he'd been marshaling his arguments, calling in the troops to win her over.

"I admit I love you," she said. "We had a great time and I'm grateful to you, but you don't seem to want to believe that part of that great time was knowing you'd go someday. Not a sweet dream of marriage."

"That's certainly complimentary."

His voice oozed bitterness and it hurt her, somehow sneaking underneath her guard to jab at her soul, but she pushed back the pain.

"Just couldn't wait to see the back of me, is that it?"

"That's not it at all," she snapped. "I would have been delighted if you stayed around for ages."

He leaned forward, his hands resting on his knees. It seemed like a full frontal assault even though she was still across the room from him. A breath, that's what she needed. A breath to give her strength to look away.

"Then why not forever?"

"Because it never is forever. Right now you think it will be; it's not really a lie. But one day some new dream will call and you'll leave. Just march right out the door without a goodbye. I can take honesty, but I can't live with the pretense."

He was on his feet, the anger blazing from him in waves that wanted to knock her over. "Dammit, Holly, Joel—"

But she was stronger than he thought. She had lessons longer than he knew. "It's not Joel we're talking about. It was my father. My kind and loving father, who walked out the door one day and never came back. Never called, never sent another birthday card. Never cared that we cried or were scared or alone." She gulped back the tears that had exploded in her eyes. The pain that had been buried so long suddenly broke through. And she saw not Zach but that little apartment, so cold and so empty without her father's booming laughter. Without *any* laughter. "I never for a moment thought he would leave, never for a second thought he didn't love me the way I loved him. Fathers are supposed to be forever, you know."

"Holly."

He didn't move, but there was something new in his voice, a calling to her soul to let him comfort her. But she wouldn't let him.

"Oh, no," she cried out, shaking her head. "Don't pity me. I don't need it. Actually, I'm grateful to my father. He made me strong."

"You're not strong, Holly," Zach said softly. "Can't you see that? You're terrified."

"Stop telling me what I am," she cried.

He took a step closer, and she *was* terrified that her weak and willing heart would act foolishly. She took another step toward the door.

"Anyway," she said, "it's over now, regardless. I could live with the idea of you wanting to travel again someday, but not with the forever you keep talking about. I couldn't live with the uncertainty." He wasn't moving, wasn't saying anything. His eyes, no longer in shadow, blazed with something she couldn't understand. It looked like pain, like gut-wrenching, agonizing pain.

"Don't you see?" she cried out in frustration. "Every time you were late for dinner, I'd wonder. Every morning I woke up to find you already out of bed, I'd get scared. I can't live with that and I'd never let Jenny. A mother's boyfriend is hard enough to lose, but losing a father devastates you."

"You don't trust me," he said. His voice was quiet.

"I don't trust anybody."

There seemed nothing more to say and she walked slowly to the door. He made no move to stop her and that, above all else, convinced her she'd done the right thing.

"It's not over, you know," he said as her hand touched the doorknob. "I'm not leaving, and sooner or later you'll have to admit that you can trust me. I can wait."

She looked back at him, at the dark eyes that reflected the agony in his soul. At the shoulders that had been so strong when she'd needed to lean on him. At the hands that knew just how to hold her in the dark. It was over; it had to be over now before her heart was broken beyond repair.

"Goodbye, Zach," she said, and left. The tears came later, much later, when she was alone in her room with the spirits of the night.

Chapter Fourteen

Holly dragged her feet up the stairs after work. Jenny had her door shut. Holly paused, then went into her room. She'd explained to Jenny about the breakup with Zach soon after it had happened, but her daughter was still angry and confused. She didn't understand and Holly wasn't up to another tearful session. She'd visit with Jenny at dinner.

Holly kicked off her shoes, then threw herself on the bed. Her eyes caught sight of the roses on the dresser and she closed her eyes to avoid seeing Zach's offering. She'd thrown them out soon after their arrival a few days ago only to have Ruth retrieve them and put them back on the dresser. They haunted her dreams, so Holly had tried moving them to the living room, claiming they were so pretty everyone should be able to enjoy them, but Ruth saw through that one and by nightfall, the bouquet was back on her dresser. Holly gave up. It was easier to close her eyes to them than to fight Ruth and endure Jenny's accusing gaze. But closing her eyes didn't stop their aroma from swallowing her up.

Why couldn't Zach just accept her decision as final? Why couldn't Ruth and Jenny understand that she knew what she was doing? Saying goodbye now was the smart thing to do, the safe thing. It wasn't as though she was happy or enjoyed Zach's distress, but it was the way things had to be.

Holly rolled over as the telephone rang, resisting the urge to pull her pillow over her head. She'd let Ruth get it. It would be Bruno. It was always Bruno.

As she turned from the phone, her hand bumped into an envelope on the pillow. She picked the envelope up, then put it down when she recognized the handwriting. She didn't need to hear any more of his arguments; she'd heard them all last Saturday, then again on Sunday, when he caught her in the laundry room. He loved her; she loved him. They belonged together. She had to take the chance that he could be trusted. He wouldn't prove her wrong.

The last few days, though, it hadn't been arguments, just little reminders he was there. That she needed no reminding of; her heart knew that all too well.

"Holly," her mother called up the stairs. "Telephone for you."

Her body tensed. Her heart told her to answer it, to hear Zach's voice again, but her common sense said not to listen to him, not to chance a weakening in her wall. She picked the receiver up carefully.

"Hello," she said.

"Mrs. Carpenter?"

Holly didn't recognize the woman's voice. She told herself she was relieved, that the faint dropping of her stomach wasn't disappointment. "Yes, this is Mrs. Carpenter."

"Mrs. Carpenter, this is Bernice Chisamore. I'm Jenny's homeroom teacher and I also have her for math."

Holly's heart scrambled and retreated before the onslaught of fear. "Yes." Holly swallowed, hoping to bury the tremor in her voice. "Yes, Mrs. Chisamore, what can I do for you?"

"You can help me with Jenny." The words were wrapped in care and a gentle sigh. "My gut feeling is that she is a very intelligent young lady. Yet she won't say a word in class, and when I have her work a problem at the board, it's as if she has never heard of any of the concepts we've covered in class."

"But she did so well in her school in New York, especially in math."

"I know," the teacher said. "In fact, I checked her transcript again this morning. That's why it's so strange. With that kind of background she still failed today's test."

Holly didn't know what to say. Her heart was sinking.

Mrs. Chisamore continued. "I tried to talk with her right after lunch, but nothing came of it. She just clammed up. Tight like a drum."

"She does that," Holly agreed. "But I'll talk to her. Maybe I can find out what the problem is."

"If you feel up to it," the teacher replied. "Otherwise I can recommend a good counselor."

A tightness spread through Holly's soul. "Why should I have trouble talking to Jenny?"

"I didn't mean to imply that," the teacher hastened to explain. "But you are a single parent with one child, are you not? Well, Jenny has a problem and I'm almost positive that it's not academic. I thought a counselor might be able to help."

Things were starting to unravel and there seemed to be nothing she could do to stop them. "I'm sorry," she said. "I know you're trying to help, but I'd like to talk to Jenny first."

"That's fine." The woman's voice had softened. "My number is in the blue book. Call me if you need help."

By the time Holly had hung up, doubt and depression had been replaced by a grim determination. The only problem Jenny had was her mother, and that was going to be fixed. She had let Zach into her life and gone all gaga, living on romance like some junior high school kid. Well, that was done, over with. She would not be distracted from Jenny again.

Holly padded down the hall to Jenny's room. She knocked and then let herself in. Her daughter had books scattered on her bed, papers on her desk and a look of caution on her face. It was obvious that she knew her teacher would call.

"Hi," Holly said.

"Hello, Mother."

Holly's heart was torn by love and she wanted to do nothing but hug Jenny tight. She swallowed that desire. "Okay if I sit down?"

Jenny shrugged. "Sure."

Holly took a white teddy bear and a yellow unicorn off a straight-backed chair and set them on the bed, then sat down, crossing her legs. Where did one start?

"That phone call was for me. It was Mrs. Chisamore. She said you're having trouble with math."

Her daughter's face bordered on the sullen. "It was just one test. I don't know what the big deal is."

"The big deal, young lady, is that you are getting below average grades on all your tests. That's a very big deal when you did so well in New York."

"Indiana math?"

"I'm not joking, Jenny."

Jenny's hopeful smile vanished so quickly that Holly knew there had been no substance behind it. "You're just doing so-so in *all* your courses," Holly said. "What's the problem?"

Jenny shrugged and played with a pencil.

"You bothered by the move?"

"Sort of." Jenny's attempt at casual didn't make it.

"Is there anything I can do?"

"No!" The answer had come out sharp and emphatic—apparently more so than Jenny had intended, for her next words came out dressed light and casual. "I have things under control. Don't worry about it."

Holly stared at her daughter a long moment. She could see the clam at work. Everything was locked up tight.

"Maybe basketball is taking too much of your time."

The sudden pain and fear in Jenny's eyes showed that Holly had struck a nerve. Holly hadn't remembered her daughter being so tied to a sport before. Was that all she had out here now? Holly wanted to remind her that lessons came before sports, but the hurt in Jenny's eyes was so intense Holly had to turn away.

She stood up and walked to the window. "I want you to be happy here," Holly said. "It seems like nothing is turning out the way I hoped, but all I really want is for you to be happy."

"I am."

The voice was soft and small. Holly turned. The eyes no longer held pain; the look was guarded, as if Jenny didn't want to let her in. Holly wasn't sure which hurt worse.

"Let me see your homework when you're done," Holly said.

Jenny just nodded and Holly left, closing the door behind her, but by the time she reached her bedroom, a total weariness seized her body. She threw herself onto her bed as if she were an armful of dirty laundry and stared up at the spots on the ceiling.

Nothing here was turning out as she'd planned, and it wasn't because they hadn't adjusted to the move. It was this damn old house. It sapped the energies of everyone who lived there. Energy that should be used to help Jenny adjust was being used to fix the roof or the plumbing.

She should never have let Ruth talk her into staying. They should have gone to a motel that first night and never come back, because after a day or two here, she'd been taken in by the timeless charm of the old place. The tower and brick and stone. The huge hedge protecting them from the outside world. Even without a moat it had been their castle.

Hot tears flowed from her eyes, burning rivulets down her cheeks. The whole thing had been stupid. They weren't fairy princesses. She was a modern career woman and single mother. Ruth and Jenny were standard, middle-class people. They'd forgotten who they were. That was what had brought all this trouble on.

Well, she was going to change all that. She was putting this damn house on the market before she left for that business meeting in New York next week.

"Mom, Mom. Wake up."

Holly blinked rapidly and sat straight up in bed. Jenny

was standing next to her bed, her robe on over her night-gown and a sweater on over that. "What is it, honey? What's wrong?"

"It's real cold in the house," Jenny replied.

Holly slid out from under her covers and met the cold air with a shock. Her slippers were useless and so was her robe. She wrapped a blanket around her shoulders. "Why don't you climb into my bed, honey? I'll go down and see if I can tell what's wrong."

"Grandma's already down in the basement looking at stuff."

"I'll see if she needs any help, then."

A light tap on the door announced Ruth's arrival. "The boiler won't go on," she said, and came across the room to sit on the bed. "I have the thermostat turned up as far as it will go and still there's no flame."

Holly collapsed onto a chair. That was the last straw. The old wreck was done for. Not only couldn't it protect them from the outside elements, but it was dying from within. It couldn't even warm them anymore. And if a house couldn't provide warmth, then it couldn't provide anything. When the heart went, everything else died.

"We could light up the fireplaces, couldn't we?" Jenny asked.

"That's what I was thinking," Ruth said, standing up. "It's only in the low thirties tonight, so I'm sure the two fireplaces will give enough heat to keep the water pipes from freezing."

Holly just sat there. This house was dead. Everything that had come with it was dead.

"I'll bring the wood, Holly," Ruth said. "Would you get some paper and light the fires?"

Holly looked up to find the two of them staring at her. "This old house is dead," Holly said. "It's time for us to get out."

Silence greeted her words. Holly saw her own weariness reflected in damp mirrors of her daughter's and mother's eyes.

"There will be time enough to discuss things later," Ruth said. "Right now we need to get this place warmed up."

"I'll get some newspapers and matches," Jenny said.

Hours later, Ruth and Holly sat on the living room floor, wrapped in their sleeping bags, leaning against the sofa and staring into the orange flames licking leisurely at the hunks of wood. Jenny was asleep upstairs in Holly's bedroom. Ruth had called Zach with a report, telling him to turn up the electric heaters in his bathroom and kitchen.

An emergency furnace man had come and gone. He hadn't needed much time to see the problem. There were some technical terms for it, but the bottom line was the boiler was dead. Kaput. They needed a new one. The tradesman had thought he could get a new one by the afternoon, but he would call in the morning. After recommending they put an electric heater in the kitchen because of all the water pipes, he had left.

"This is actually rather cozy."

Holly didn't turn to look at Ruth. She knew that her mother's eyes would be bright with excitement. Her mother had always been an incurable romantic. Open fires in the fireplace were high on her list. Holly said nothing. What was there to say?

"These old houses are really built to roll with the punches," Ruth said.

"They should," Holly grumbled. "They've already taken a lot of punches in their time."

"Aw, come on, Holly. A furnace could have gone out in a newer house. What would we have done then? The newer houses don't have fireplaces on each floor."

"A newer house would have been smaller and more compact, so a few electric space heaters would have done very nicely."

"Space heaters aren't in the same class as fireplaces," Ruth sniffed. "They are totally lacking in charm."

A quick glance from the corner of Holly's eye was enough to read the other messages Ruth wore on her face. Stubbornness. Devotion. It was a strange collage. Holly set her jaw firm. She wasn't turning back. This house wasn't for them.

"I'm going to put the house on the market," Holly said.

All emotion left Ruth's face; it seemed to turn to stone. After a long moment words followed, words without emotion or feeling. "You're the owner. You can do what you want."

"I was going to talk it over with you guys in the morning," Holly said. She hadn't wanted to include the defensive whine in her voice, but it was out and there was nothing she could do about it.

"You really don't have to if you don't want to."

Tiredness was again storming Holly's defenses, taking over her body, her mind, her soul. It was best for them, for all of them, to leave this house.

"But I want to discuss it," Holly said. "I don't like to make unilateral decisions."

"Then don't. Wait until you aren't squabbling with Zach anymore."

"Zach doesn't fit into this at all," Holly argued. She would not get sidetracked into yet another explanation of her breakup with Zach. "This is purely a family matter. You, Jenny and me. That's it."

Ruth turned to look at Holly, soft eyes searching her face. Holly finally had to look away. She felt very uncomfortable under this inspection.

"I thought Zach was close to being part of the family," Ruth said softly.

"Mother, close only counts in horseshoes and hand grenades."

"I see. And which one was Zach?"

"Neither." She hadn't let him get close enough to be either. Loving him wasn't close enough? a little voice mocked.

Her mother went on as if she hadn't heard Holly at all. "He's very tender and gentle, but I'd say he was a hand grenade."

"Mother, this is ridiculous." She turned off her mind refusing to listen to little voices.

"He knocked some of the barnacles off your heart."

"He's just a tenant."

They stretched the silence between them, staring into the flames and watching as the spirits danced and threw bouquets of warmth at them. Though the fire warmed Holly's toes, it didn't even begin to thaw out her heart.

Finally Ruth rose. "I'm going upstairs to be with Jenny."

"All right," Holly said wearily. "I'll stay down here and keep an eye on this fire."

Ruth walked away silently. Holly couldn't remember the last time they hadn't wished each other a good night. The tears came again, following age-old paths down the sides of her face. Where did all these stupid tears come from? Her well of tears should have dried up long, long ago.

Zach snatched up the telephone and pressed the intercom buzzer. "Yes?" he demanded.

"Dr. Philips, there is a young lady here to see you."

Hope jumped alive. "A student?"

"Of course she is."

Damn. Of course it would be. Holly wouldn't come here to see him, not when she could see him anytime at home, but wouldn't.

"Tell her to make an appointment," Zach said wearily. "During my normal office hours."

"I'm sure she has an urgent matter that needs to be discussed now."

Zach sighed. Lucille wasn't going to let him off the hook. What had this student done, shed a few tears? "All right, send her in." Maybe it was better to have an unscheduled trauma than sit around here thinking of Holly.

The door opened and a miniature Holly came in. "Hi, Zach."

"Jenny?"

"It's me all right."

Zach shook his head. "I'm sorry. That was a dumb question. I can see it's you. I was just surprised, that's all. Sit down."

Jenny sat down and stared at the toes of her boots flicking up and down. He didn't know what to say. In the past week and a half, he'd seen Holly for only the briefest of passings. They weren't ships in the night anymore, but two distant planets never even acknowledging each other's presence. How could they have got so far away after being so close?

"Lucille announced you as a student."

"I am," Jenny said firmly.

He nodded. "That's true." He paused a moment. "She also said you have a problem."

"Yep." The vigorous nod flapped the pigtails back and forth.

"Anything I can help with?"

"I don't know," Jenny said with a pronounced shrug.

The silence descended again until Zach roughly pushed it away by clearing his throat.

"Mom's going to sell the house," Jenny burst in.

Zach was suddenly filled with pain, the pain of defeat, the pain of loss.

"We're going to buy a motel."

"What?"

Her eyes glistened and she was holding her lower lip firmly with her teeth. All she could do was shrug.

"Do you mean a big building with a lot of rooms that you rent out to other people?"

Jenny shook her head. "No way. Mom said that we're never, ever, going to rent our house out to anyone again."

"Then what kind of motel are you guys buying?"

"I don't know." Her voice was raised in a don't-blame-me tone. "That's what Grandma said it was going to be. Just a plain old motel for the three of us." Jenny shrugged again. "She said it would probably be a ranch motel, but I haven't seen any ranches around here."

The picture was starting to take shape. Holly had put the house up for sale, but Ruth didn't want to. They were going to move into a newer, tract type of house, though Jenny didn't seem overjoyed by the idea.

"Well, if you're not happy with the house, you should find another," he told her gently.

"I thought we were happy with it," Jenny said. It was almost a wail that lingered in the air.

"Maybe your mother thinks you'll do better in school in another house."

Her jaw set in that firm line that Zach had come to know in her mother. "I'm going to do a whole lot worse," she vowed.

She was so much like Holly. Tough. Determined. Stubborn. Especially stubborn.

"Why aren't you doing well in school now?"

Again the shrug. "I don't know. I must be having difficulty adjusting to the move."

"Don't con me, kid. I've got experts twice as old as you pulling that kind of stuff on me every day." This time she didn't bother with a shrug at all, just a glare. "You're not doing well on purpose, right?"

Like the fog rolling in, silence returned. Zach let it lie there. Jenny would break it herself when she was ready. And she did. "Most other kids don't like kids who are too smart."

"Are you too smart?"

The shrug had returned. "Maybe."

He made his hands into fists, then set his chin on top. "In the long run it's best to just be yourself."

"I guess."

"Then the people who like you will like you for yourself. Those who don't like you don't matter anyway."

"I guess."

"Your mother would like it if you did your very best."

"I know."

"Are you going to?"

"I might."

This time Zach gathered the silence to him. He knew from counseling college students that you could only plant a seed; you couldn't force it to grow. The old philosophy of you can lead a horse to water, but you can't make him drink.

Jenny was back to looking at the toes of her boots. "Don't you and Mom like each other anymore?"

Once the last word was out, the eyes came up. Earnest, appealing eyes. Eyes looking for the truth. Eyes filled with hope. A little voice laughed at him. Were the child's eyes filled with hope or were they just a reflection of his own feelings?

"We don't dislike each other."

"But you're not going out anymore, right?"

Anymore. That was so final but most likely true.

"Sometimes things don't work out, Jenny. It's not the fault of either person. It's just something that wasn't meant to be."

"How do you know what was meant to be unless you really try?"

Zach could feel his left cheek twitch ever so slightly. He had tried; he had really, really tried. "When you're a grown-up," he said, "you just know."

"I don't want to move," Jenny said, jumping back to the first subject like a little girl on a hopscotch grid.

Zach bit his lip. There was nothing he could do. Her mother had a right to decide where the family would live.

Jenny stood up. "Well, goodbye."

"Goodbye, honey," he said gently.

At the door, she paused and looked back. "I'm going to talk this whole thing over with Pokagon. He'll figure something out."

A huge, painful bubble came up in his throat. What had he done? It was all right to make jokes but not to rely on something that wasn't really there. Like Holly's love for him?

By the time he swallowed his own lump of disappointment and pain, Jenny was gone. He hadn't wanted to believe it was over, that it would ever be over, but maybe it was. Maybe he'd just been clinging to pipe dreams, refusing to see that they were only smoky illusions of the night.

Chapter Fifteen

You've done splendidly in Indiana," Ben Mitchell said. "The initial figures are much better than we'd hoped."

That was the only thing then, about the whole move that had turned out better than hoped, Holly thought morosely. But she only said, "Thank you."

Ben's phone buzzed, and with a half glance of apology he reached to pick it up. Holly let her eyes wander out the window to gaze at the dull and dirty building across the street. She was back in Manhattan, where the only way to see the sky was to lie on your back on the sidewalk and stare straight up.

"Sorry," Ben said as he hung up the phone. "How was your trip in?"

"Fine. I had a—" No, he wouldn't care she'd had a friendly cabdriver and worried the whole ride in. He wouldn't understand. "I had a nice flight."

He stared at her strangely, then shuffled some papers on his desk. "You're probably wondering why we called you back here when things are just getting started on the new office," Ben said.

"Yes." Though she hadn't really thought about it. There were a few million other things on her mind lately. Like selling the house. Like getting Ruth and Jenny to smile again. Like forgetting Zach. She stared at the silver pen-and-pencil stand on Ben's desk and wondered if her heart would ever be cool and distant again.

"Gerry Longren had a heart attack last week," Ben said.

Holly came back to attention with a thud. "How is he?"

"Should be out of the hospital in a few weeks, but then it's rest and rehabilitation. A hell of a mess."

"For Beth, you mean?" Holly remembered meeting Gerry's wife at a company picnic, a gentle, quiet woman whose life centered on her husband and family. "How's she taking it?"

"More important, how are we taking it?" Ben asked. "Gerry was heading that Newport project and it's at a crucial stage. God knows when he'll be back to work, if ever. We've got to get somebody on the job immediately. Yesterday, if possible."

"Who'd you have in mind? Dailey? Davis?"

"You."

Holly stopped. He was kidding. She had misunderstood him. No, he was staring straight at her, waiting for a reaction. "Me heading the Newport project? I just started a branch office and you're offering me a project that's been touted as the future of the company?"

"You can do it. We all think you can or we wouldn't be offering it."

She shook her head to clear it. She would have thought it all a dream, except that Zach wasn't around, and he had figured in all her dreams lately. "But I've barely begun out in Indiana."

Ben waved her objections away like flies. "You've got it going. Anyone can take over from here." He leaned forward for the hard sell. "I know it'll mean another move in a short time, but you'll be coming back here. It won't be relocating your family so much as bringing them home."

Home. The image of a ramshackle castle came to mind, not that apartment on Fifty-fifth Street. But would coming back to New York be the answer for Jenny? Would going back to her old school solve her problems with "Indiana math"? "I just don't know, Ben. I never expected—"

"Well, hey, we haven't covered the important parts yet." He was all smiles and went on to discuss her new salary—substantially higher—and the bonus they'd throw in to cover the emotional adjustments of another move.

She could use the extra money; their savings account could never be too full as a hedge against a rainy day. But still . . .

"Look, go back to the family," Ben said. "Talk it over with them. You guys are New Yorkers. Once the city's in your blood, you gotta come home. See if your mom can handle the details of the move so you can get back here by the beginning of next week."

"Next week? But that's only a few days."

"We need you here, Holly. REV is all revved up to bring you home." He chuckled as she left the office, heading down the hall to another round of meetings. Each one should have made the decision easier as she was surrounded by old friends and co-workers, but she no longer quite felt as though she belonged. They went for lunch to that wonderful delicatessen three blocks over, and they all ordered the same thing they'd been having three months ago. It was as though she'd never left. Almost. Her heart had a new set of scars.

When she was invited out for drinks after work, she politely declined. She needed time for herself. The hotel wasn't the answer, though, and even as the cabdriver was pulling up to the main entrance, she changed her mind and directed him to Fifty-fifth Street.

Now, this was home, she thought as she got out of the cab at her old apartment building. There was garbage at the curb, people milling out of the subway entrance and practically no snow in sight. No grass, either, she noticed, or trees.

"Holly?"

Holly spun to find a young black-haired woman coming down the steps of the building toward her. "Sarah! How wonderful to see you!"

"I thought it was you," Sarah said. "I looked over here and said, 'That's got to be Holly, strange as it seems.'"

"And it was." Holly escaped her embrace and walked toward the apartment building with her. "So how are things in the neighborhood?"

Sarah shrugged. "The same. The couple that got your apartment are the pits. Music blaring all the time and I swear they got a dog. But who listens to my complaints?"

"I always did."

Sarah grinned. "Yeah, but what good did it do? What are you doing here? No, wait. Don't answer. You're coming up for dinner and then you can tell me and Tony."

Before she could agree or disagree, Holly was swept up into Sarah and Tony's apartment. Their living room was the size of the library in her home; their kitchen was barely big enough to blink in. Had the building shrunk since she'd left?

"We might be moving back," Holly told them over plates of spaghetti. "I got a very tempting offer today."

"Is he tall, dark and handsome?" Sarah asked.

Holly smiled. "Job offer. A promotion."

"I should have known." Sarah turned in her chair to reach the coffeepot off the stove and refill their cups. "I was just hoping you'd got lucky."

She had for a while there. Holly shook off thoughts of Zach. "I have to talk things over with Mom and Jenny. I'm just not sure."

"If it was up to me, you could have your old apartment back," Sarah said. "Then it would be like you'd never left."

Except for the ache in her heart.

"You don't need your old apartment," Tony said, and turned to Sarah. "Aren't the Wilkersons moving out next month? Bet she could get their place."

"That's right," Sarah squealed. "It's a big one, like ours, too. Wouldn't that be great? Just like old times."

Just like old times. The thought echoed through her head all evening, lasting until she propped herself up on the pillows in her rented bed for the night and dialed home. Just how good were the old times? And could you ever really go back? Zach had been a part of her life. Could she pretend that he'd never meant anything to her? It would be easier, but it also would be impossible. Ruth answered the phone.

"Hi, Mom."

"Holly! How's New York? You get in all right?"

"Fine and yes." She stared ahead of her at the beige wall. Smooth surface, perfectly even color. No excitement, no character. An easily forgettable framed print graced the space opposite the closet. A room that would fit perfectly in their new "motel" home. Was this what she wanted to live with day in and day out?

Holly closed her eyes and concentrated on her conversation. "How's everything at home?"

"All right. Jenny's upstairs doing her homework. Want me to call her?"

"Yes, that would be great." She'd sound Jenny out about returning, maybe work a little bit of warmth back into her voice.

But in a few minutes, Ruth was back. "Sorry, hon, she's in the shower."

Holly sighed from deep in her heart. "She still mad at me?"

"No, she's really in the shower," Ruth assured her. "She's disappointed about the house, but she's not mad at you. Neither of us is."

Holly could hear the weariness in Ruth's voice. Would moving back to New York cheer her up? But somehow she couldn't say the words. She couldn't tell Ruth about the job offer. No matter; she'd keep it as a surprise for when she got home.

"A realtor came to see the house today for some out-of-town client," Ruth told her.

Holly opened her eyes. "Oh? He seem interested?"

"Who can tell?"

The silence joined them again. Finally Holly spoke. "I went by the old neighborhood and saw Sarah and Tony tonight."

"Oh, yeah? How are they?"

"The same. Everything seemed the same."

"I guess nothing ever changes that much."

"No." Did that mean this pain would go on forever?

"I hate to cut you off, honey, but Bruno should be here any minute and I've still got to change."

"Sure, Mom. Not much to tell anyway. I'll call again tomorrow night and see you on Thursday. Give my love to Jen."

"Sure thing."

The dead line echoed in Holly's ear, and she slowly hung up. From far down the street she heard a siren wail, but it brought back no memories this time. Just the weary realization that she was back in the city with all its noise and commotion. Had this ever been home?

"Evening, ma'am. Need a cab?"

Holly forced a smile for the round little man with the Yellow Cab cap on. "Yes, thank you."

She hadn't really been hoping Zach would be here. She didn't want to see him again. Why, then, was her heart so heavy? But she'd grown used to ignoring such inner voices and she climbed into the cab, answering the driver's chatter with stock empty phrases as he drove toward home. No, toward her house.

She'd just about decided to take the new job. After all, what was holding her back? Not the house. Not Zach. Jenny and Ruth hadn't really wanted to move out here in the first place. Oh, Ruth had hoped to get out of the city, but she'd missed the conveniences they'd left behind. It would be fine. She'd been wrong to uproot them, and going back would right that wrong. They'd both jump for joy when she told them, and in a few weeks life would be back to normal.

Normal. Lonely, overworked and underslept. That was what she wanted?

She looked out the window and saw blue sky. Wide open blue sky that never stopped. Big yards with kids playing catch. Dogs racing along with kids on bikes. An elderly couple strolling hand in hand. Her mind saw the cramped apartment in her old building and she shook the image away.

"So how's the weather been here?" Holly asked the driver.

"Just beautiful. Warm and sunny. You'd think it was summer."

She'd had her summer already, back in February and early March in Zach's arms. Stop it. That wasn't the way to think.

The driver pulled up in front of the house. She paid him quickly and carried her luggage up to the gate, then stopped in surprise. She'd been gone only a few days, but little bits of color were smiling at her from the flower beds. She came through the gate. White and purple crocuses were lifting their faces into the sunlight, promising that the best was yet to come.

She turned away. Maybe the best of the garden was yet to come, but not the best for her. She took a deep breath, pasted a bright smile across her lips and went inside.

"Mom. Jenny. I'm home."

Jenny came from the kitchen. "Hi, Mom. How was your trip?" Her voice was listless, her eyes tired.

"Just great." Holly reached down to give Jenny a hug and was rewarded with a weak one in return.

"Hi, Holly." Ruth came along the hallway, wiping her hands on a towel as Jenny took Holly's suitcase and started up the stairs.

"Hi, Mother. Boy, you guys look cheery. Wait until you hear my news."

"We've got news, too," Jenny said. "Somebody bought the house."

A hollow emptiness bit at Holly's stomach. "Already?" The smiles her heart had worked so hard to grow all drooped and wilted. Winter was back.

"They met your offer," Ruth said. "No bargaining or anything."

Stop it, Holly scolded her heart. It was reason to celebrate. They were free of this old place. No more leaky roofs, no more climbing in cobwebby cubbyholes, no more ghosts.

"Well, hey, that's great," Holly said, though a part of her questioned if it really was. She dredged up a smile. "It makes my news even better, then. I got a new job offer. If we want to, we can go back to New York."

Ruth and Jenny just stared at her. "Why?" Jenny said.

"I thought you'd want to. You could go back to your old school, be with your old friends."

"I like my friends here," Jenny said, a quiver in her voice.

"But you don't like the school," Holly pointed out. "You're doing terribly."

"But I've got my basketball team here. I was voted player of the week for our last game." The quiver turned to tears, a slow trickle running down each cheek, which just about broke Holly's heart.

"I thought you'd want to go back."

"I just want to stay here," Jenny cried.

Holly didn't know what to say and stared at Jenny in silence. Ruth stepped in. "Jen, take your mom's bag upstairs. Time for big people's talk."

Jenny wiped her cheeks with her sleeve and trudged up the stairs. Holly, in turn, trudged into the living room and sank into the nearest chair, bracing herself for another argument. Ruth sat down across from her. What if her mother didn't want to go back? She had Bruno now.

"Whatever you want to do is fine with me," Ruth said quietly. "I know things haven't been easy for you and you're only trying to do the best for us."

Holly shook her head. "I thought you were going to try to talk me into staying. What about Bruno?"

Ruth just shrugged. "What about him? We've had some fun, but we're both too old and too set in our ways to make a go of it."

Why didn't Holly believe her? But rather than argue, Holly leaned back in the chair and stretched her legs out, kicking off her shoes. "I wish I knew what to do," she said with a sigh. "I thought going back was the answer, but it didn't feel like home anymore. Nobody understood about friendly cabdrivers or Indiana math."

"Are you running away because of Zach?"

Holly said nothing for a time, tossing the question about in her mind. "No, I don't think so. That's over and done with. I rarely even think about him anymore." Would her mother buy that out-and-out lie?

There was dead silence for what seemed like several millennia. "A mother can always tell when her child is lying," Ruth said softly. "No matter how old the child is."

Holly looked over at her with a frown. "All right. So I do think of him. It wouldn't matter whether I thought of him constantly or never. It's still over between us, and my decision about the job has nothing to do with him."

"I hope not." Ruth got to her feet, moving stiffly—from age or weariness or both? Holly wondered. "Do what you feel is best, Holly. But make sure it's what you really want to do." She went back into the kitchen, leaving Holly alone with her thoughts and her memories.

The house was suddenly too still and accusing. Holly got to her feet and wandered out into the yard. The statues in the garden were finally free of their coats of snow, and chubby little cupids smiled coyly at her. She ignored them and sat on the stone bench, staring back at the house.

Did the buyer know about the leaky roof? Or that the grout could crack and cause leaks? They'd never had a chance to replace the dancing coffeepot wallpaper. What would she have chosen? Maybe yellow flowers that would be bright and sunny and welcoming on groggy mornings.

This moping was nonproductive, her common sense scolded, and she turned her gaze from the building. But then her eyes found the spot where she and Zach had made angels in the snow. Would he come out here next winter and remember how silly they'd been? Would he even be here next winter? He might be watching the dawn in Paris or have to find a new apartment if the buyer didn't want to let him stay. She felt badly about that. Their moving shouldn't have to mean he moved, too.

While the spirit of compassion was still stronger than her fear of loving Zach, she went up to his apartment. The third floor seemed silent and empty. She shivered even in the thin stream of sunlight coming through the hallway window, but she couldn't remove the chill from her heart.

She knocked loudly once, twice, three times, but there was no answer. It was still early. He was probably at the university. As she turned away from the door Ruth came up the stairs with a small watering can.

"Holly, what are you doing up here?"

Holly stammered like a kid caught at the cookie jar. "I just wanted to see Zach, tell him I hoped the new owner will let him stay."

Ruth shook her head as she unlocked Zach's door. "Zach's gone. He went to a history conference in California. Won't be back until a week from tomorrow."

"The end of next week?" If they went back to New York she wouldn't even be able to say goodbye.

Unable to think clearly, Holly followed Ruth into the apartment and stood in the doorway as her mother went around watering Zach's plants. Holly stared at the arrowhead collection and the humidifier filter still on the hutch. At the stack of magazines that had grown taller but no neater. At the memories that circled around her, diving in to tease her with bits of ecstasy, bits of laughter, bits of belonging totally to another. She sighed and turned away.

A stack of newspapers was on a small table near the door and she opened the top one, paging through as if she cared that St. Joseph's Hospital had bought up another block of property for its expansion or that the bridge on Auten Road was going to be widened.

Zach had argued with his father and had left, but he'd come back. He'd come back when the old man had needed him. *A grudge is very heavy*, he'd said. *It takes two people to carry it*. He wouldn't leave her, not in anger, not in boredom. Why, then, was she ready to leave him, pack up and leave without a word? Oh, she could write him a polite letter and Ruth would make sure he'd get it, but what did a letter mean? Would a letter from her father have cut the hurt, have eased the loneliness? Was she really protecting Jenny as she claimed, or was she playing follow the leader after her father?

The thoughts nagged at her and she focused her gaze on the newspaper to avoid the pokings of her conscience. But then the picture at the top of the page jumped out at her. The pet-of-the-week column featured a golden retriever named Duke. It was Jenny's dog, just as surely as if they both were in the picture together. Holly closed the paper. What was she doing to everyone she loved?

Holly parked the car at the curb, got out and, leaving the car door open, scanned the meager crowd for any sign of Zach. A couple came out of the terminal and took one cab, then a businessman took another. She glared at the remaining two taxis, willing them to get flat tires or flooded engines. She didn't want any other vehicles here for Zach to take. But then he was coming out the far doors, suitcase in hand, striding briskly toward that evil taxi at the end.

"Zach!" she cried, and waved. Either he didn't hear her or he was ignoring her. She slammed the car door and sprinted down the sidewalk. "Zach, wait."

He stopped, his eyes none too friendly. Somehow she hadn't expected that response from him. "I've got the car down there," she said, waving her hand down the row of cars. "I came to pick you up."

"Why?" he asked, but motioned the approaching cab-driver away and followed her to her car.

She ignored his question. Now was not the time or place to pour her heart out. To tell him she'd been scared and foolish and wanted to correct whatever mistakes she could. "How was your conference?" she asked.

He looked at her, but his eyes didn't see into her heart as they used to. They flickered over her face as if her surface revealed more than her soul. "Fine," he said after a moment.

They reached the car and he tossed his suitcase on the back seat and climbed into the front next to her. His silence was intimidating; her courage ebbed slightly. Maybe some mistakes couldn't be undone. She started the motor and pulled into the traffic lane.

"I was offered a new job in New York," she told him.

"Must have made you happy."

"Not really. I turned it down."

"Why?"

She was starting to get annoyed. She hadn't expected that crawling back would be easy, but somehow she'd thought it would be her pride that would stand in the way, not his irritation. What was he mad about?

"I turned it down because I didn't want to go back to New York." She stopped at the highway and waited for a break in the traffic. "We like it here." She made her turn and concentrated on the road, trying hard not to think about Zach even sitting there next to her.

"I knew that Ruth and Jenny did, but I hadn't noticed you being too overjoyed about things."

"That's not fair. That house was a bit of a shock."

"I wasn't talking about the house, but about your whole attitude. What can you say you've really enjoyed since you came here three months ago?"

You, was what she wanted to say, but his tone had stung her. "That's a lousy thing to say. If it's so distasteful to ride with me then I'll pull over and you can get out." But she didn't make a move to go to the right-hand lane and he didn't ask her to.

"Maybe I'm just tired of the way you walk all over people," he snapped.

"I do not."

"No? You up and sold that house right from under Jenny and Ruth."

"They knew it was for sale."

"But did they want it to be?"

"It ate money. Everything that could go wrong with a house went wrong with that one. I'm lucky someone was willing to buy it."

"Maybe the house is lucky and finally got someone who'll care about it."

She drove through the downtown section and turned north along the river. She was sorry about the house; it was just one of a number of things she'd handled wrong in the last few weeks, but one she couldn't do anything about.

She'd signed a contract and someone was willing to pay her asking price. She legally couldn't back out, even though she would have liked to. Ruth and Jenny had forgiven her, so why couldn't Zach? In his present grumpy mood, she wasn't about to explain anything. All her carefully prepared speeches were floating in the wind back at the airport.

"Jenny and Mother aren't angry at me," she told him. "I don't see why you should be."

"Neither do I," he said, but there wasn't any laughter in his voice. "You didn't want to get involved with me or the house right from the beginning. You were honest about it, so anything that followed was my own fault."

There was pain in his voice, and some of her answering anger faded. "Zach."

But he went on. "I did a lot of thinking when I was away, real thinking. I'd thought at first that there was a chance we could still work things out, that I could be patient and give you time, but then it suddenly dawned on me that I had never really loved you."

Her heart just about stopped, except that real stopping would be an end to her pain and the fates wouldn't let her escape suffering. "I see."

"I fell in love with an illusion," he said. "I'm at that age where men get tired and start looking to make a home. You were convenient and I decided you were my ideal."

Her hopes were gone. Dead, buried and ready to be mourned. "Sorry I wasn't."

"We can't change what we are."

She turned onto Pokagon Street, then into the alley, holding her heart and her tears in careful check. A few more minutes and she could escape, a few more minutes and she could watch her dreams vanish. She hit the garage door opener and it creaked slowly upward. Inched upward, it seemed, as her heart threatened to burst. She blinked back her tears. Not yet, fellows. Give me a few minutes more. A few hours more, at the rate that garage door was moving. It was finally up and she pulled the car in, hitting the controls to close the door.

"Thanks for the ride," Zach said stiffly as he got out of the car.

"No problem." If only she hadn't fled in panic when he proposed to her. She got out her side as the garage door thudded closed. Lord, her pain made even the sound of the door closing seem loud.

"The door's closed," Zach said.

"What?" She frowned at him, thinking for a wonderful split second that he was reading her mind again, but then realized he was talking about the smaller door. The one that always jammed.

"I know now that there are other ways to get out," she said. She'd learned a lot since that first day, when she'd gotten locked in here with him.

He hit the garage door control on the wall. Nothing happened.

"Damn." He hit it again. There was a grinding noise and the door lifted an inch, two inches, six inches, then fell back down with a squeal.

"Now what?" Zach snapped, and strode over to the door. "Damn. The door's off the track."

She stared at him. "What does that mean?"

"It means this door won't open. We'll have to pound on the other door and hope Ruth or Jenny hears us."

Holly stared at him, at his back so rigid with obstinacy. She suddenly knew he was lying. He did, too, love her. He was hurt, and he was lying to cover his hurt. The old Zach, the one she'd been locked in the garage with that first day, would be teasing and joking. Maybe if he was annoyed with her the jokes would be a bit sharper. But there had been no jokes, and the only reason she could think of for that was he was hurting.

The tears that had been threatening were ordered to retreat. She'd never been one to indulge in self-pity; action was much more her style. If she wanted Zach, she'd have to fight for him. She leaned against the door, bracing for her siege.

"Jenny and Ruth aren't home."

He spun slowly toward her. "Not home?"

She shook her head. "They took Duke to obedience school and I'm supposed to pick them up in an hour."

"Who's Duke?"

"Jenny's dog."

He said nothing. She'd surprised him with that one. A minor victory.

"I'd say we're stuck here for a while," she went on after a long silence. "They're bound to wait at least a half hour before even calling home for their ride, and then when they get no answer, they'll assume I'm on the way. It could be hours before they actually get here to let us out."

He looked as she must have when she got locked in that first day, and she bit back a smile.

"It's not that cold," she told him. "We won't freeze."

"But it's not that warm, either." He walked back to the garage door. "Maybe I can get this thing back on the track."

He took off his raincoat and tossed it onto the front seat of the car, then leaned his shoulder into the door. Nothing budged.

"Guess that's not going to work," he muttered, and stepped away.

Holly looked to see a wide streak of grime down the side of his white shirt and tan slacks. Since the garage was built after the house, it might have been only sixty years' worth of grime instead of a hundred. "Sorry," she said softly.

He grimaced and tried sliding the door back into place. All he got was a matching streak of dirt down the other side. "I'll get them cleaned," Holly said.

"That's not necessary."

"It's my garage. I'll pay the cleaning bill."

"You sold it along with the house, remember?"

"It's mine for another month."

She glared and he frowned. A standoff for the moment.

"What I need is some sort of crowbar," he murmured, and glanced around the garage, finally settling his gaze on the rafters over their heads. "I wonder if anything's up there."

"I imagine there are lots of 'anythings' up there, but probably not a crowbar."

He climbed up gingerly onto the hood of his car and tried to peer over the edge of the planks that made up the flooring where things were stored. He couldn't quite see over the edge and had to pull things out blindly. He dragged his first treasure forward. An old canvas awning. He tossed it to the floor.

"So Ruth got Jenny a dog?" he asked suddenly.

Holly had the urge to stick out her tongue at him but restrained herself. "*I* got Jenny a dog. I'm not a monster, you know."

"I never thought you were."

Was it her imagination or had his voice softened just a fraction? "Anything I can do to help?"

"No."

He pulled out another awning, sliding a box out with it. "Wonder what's in here?" As he said it, the bottom of the box gave way and dust and dirt rained onto the car.

"Careful," Holly cried, and darted over to the car to sweep the dirt clods off his car before he stepped on one.

"Ah, just what I wanted."

"A crowbar?" Holly fought back disappointment. How was she going to win him back if he got the door open and left?

"Close enough to one." He jumped down from the car with part of an awning brace.

She watched in growing silence as he fiddled with the brace and the garage door track. "I hope the new owner doesn't make you move," she said suddenly.

"I've already packed." He stepped back and wiped his hand over the back of his neck. Maybe she should call a halt to this little game. But then, was it really a game? Wasn't she fighting for their future together?

"Damn. This isn't going to work, either."

He was talking about his makeshift crowbar, but she read other meanings into it. Time for a stronger assault. "Why'd you ask me to marry you if you didn't love me?" she asked.

"Insanity." He kicked at the track in frustration, then turned to look at her. In the dim light of the garage, she could read nothing in his eyes. "Why'd you sell the house?" he asked.

"Insanity." She tried a grin. "Hey, I was mad at you for spoiling all my carefully set plans, and when the boiler went out, it was the last straw."

Her smile wasn't returned. "Great reasons for hurting people who care about you."

That stung. Some of her hope and good spirits drained away, irritation filling their place. "What about me? You think I wasn't hurt, too? And for all your great talk about communication, you neglected to communicate with me on a few vital topics."

"Like what?" he demanded, running his fingers through his hair.

"Like the fact that you'd changed your mind about your life-style," she pointed out. "First you tell me how you love to travel and how you can hardly wait to leave this place, then I'm supposed to believe you've suddenly announced you've changed your mind."

"Well, I stopped talking about it. That should have been a clue."

"Great." She waved her arms in exasperation. "So anytime in the future that you stop talking about something, I'm supposed to know how you're thinking."

His eyes narrowed. "What do you mean, 'anytime in the future'?"

"What do you think I mean, you stubborn idiot?" She took a deep breath. You catch more flies with honey, Ruth always told her. Why couldn't she remember it when she needed to?

"If I remember correctly, you quite emphatically turned my marriage proposal down." He came a step closer as if to see her better.

"Luckily as it turned out, since you realized you never loved me." She took a step backward and found herself up against the side door again.

"Love is a scary thing," he said.

"No, being without love is what's scary."

He stopped and somehow everything changed. It was as if the snows had melted and tiny flowers were poking up through the earth. "You're right," he said. "Being in love was wonderful. The bad part started when you left me."

His words hurt. She *had* left him, not so much physically as emotionally. She'd pulled away without very apparent or sensible reasons, just as her father had. Her eyes could no longer meet his and she stared down at her hands. "I'm sorry about that."

"What does that mean?"

He was closer, much closer. She looked up to find him barely a breath away. She wasn't sure what to think.

"It means I'm sorry," she said slowly.

"But is that an apology or an I-wish-I-hadn't-done-it remark?"

She looked into his eyes and saw life there. Smiles and hope and laughter. "Both," she said softly. "I was a jerk and I'm sorry."

He reached for her and suddenly she was back in heaven, tightly held and in his arms as if he'd never let go. "And I lied when I said I'd never loved you."

"I knew that. Not at first, but pretty soon afterward."

He pulled away slightly, just enough to frown at her. "You did? How did you know that?"

"You never once mentioned Pokagon. If you'd figured you'd escaped a close call, you would have given him credit."

His smile returned. "Is that so? And should I give him credit now or blame?"

"Depends on whether your offer is still open. I've made some stupid mistakes in the past few weeks. Is this one correctable?"

She was in his embrace, surrounded by love and Zach. "Always," he whispered into her hair. "Always."

They kissed, first to celebrate the magic of the moment, the splendor of finding each other again. But then the kiss deepened, and the winter turned to spring. Birds sang, flowers bloomed and the sun smiled on them.

"I'm sorry about the house," she said a moment later, leaning against his chest. "I knew I'd made a mistake when I came back from New York, but it was too late. The realtor and my lawyer said I couldn't get out of the deal."

Zach's hands soothed her back, moving with slow possession over it. "I'm not," he said. "I'm glad you sold it."

She freed herself from his hold and stared up into his eyes. They were gentle and laughing. "You really are insane. I was right that first day to be suspicious of your friendliness. After all your moaning about the house, you're glad I sold it?"

He nodded and leaned forward to plant a kiss on her lips. "Because I bought it. Now you and Jenny and Ruth will come and live in my house and be my family."

She shook her head in confusion. "But ... but, why were you packing?"

"To move downstairs."

She sighed, her confusion sinking into a laughing thirst for revenge. "Why, you—"

His laughter surrounded her and he caught her up in his arms, swinging her toward the heavens and forever happiness. She gazed into his heart and knew real peace at last. He wouldn't leave. He was putting down roots. "I love you so much," she told him.

"And that's only half as much as I love you." Their lips met in a blaze of sunlight but ended in smiling, grinning joy. "Now, if we could just get out of this blasted garage," Zach moaned. "What a place to discover love."

"Sort of fitting, don't you think?"

"I suppose, but I'm ready to be rescued. I can think of more comfortable places to spend the rest of the hour before you pick up Duke and his gang."

"Well, I suppose we could tackle the small door. Maybe we could take the hinge pins out and—" Even as she was speaking though, she'd tried the old, broken knob and it worked! The door opened easily, as if the latch was brand new.

"How did you manage that?" Zach asked. "It's never worked."

From outside in the yard, the sounds of spring could be heard. The wild singing of the birds, the rustling of the newborn leaves in the gentle breeze, and something else. Something not quite so easy to define. Could sunshine hold laughter and happiness?

"Maybe the house is healed along with me," Holly said with a grin.

Zach smiled back. "Pokagon to the end, eh?" He swept her into his arms. "Welcome home, love. Welcome home."

Epilogue

Holly let a broad yawn run its course as she stepped into the kitchen. She'd better get to bed and get her beauty sleep or Zach would leave her at the altar tomorrow. A grin crossed her face as she put her cup in the dishwasher. She wasn't worried, not anymore. They loved each other too much for either to want to live without the other.

A creaking on the servants' stairs made Holly's heart jump into her throat. What in the world was that?

"Jenny?" she called softly, but there was no answer.

Holly crept over to the stairs, but no one was there. She peered down the basement steps. A square of light was splattered across the floor. "Jenny? Ruth?"

Still no answer. She forced her feet down the steps. Maybe it was Zach playing a trick on her. "Zach?" But only silence answered her. All rooms were dark except the tool-room off to the right side of the steps. Holly peeked in. Everything looked in order. The tools were on the bench and—

Holly blinked in surprise. A glass of orange juice and pieces of apple? Holly walked into the toolroom. There was a note under the glass and she picked it up.

Dear Mr. Pokagon
Thank you for making Mommy happy and for bringing back Zach to us. Attached, sort of, you will find one glass of orange juice and three pieces of apple. I had one piece myself. It was good. Mommy and Zach would like some little kids. Twins or triplets would be nice.

Respectfully yours,
Your friend Jenny Carpenter

P.S. I know that you prefer rum, but orange juice is much better for you. It is very nutritious and packed with vitamin C, which will help you not get a cold.

The neatly written letters swam before Holly's eyes as she tried to swallow the lump in her throat. Resolutely, she snatched a pencil from the toolbox and began writing at the bottom of Jenny's letter.

P.P.S. This is to inform you that I am now completely healed, so you don't have to break anything else in the house.
Thank you.

Holly Carpenter

P.P.P.S. Forget about the twins or triplets. Zach and I can handle that ourselves.

Then she laid the letter back down on the bench and ran upstairs. Jeering laughter, common sense and sixteen-plus years of education followed her up, but she didn't care. She knew in her heart that Jenny was right. Orange juice was much better for a person than rum.

*   *   *   *   *

Silhouette Desire®

CHILDREN OF DESTINY

A trilogy by Ann Major

Three power-packed tales of irresistible passion and undeniable fate created by Ann Major to wrap your heart in a legacy of love.

PASSION'S CHILD — September

Years ago, Nick Browning nearly destroyed Amy's life, but now that the child of his passion—the child of her heart—was in danger, Nick was the only one she could trust....

DESTINY'S CHILD — October

Cattle baron Jeb Jackson thought he owned everything and everyone on his ranch, but fiery Megan MacKay's destiny was to prove him wrong!

NIGHT CHILD — November

When little Julia Jackson was kidnapped, young Kirk MacKay blamed himself. Twenty years later, he found her...and discovered that love could shine through even the darkest of nights.

To order any of Ann Major's thrilling Children of Destiny, send your name, address and zip or postal code, along with a check or money order for $2.50 for each book ordered, plus 75¢ postage and handling, payable to Silhouette Reader Service to:

In Canada

P.O. Box 609
Fort Erie, Ontario
L2A 5X3

In U.S.A.

901 Fuhrmann Blvd.
Box 1396
Buffalo, NY 14269-1396

Please specify book title with your order.

SD 457

ATTRACTIVE, SPACE SAVING BOOK RACK

Display your most prized novels on this handsome and sturdy book rack. The hand-rubbed walnut finish will blend into your library decor with quiet elegance, providing a practical organizer for your favorite hard-or soft-covered books.

Only $9.95

Approximately 16" x 8" when assembled

Assembles in seconds!

To order, rush your name, address and zip code, along with a check or money order for $10.70* ($9.95 plus 75¢ postage and handling) payable to *Silhouette Books*.

Silhouette Books
Book Rack Offer
901 Fuhrmann Blvd.
P.O. Box 1396
Buffalo, NY 14269-1396

Offer not available in Canada.

BKR-2A

*New York and Iowa residents add appropriate sales tax.

Silhouette Special Edition

COMING NEXT MONTH

#493 PROOF POSITIVE—Tracy Sinclair
Tough divorce lawyer Kylie O'Connor privately yearned for a happy marriage and bouncing babies. But cynical Adam Ridgeway wasn't offering either, and Kylie's secret couldn't keep for long....

#494 NAVY WIFE—Debbie Macomber
Navy officer Rush Callaghan placed duty above all else. His ship was his home, the sea his true love. Could vulnerable Lindy Kyle prove herself the perfect first mate?

#495 IN HONOR'S SHADOW—Lisa Jackson
Years had passed since young Brenna coveted her sister's boyfriend. But despite recently widowed Warren's advances, Brenna feared some things never changed, and she'd forever be in Honor's shadow.

#496 HEALING SYMPATHY—Gina Ferris
Ex-cop Quinn Gallagher didn't need anyone. Yet sympathetic Laura Sutherland saw suffering in his eyes—and her heart ached. She'd risk rejection if her love could heal his pain.

#497 DIAMOND MOODS—Maggi Charles
Marta thought she was over Josh Smith. But now the twinkling of another man's diamond on her finger seemed mocking...when the fire in her soul burned for Josh alone.

#498 A CHARMED LIFE—Anne Lacey
Sunburned and snakebitten, reckless Ross Stanton needed a physician's care. Cautious Dr. Tessa Fitzgerald was appalled by the death-defying rogue, but while reprimanding Ross, she began feeling lovesick herself!

AVAILABLE THIS MONTH:

Silhouette Intimate Moments

JOIN BESTSELLING AUTHOR EMILIE RICHARDS AND SET YOUR COURSE FOR NEW ZEALAND

This month Silhouette Intimate Moments brings you what no other romance line has—Book Two of Emilie Richards's exciting mini-series Tales of the Pacific. In SMOKE SCREEN Paige Duvall leaves Hawaii behind and journeys to New Zealand, where she unravels the secret of her past and meets Adam Tomoana, the man who holds the key to her future.

In future months look for the other volumes in this exciting series: RAINBOW FIRE (February 1989) and OUT OF THE ASHES (May 1989). They'll be coming your way only from Silhouette Intimate Moments.

If you missed Book One of Tales of the Pacific, FROM GLOWING EMBERS (IM #249), you can order it by sending your name, address and zip or postal code, along with a check or money order for $2.75 for each book ordered, plus 75¢ postage and handling, payable to Silhouette Reader Service to:

In Canada

P.O. Box 609
Fort Erie, Ontario
L2A 5X3

In U.S.A.

901 Fuhrmann Blvd.
P.O. Box 1396
Buffalo, NY 14269-1396

Please specify book title with your order.

IM261